"Slow dances we~~re~~ confessions…"

Lily swiveled in her seat. "I shouldn't be dancing. Or having fun. I just left a man at the altar."

"Technically, he never stood on the altar." Conner took Lily's hand. When they were together, it was easy to forget all the reasons they shouldn't be. "Dance with me, Lily."

She didn't move.

Emotions were spinning in Conner's chest, trying to break free. "Sometimes, you have to go with your gut, even if others might raise their eyebrows. Sometimes, you have to honor your feelings, because they don't fit into a polite box. But following those feelings makes you feel more like yourself."

Being with Lily made Conner feel all kinds of emotions he'd kept locked away since his accident—guilt, tenderness, duty, joy. "Let's dance, Lily. Just you and me."

Because they'd be in Falcon Creek tomorrow and go their separate ways. Because feelings got in the way of responsibilities. *Always.*

Dear Reader,

I enjoy writing about characters that have made bad decisions in their past and suddenly wake up to find themselves in a bind. How did their lives come to this? And what are they going to do about it now?

The key players in this story each find themselves at a crossroads. Old Elias Blackwell has just found out he has a son and a set of five granddaughters. Lily Harrison, one of said granddaughters, is having doubts about marrying her childhood best friend. And Conner Hannah is realizing there might be more to life than working on the Blackwell Ranch. The decisions these three make, the emotions they sort out... they impact the entire Hannah, Harrison and Blackwell families.

I hope you enjoy this installment of The Blackwell Sisters, as well as the upcoming books in the series. It was a joy working on another project with my writing sisters—Amy Vastine, Anna J. Stewart, Carol Ross and Cari Lynn Webb. Yes, this wasn't our first writing rodeo, so to speak. And yes, we're something of a family. We all share a love of handsome heroes and a sense of humor, one we wield on the sometimes painful journey to a happily-ever-after.

Happy reading!

Melinda

HEARTWARMING

Montana Welcome

———

Melinda Curtis

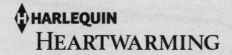

HARLEQUIN
HEARTWARMING

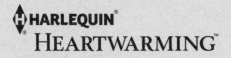

ISBN-13: 978-1-335-88981-2

Montana Welcome

Recycling programs for this product may not exist in your area.

For questions and comments about the quality of this book, please contact us at CustomerService@Harlequin.com.

Harlequin Enterprises ULC
22 Adelaide St. West, 40th Floor
Toronto, Ontario M5H 4E3, Canada
www.Harlequin.com

Printed in U.S.A.

Melinda Curtis is the *USA TODAY* bestselling author of lighthearted contemporary romance. In addition to her Mountain Monroe series for Harlequin Heartwarming, she's published independently and with Forever Romance. Look for a TV movie based on her Harlequin Heartwarming title *Dandelion Wishes*. Between books, Melinda spends time with her husband remodeling their home by swinging a hammer, grouting tile and wielding a paintbrush.

"You'll laugh, you'll cry, and you'll want to visit again soon!" says Brenda Novak, *New York Times* bestselling author, about *Can't Hurry Love*.

"A small town brought to life with wit and charm," says Sheila Roberts, *New York Times* bestselling author, about *Can't Hurry Love*.

Visit the Author Profile page
at Harlequin.com for more titles.

To Carol Ross, Cari Lynn Webb, Amy Vastine and Anna J. Stewart. I know I often scare you with my writing ideas—"Come on! Let's write another set of Blackwell books!" Thanks for having my back so I don't face plant on a public sidewalk. Love you, ladies!

PROLOGUE

SEVEN WAS A magical age for Lily Harrison.

Six had been pretty good, too. But seven…

It was the first year she hadn't been in the same classroom as her triplet sisters, Amanda and Georgie. The first year Mom had called her a big girl and it felt like she meant it. Before that, her older sister, Peyton, had been the big girl.

Being seven was cool. It was nothing like being five, like Fiona, the baby in the family, who could barely tie her shoes.

Lily was seven when Danny Belmonte moved in next door. He was seven, too. And in her class.

From her perch on top of the backyard swing set, she watched his family carry boxes and furniture into the house. From there she could see Danny's driveway and his back porch. The Belmontes were navy, same as the Harrisons. But they had three boys, all of whom had dark, curly hair and rich, loud laughs. Lily had wondered what they'd think of their new neighbors—five girls who, according to Dad, shrieked and shouted and generally "carried on" nonstop.

While Lily was enjoying her bird's-eye view of the Belmontes moving in, Danny stepped out onto the rear deck with a plastic baseball bat and a Wiffle ball. He took a swing and whacked the ball over the fence into Lily's yard.

"Gahhh!" Danny stomped off the deck and onto the grass, out of sight.

Lily didn't think twice. She swung to the ground, picked up the ball and threw it back over.

"Hey. Who did that?" Danny ran to the fence and pressed one eye to an open knothole. "A girl?" He made a sound like she did when presented with beets on her dinner plate.

"Yeah." Lily scrambled to the first branch of the apple tree and looked down on him the way Peyton looked down on her sometimes. "So?"

Danny scrunched his face. "Girls don't get ta play baseball."

"Who says?"

"Everybody."

"Well, that's stupid." Lily pointed her thumb at her chest. "I play everything." That was true. She wasn't much of a reader, like Georgie and Peyton, and didn't like to sew and stuff, like Amanda and Fiona. "My dad says I'm the sporty girl."

Danny pounded his bat in the dirt. "Prove it."

"How?"

A grin spread across his face, a grin she recognized since it was much like her own. "You wanna do something super fun?"

"Yeah!" Because shrieking and shouting and carrying on weren't really super fun.

And so started an instant friendship based on Danny's wild ideas and Lily's determination not to say no.

Lily was close to her sisters, but Danny was truly like her brother from another mother. During their first year of friendship, they shrugged off skinned knees and stubbed toes. They laughed at clothes they'd torn from climbing trees. Together they egged each other on and got away with a lot.

And then the day before Lily, Amanda and Georgie were going to turn eight, Danny came up with the best plan—they were going to launch themselves in a homemade rocket. Lily couldn't wait.

In reality, the supersonic rocket was the box the Harrisons' new dishwasher had come in. Their launching pad was the top of the slide attached to one end of the swing set. Danny had made holes in the box for their heads and feet to stick out. Lily had drawn red stripes on each side of the box with a marker because she refused to let him do all the work.

They pushed their boxy rocket to the upper platform and looked down.

"Don't rockets shoot up?" Lily asked.

"We're going to take off like a plane." Danny sliced his hand down through the air and then up toward the sky. "Whoosh!"

Over at the picnic table, Amanda clasped her hands and Georgie hugged her first-aid kit. Fiona sat in the sandbox. She'd arranged a row of dolls in front of her to watch. Peyton had left a book on the picnic table and gone inside, probably to get Mom or Dad.

"It's not high enough." Danny frowned. He pointed to the shed Dad had built last weekend, the one that was within touching distance from the slide. "We'll start up there and fly over here. It'll be cool."

Of course, Lily agreed. When had Danny ever led her wrong?

While they wrestled the box up to the roof of the shed, Amanda came forward and wrung her hands. "Don't. It's too high."

"It's not," Danny scoffed. While Lily held the box, he scrambled inside, using his feet to hold the rocket at the roof's peak.

"You'll break something!" Georgie still hugged her first-aid kit.

"Will not!" Danny snapped.

Fiona started to sob in the sandbox.

Deep inside Lily, something didn't feel so good. Just last week Dad had told her she had to slow down and think. Danny said slow was boring. Nothing was boring when Danny was around. But that didn't make the sick feeling in her tummy go away. Lily wished Peyton would hurry back with Mom.

"Ready?" Danny grinned.

Lily crawled into the unsteady box and poked her head out the top.

"Here we go!" Danny drew his feet in.

The box slid down the roof and off the edge. For one exhilarating moment they were flying just like Danny had promised.

But that moment was short-lived. The rocket never made it to the slide.

They dropped.

On the way down, Lily's head whacked something hard and then they landed in a heap.

The next thing Lily remembered was Dad telling Danny he had to cut out the shenanigans and watch out for Lily.

All the time.

CHAPTER ONE

"OF COURSE I'LL take care of Lily." Danny's voice drifted down the hallway. "But I don't need to marry her to do that."

Lily froze at the corner of the church corridor in San Diego with a soft rustle of tulle.

She'd left the bridal vestibule to find Danny and ask him if this was something they shouldn't be doing, like that rocket ride from long ago. Because it didn't feel right. Their engagement. This wedding. Things had happened too fast. He hadn't even told her he loved her!

"Oh, you need to marry her." The man Lily had called Dad for twenty-nine years, the man whose name she'd just discovered was *not* on her birth certificate, spoke in the commanding tones of a naval officer to his subordinate.

"She had a scare," Danny said respectfully to his boss. "But this is all just…rushed."

Danny has cold feet, too?

Lily held her breath, waiting for her heart to break.

It didn't.

It should, right? If I love him?

"Aren't you the one who always cautions Lily and me to stop and think before we act?" Danny said in a much louder voice, the timbre resonating with annoyance. "We need to take a breath, sir."

"We?" It was a good thing the man who'd raised Lily and her sisters was wearing his dress whites and not his weapon. Rudy sounded like there was just cause to use deadly force on Lily's fiancé. "*We* lost Susan six months ago. *We* nearly lost Lily a week later when you took her skydiving."

"Something wild always makes her feel more alive," Danny retorted.

Not always.

Lily steadied herself with one hand against the wall as the memories intruded.

Being tossed by currents of wind. The earth rushing up toward her. The mind-numbing fear. If not for Danny, she would have plunged to her death.

"You're the reason she's the way she is," Dad—*Rudy*—said harshly, referring to their childhood. "Don't forget that."

Lily stared at her hands, feeling numb.

She loved Danny. Truly, she did. He always had her back. But she wasn't sure she loved him the way you were supposed to love a husband. They'd been best friends for over twenty years and had only kissed for the first time when Danny proposed to her—the day after she'd nearly died skydiving. He was good at the kissing thing and Mom had just died of an aneurysm and she'd said yes, except…

I don't love him to the tips of my toes.

Lily swallowed thickly; sad, but not heartbroken. Sad, but oddly…relieved.

We shouldn't be getting married.

As quietly as possible, Lily turned in her ball-gown wedding dress and made her way back down the church corridor, wondering what she was going to do.

Stop the wedding.

But…

Dad—*Rudy*—had spent a fortune on it.

Lily opened the door to the bridal vestibule and eyed her four sisters in their lilac bridesmaid dresses. They were smiling and laughing, so carefree.

The champagne might have had a little to do with that.

Lily, who hadn't drunk anything, was a wreck.

The Harrison sisters surrounded Lily, chattering excitedly, perhaps eager for the upcoming nuptials, perhaps sensing her uncertainty.

Was Lily uncertain? No. She knew what she should do. And it didn't involve walking down the aisle on the arm of a man who wasn't her father to pledge herself to a man who didn't want to marry her.

"I need some time alone." Time to work up the courage to stop the wedding. Lily tried to smile at her sisters.

Peyton, the oldest, frowned. "Now isn't the time to be alone."

Fiona, the youngest, moved toward the door. "If Lily needs a few minutes to collect her thoughts, we should leave."

"What can I get you? A stiff drink? Aspirin?" Dr. Georgie Harrison, one of the triplets, would never stop trying to make things better for everyone around her.

"I don't think you should be alone." Amanda tenderly touched Lily's ornate updo. Of all her sisters, Lily was closest to Amanda. "There's something about your mood today that worries me."

"I just need a few minutes." Refusing to be

put off, Lily opened the door. "Please go... find Dad."

As was usual with the Harrison sisters, it took more than a little effort to shoo them out the door.

Finally, Lily was alone with that familiar feeling of unease, the one that preceded an activity Danny would consider perfect and Rudy would consider rash. She had to find the strength to stand behind her decision to stop the wedding.

Her decision would be challenged. To be honest, most of her decisions were challenged by her family.

Stay out of trouble. Rudy's words echoed in her head. *Honor your word.* Live up to the military code of conduct. *Do the right thing.*

Canceling the wedding, refusing to get married... Her word would be broken, and mayhem would ensue.

Mayhem. The ripple made by my life.

Rudy's anticipated displeasure descended upon her like a cold, wet blanket.

Lily drew a deep breath, and—

The door opened behind her.

She spun with a swirl of voluminous skirt, the momentum of which nearly carried her in a complete circle.

A cowboy stood in the doorway. A handsome cowboy.

Lily blinked. This was San Diego. Cowboys didn't just mosey on by.

Tan cowboy hat, black cowboy boots, a blue checked shirt and dark blue jeans. Yep. It was a cowboy. His body was lean, his features chiseled, and his expression said he was uncomfortable being here.

That makes two of us.

"Can I help you?" Lily asked.

The cowboy stepped aside to allow an elderly man through. And then the cowboy closed the door and leaned against it.

"Lily Harrison. You have doubts." The old man's white hair was thinning. His brown cowboy boots were scuffed. His face was wrinkled and lined from years of sun exposure. His blue wool suit was rumpled and worn at the elbows. Everything about him looked washed out. Everything, that was, except for his eyes. Those dark orbs were focused on Lily. "You have doubts," he repeated. "About who you are. About getting married."

"How did you...?"

Who am I if not Rudy Harrison's daughter?

She'd been asking herself that question for a few weeks now, ever since she'd requested a copy of her lost birth certificate from the county clerk and had noticed Rudy Harrison's name wasn't on the line labeled *Father*. She would have asked Rudy about it except he'd been in overprotective mode ever since Mom's death and Lily's near accident.

And her four sisters?

They weren't as close as they used to be now that they didn't live under the same roof. Lily and Amanda were always in touch since they were the ones still living in San Diego, but mostly Lily felt like the loose end the family wanted to wrap in cotton so they could carry on with their own lives. So she'd kept the birth certificate revelation to herself.

The two cowboys stared at her, waiting for a reply.

She'd be darned if she was going to tell these strangers about her intention to call off the wedding.

Lily drew herself up tall. "Everyone has doubts." Even Danny.

"That sounds like a bad fortune in a fortune cookie." The old man gave her a wry half smile. "If you were meant to get married today, you'd have a clear mind. True love tends to trump any worries."

"I never admitted I'm having second

thoughts." But this stranger... He'd known. Lily's stomach dropped to her toes, currently housed in white sequined sneakers. Was this man related to her fiancé? If so, she had to keep up appearances until Danny knew she was backing out. "Danny and I make sense. We never fight." She generally accepted whatever challenge he threw her way. And if there weren't any fireworks when they kissed... Well, she hadn't met a man yet who sparked something inside her.

The younger cowboy at the door shifted, just a scuff of those black boots.

Unexpectedly, something sparked inside her.

Lily blew out a breath and asked them both, "Do I know either of you?"

"This is Conner, one of my ranch hands." The old man pointed toward the guy leaning against the door. "And I'm Elias. But folks call me Big E." He strode forward with confidence, as if intent upon a handshake. Instead, he took both of Lily's cold hands and held them out so he could get a good look at her. "You're beautiful. We've never met, but your father... *My son*..." There was a rueful slant to his dark eyes. "I had no idea I had another son, much less five granddaughters, until a few days ago."

Lily tried to smile past her confusion. "My paternal grandfather's name is *Charles*. Charles Harrison. And I hate to disappoint you, but I'm not your granddaughter. This is the Harrison-Belmonte wedding. I heard there was a small ceremony earlier. Perhaps your long-lost granddaughter was married then?"

"I'm in the right place, honey. Charles Harrison is your *step*grandfather. Rudy Harrison is your stepfather. And…Susan was your mother, may she rest in peace." He sighed mournfully. "And from what I've recently learned, your real father is named Thomas. Thomas Blackwell."

Thomas Blackwell. The world tilted. Lily recognized the name from her birth certificate. But she hadn't shown it to anyone.

The younger cowboy's boots creaked.

"I never had the honor of meeting your mother or knowing my son Thomas," Big E continued with that reassuring, yet slightly vulnerable smile. "Fifty-some-odd years ago, I fell in love with a woman when she and her family visited distant relatives in Falcon Creek, Montana." His expression turned mischievous as he straightened his black bolo tie. "I was a fine young rancher and she wanted to be a photographer. She took a picture of me leading my horse across an old wooden bridge on our ranch."

This was surreal. "I've seen that picture." There were grand mountains in the backdrop. "I've seen that picture," Lily repeated, frowning. "At Great-Aunt Pru's house." Great-Aunt Pru, who Mom had said was a dear family friend, not a relation. Hence the title was honorary.

"Yes, Prudence." Big E's tone turned sentimental. "She had a beauty mark right here." He touched his cheek. "A sharp wit, a laugh that made a man smile and a father who didn't approve of me."

Great-Aunt Pru had indeed had a beauty mark, a Victorian home full of photographs and apparently a secret, if Big E was to be believed.

But there was a flaw in his story. "Great-Aunt Pru doesn't have any children." At least none living. There was a picture of her son on her mantel, a handsome man. He wore a military uniform and a roguish smile. And his eyes... They bore a striking resemblance to Big E's. But if that were true... It would mean they were related. It would mean the birth certificate hadn't been a misprint. And that Dad—*Rudy*—wasn't really her father. Lily's stomach did another free fall. She wasn't ready to believe it.

"Haven't you ever wondered where you got your adventurous spirit?" Big E asked softly.

"Well, I…" *Yes.* But still, coming on the heels of Rudy strong-arming Danny to marry her, this was too much. "I can't be the person you're looking for."

"I think you are." Big E pinned her with an honest glare. "Because recently, one Lily Rose Harrison requested a copy of her birth certificate, a document that listed Thomas Blackwell as her father." When Lily opened her mouth to say something—*anything*—he held up a hand. "I have protocols in place to notify me when the Blackwell name hits public record. I don't put much stock in coincidences. Blackwell isn't an uncommon name. Though a trace of the lineage of Thomas Blackwell proved interesting. Guess who was listed on *his* birth certificate? His father. Elias Blackwell." Big E tapped his chest. "And his mother, Prudence Williams."

"Great-Aunt Pru," Lily rasped. *Grandmother Pru?* Wait until she told her sisters. "When I saw the name Thomas Blackwell on

my birth certificate, I figured…" She picked up her pearl-studded pouch from the side table. Her fingers fumbled at the latch and slipped while pulling out the earth-shattering document. She stared at the names listed on her birth certificate—Susan and Thomas Blackwell. Lily wished Mom were alive to explain this away.

She lifted her gaze to the man claiming to be her grandfather. "Who are you really? And why are you here today? Now?"

On what was proving *not* to be the happiest day of her life.

"I came here to meet you." Elias led Lily to the antique love seat and they both sat down, not saying anything until she'd properly angled her broad hoop skirt so she could face him. "From the moment I came through that door, I knew I'd arrived at just the right time—the moment when you were realizing this wedding might be ill-conceived."

"Danny's my best friend," she protested, albeit weakly. She set her birth certificate on the small end table. "I don't want to hurt him." But she no longer wanted to marry him, either.

Big E waved her words aside. "Notice you didn't say you loved him."

Oh, she'd noticed, all right.

"I can't call off the wedding." Although she wanted to more than anything. The longer she delayed, the harder it would be. All the repercussions… She had to talk to her family. Make them understand that she was about to make another mistake, create another wave of mayhem. Lily tried to dislodge the guilt, the nerves, the tantalizing urge to run. "This dress… The flowers… The people…"

"A wedding isn't like a play." Big E's voice was gentle, soothing. "The show doesn't always have to go on."

"But my father… Rudy, I mean…" Lily blinked back a sudden onslaught of tears, looking toward the hot cowboy but fixated on the door behind him. "I can't marry Danny. I know that now." She loved him, but he deserved someone who loved him to the moon and back. "But how can I stop the wedding?"

The old cowboy straightened, drawing her attention to his resolute posture, the firm line of his jaw, the air of strength. He'd never run from responsibility.

Yet he didn't have Rudy and Peyton to contend with. They'd argue. They'd wear her down. She knew it. Look at the way Rudy had convinced Danny. The only way for Lily to avoid getting married today was to flee the scene.

"I need to leave." Once she got free, Lily could call her family. She sprang from the couch, scanning the room for her cell phone, which was…

Back at her apartment. Peyton had told her it was the worst wedding faux pas to carry your phone on your wedding day. The only thing Lily had in her tiny purse was a roll of antacids, her driver's license and her birth certificate.

"I can't go without telling someone." Her breath caught in her throat. "How am I going to break this to—" *Dad* "—Rudy?"

"You should leave a note explaining that you need time to think and to discover who you are." Big E produced a pen from the interior pocket of his jacket and held it toward her.

She didn't raise a finger to accept it. "They won't understand."

"They will. Eventually," Big E said. "Knowing where you come from helps you see the path ahead of you."

Lily understood nothing.

Stay out of trouble. Honor your word. Do the right thing.

The feeling of unease returned. She rubbed her chest. "Where would I go?" As soon as she left, everyone would converge on her apartment in downtown San Diego.

"Back to your roots. To the Blackwell Ranch in Falcon Creek, Montana." Big E made it sound so simple. "You might find the piece of yourself you're looking for."

She studied the old man—*my grandfather*—and in her muddled, panicked brain, she thought, *Why not?*

Lily glanced at the handsome cowboy still standing at the door. Did he think her foolish? His expression gave nothing away.

"I'll explain to your family." Big E put an arm around Lily's shoulders. "Conner will take you to Montana."

Make her escape with the cowboy?

Lily sorted through the repercussions of such a thing.

What would it look like to leave my wedding with a hunky cowboy?

Bad.

What would it look like if I bolted while walking down the aisle?

Worse!

Lily scribbled a note on her birth certificate and left it on the table with her engagement ring.

I need to know who I am.

CHAPTER TWO

"CONNER, WE HAVE a slight change in plan."
Big E eased the door to his motor home closed
with Lily inside. He lowered his voice. "Obviously, I have business to take care of here."
The old man nodded toward the church.

"Yes, sir." Conner Hannah shifted his stance
the way a good cutting horse shifted its weight
in anticipation of a steer making a run for it.
His new boots groaned.

Behind him, the motor home tilted as Lily
walked toward the back in that bell-shaped
wedding dress, the one that kept everyone a
good three feet away. She was tall and willowy, delicate in appearance, like the porcelain figurine of Little Bo Peep in his mama's
curio cabinet. The dress was as bad a choice
as that cold-footed groom of hers. When he
and Big E had entered the church, they'd heard
him try to wheedle his way out of marriage.

"You still want me to pick up Pepper and
Natalie in Vegas?" That had been the main

reason Conner had come along with Big E in the first place—to transport and entertain Big E's stepgranddaughter and friend to the Blackwell Ranch. "And swing by the wild-mustang auction?"

Not being one to waste time or effort, his boss nodded. "Deliver everyone to the ranch as planned. It should be easy. And, Conner..." Big E gave Conner a cagey look. "I need to know I can count on your discretion. I want to be the one to break the news about my son and granddaughters to the family."

To Conner's childhood friends, the older man meant—Big E's five grandsons and Big E's wife, Dorothy.

In fact, Big E wanted Conner to lie. Or at the very least, be as guarded and evasive as the old man himself.

Not stinkin' likely.

Conner removed his cowboy hat and ran a hand through his hair, sweating in the August midday heat. "And just what am I supposed to tell everybody about who she is?" She. Lily.

The curtains near the end of the motor home twitched.

"That she's a guest of the Blackwell Ranch." End of story, if Big E's tone was any indication.

Like it's that easy.

But Conner was being paid a sizable bonus to help Big E on this trip. And his boss didn't like to be disobeyed.

"Yes, sir." Conner resettled his hat on his head, accepting the hard road ahead. "When should I tell everyone to expect you home?"

Staring at the church, Big E took his time answering. "I'll be back in time for Pepper's wedding next weekend."

A commotion arose inside the church. Most likely, Lily's family had discovered the bride was missing.

"That's my cue to leave." Keys in hand, Conner turned toward the motor-home door.

"She'll be questioning herself." Big E caught Conner's arm. He may have been old, but he wasn't frail. "You're as good with people as you are with horses, Conner. I'll double the bonus we agreed on if you can take care of things until I return to Montana."

Double meant Big E expected Lily to have more than doubts. He expected her to have regrets. *Double* meant Conner had to make sure her regrets didn't send her running back to an ill-conceived marriage. *Double* meant Conner could pay the second mortgage on the Rocking H this month and the feed bill in full.

He nodded.

"Now, git." Big E strode back toward the church, where four bridesmaids, the father of the bride and a soon-to-be-jilted groom were spilling out the back door.

Conner hopped into the motor home and started the old tank up.

"Wait. I see my sisters." Lily emerged from the bedroom with a noisy rustle of voluminous material. "And there's Danny! And my...my stepdad."

"Big E's taking care of your goodbyes." Conner gunned the motor home out of the parking lot.

"But...*oof*." Lily fell into the dinette, skirt groaning louder than Conner's stiff new boots. "They'll think you're kidnapping me."

"Big E knows what he's doing." Oh, if his Blackwell friends could hear him now. Their laughter ricocheted in his head.

"But..." Lily righted herself and stumbled forward to stand next to Conner, or as close as she could, given the girth of her wedding dress. "What if *I* think you're kidnapping me?"

Conner braked sharply at a yellow light, bringing the old motor home to a premature stop. He gaped at Lily. "In case Big E's intro didn't sink in, I'm Conner Hannah and I'm not a kidnapper. I'm a cowboy." Mental cringe. One didn't necessarily cancel out the other.

Lily knew it, too. She smirked.

"I mean…" Conner turned his attention back to the intersection. "This isn't a hostage situation. I wrangle cattle for the Blackwells and guests on their dude ranch." Instead of running his family's place, which his pay barely kept afloat.

Double bonus. Some might call that abduction wages.

Conner's temples throbbed.

The light changed and he sent the motor home lurching ahead, like a bull charging out of a rodeo gate.

"You're driving like a kidnapper." Lily may have been the prettiest lady he'd ever laid eyes on, but she wasn't the prettiest lady to listen to, given kidnapping was a serious crime.

If Conner dwelled on her words much longer, he might convince himself to head toward the nearest police station and drop her off. But that wouldn't help him pay the mortgage or keep a roof over his mother's head.

"I apologize. This old RV has a hard time shifting out of first gear. I'm slowing down."

He took a deep breath and eased the pressure off the accelerator.

The bell of her skirt crowded against his seat, his leg and the three-foot-high center console.

Motor homes weren't made for wedding dresses.

"Could you take a seat?" Without shifting his gaze off the road, he gestured with his head toward the dinette behind him.

She moved in the direction of the passenger seat instead, hindered by the circumference of her gown. A huffing fit ensued. Lily sounded like a wild mustang being penned in for the first time. She bent down, grabbed the hem of her skirt, picked it up like a collapsed Slinky and then sat in the passenger seat. The hooped skirt rose above the back of her head like an albino peacock's feathers in full spread. "I never should have let Fiona talk me into this dress."

"Fiona being one of your sisters?" He'd seen them file out of that room she'd been in. The family resemblance was strong.

She nodded. "We found a picture of our mother on her wedding day in a dress like this. And since I was the first of five sisters to get engaged, she thought it'd be a good way to honor our mother's memory."

"Nice."

Her skirt had so much hardware working noisily to keep it intact, it practically grunted with effort.

He and Lily exchanged a quick glance.

"I should get out of this dress before it explodes."

"There's just one problem with that idea."

They exchanged another quick glance, and then both said, *"Clothes."*

"Big E's clothes are in the bedroom, but they…uh…" They smelled like old man. "You could borrow one of my shirts, but…" His jeans would drop off her slim hips.

"Are you a boxer or brief man?"

Conner brought the motor home to a hard stop at a yellow light, sending Lily's skirts flouncing over her head like a porch overhang. "Beg pardon?"

"Obviously, I'm not going to don your briefs, but as it's an emergency, I could wear a pair of your clean boxers." She eyed his beltline. "Unless you go commando."

Sweat broke out on the back of Conner's neck. He cranked up the air conditioner. "I'd prefer to keep my secrets secret."

"Are you blushing?"

He was. Despite the air blowing on him,

sweat popped out on his brow, too. He wasn't cut out for chaperoning runaway brides.

She grabbed her skirt and tried to rearrange herself. "You know what they say, cowboy—commando by day is commando by night." Conner didn't have to turn his head to see Lily's smile. It was there in the teasing tone of her voice. "That's a shame."

Conner swiped at his damp brow. Had he been worried about what he'd say to the Montana Blackwells regarding Lily? He should have been worried about a twelve-hundred-mile trip with Lily beside him.

"I could have worn a pair of men's pajama bottoms," she said. "That is, if you weren't a commando cowboy."

He was afraid his burning cheeks were a fiery red. They felt hot enough to roast a campfire marshmallow. "If it's jammies you're looking for, you can wear Big E's." Regardless of eau de old man.

She chewed on that for a moment. "I'll pass."

But she would have worn his boxers?

He swallowed. Hard.

Lily Harrison was so far out of his league, he couldn't remember what his league looked like. She was an elegant bride. Her dark blond hair was done up with strings of tiny pearls.

The simple wedding dress hugged her tall frame from the waist up. She was a beautiful woman, blotchy cheeks and reddened blue eyes excepted, and as sharp as Big E.

The light changed. Conner saw the freeway ahead. He eased down on the gas pedal this time. The old RV rocked into motion.

"Did you guys drive this all the way from Montana?"

"Yes, ma'am."

"You could have flown."

"The plan was to pick up Big E's stepgranddaughter and her friend in Las Vegas and drive them to Montana with a couple of stops along the way." Conner clenched the steering wheel tightly. All those stops. Lily could bail on him at any time. And then there was Big E's stepgranddaughter Pepper, who had more energy than a child on Christmas morning. He knew nothing about the friend she wanted to bring along. What if Lily didn't like them?

Apprehension filled the space between his ears.

Three city gals. One long road trip in an unwieldy vehicle. He tried to tell himself it would be easy.

Tried, and failed.

I should have asked for a triple bonus.

"And then Big E heard about me," Lily said. "And had a change in plans?"

"Yes, ma'am." The important thing was not to panic. He had this under control. Big E trusted him to do this alone.

A car cut him off. Conner hit the brakes. Lily's skirts whooshed and flipped up against the back of her head once more.

"Can you remove those hoops?" One more hard stop and that dress was flipping inside out, exposing...

Do not think about what would be exposed!

Lily sighed. "When it comes to this dress, I'm afraid it's all or nothing."

Commando Cowboy gulped.

"Do you think I'm a bad person?" Lily's question lacked her previous spunk.

"No, ma'am." Conner eased the motor home onto the freeway ramp, pleased at his smooth acceleration, until he noticed the traffic was at a standstill ahead.

"But I left my groom at the altar."

Inwardly, Conner cursed Big E, wishing their roles had been reversed. It might be easier to tell Lily's family she'd fled the scene than to weather Lily's uncertainty. "I...uh... heard what your fiancé said about marrying you." Or not wanting to. Conner spared Lily a glance. "You know. In the hallway. To your dad." He'd seen Lily sag and lean against the wall. But she hadn't cried, and Conner respected her for that.

"You're probably the only person who'd defend me running away." A statement made in the smallest voice yet.

"Me and Big E."

"I'm going to be explaining this for the rest of my life." She heaved a sigh. "Who'll want to marry me now? I mean…" She raised her hands in the air, curling her fingers into loose fists and then dropping them to her lap. "Who could trust a woman who left her last fiancé on their wedding day?"

Lily was right, but it was best not to answer that question and fuel her regrets.

Still, the way she was talking, Conner supposed he'd be dodging quick quips and rhetorical questions all the way to Montana.

"On the bright side, I did get to wear a wedding dress once in my life." She made a sound suspiciously like a choked-off sob. "Check that off my bucket list."

He was stuck in a motor home with a runaway Blackwell bride and traffic on the freeway was at a dead stop. The only thing that could make this worse was if she started to cry.

Lily sucked in air sharply.

Oh, no. Here it comes.

"Can you...?" Her head bowed. Her nose reddened. She wouldn't look at him. "I should..."

No tears. Please.

He'd driven Lily away from her family, which was akin to rounding up a wild horse and removing it from its herd. Of course Lily was upset. But he was here. Ready to offer what comfort he could. *If she just doesn't cry.* He willed Lily to glance his way, to acknowledge his presence, to join the "herd"—his herd. Just until they reached Falcon Creek. Was that too much to ask?

"There's so much my family does for me," she said softly. "I should go back."

Big E wouldn't be happy to hear that. Heck, Conner's bank balance wasn't happy to hear that. But at least she wasn't crying.

"You want to go through with the wedding?" If that was what she really wanted, he'd for sure be a kidnapper if he didn't return her to the church.

"I don't want to marry Danny. But I should at least have told my family..." Her hands twisted loosely in her lap. "I don't have my cell phone. Can I borrow yours?"

Conner hesitated, feeling the press of a rock against him and a hard place. "Sure." He tugged his phone out of his back pocket and handed it to her.

"What's this?" She flipped it open. "I had one of these flip phones in middle school."

"What a coincidence." Conner smirked. "Me, too."

She stared at his outdated device. "I don't know anyone's phone number. Not by heart. They're all in my phone's contacts folder."

That's too bad.

She pressed his buttons with slow, exaggerated movements and read off a number. "Whose is that?"

"My mother's cell phone."

"There are no other numbers in your recent file." Lily frowned. "Didn't Big E call you?"

"No. Why would he? We've been on the road together for days."

She pressed more buttons, again with those overexaggerated movements. "You don't text anyone, either." She glanced up at him and then tried to look past her hoops to the rear of Big E's beloved, dated motor home. "Are you sure you didn't step out of a time warp?"

He chuckled and tipped back the brim of his hat. "Did I mention I'm a cowboy? Those fancy phones don't last very long in the high country." Whereas his flip phone was going on forever.

"What am I supposed to do?" Panic edged her question.

"Trust Big E?" If Big E's grandsons could hear him now, they'd be hooting it up like they were at the Silver Stake bar and it was payday.

"Trust a man I just met who claims to be my grandfather? Trust a cowboy heading for Montana in an old motor home?"

"Yes, ma'am." It would make the next few days that much easier on Conner.

The traffic inched forward.

"I suppose I set myself up for this," Lily muttered. "My dad always says I never look before I leap. Always. And because he won't let me live anything down, I always stood behind my choices, no matter how foolish."

"Conviction says something positive about a person." In Conner's book anyway.

"Not if you're a runaway bride." She scoffed. "Or a cowboy kidnapper."

CHAPTER THREE

JUST WHEN THEY finally broke free of Southern California bumper-to-bumper traffic and Conner could breathe easy, Lily's stomach growled louder than the motor-home engine.

"I'm going to need a pit stop." Lily's dress quivered.

"But we just…" Conner caught the subtle, concerned change in Lily's expression and rephrased. "There's food in the kitchen and a bathroom if you need it."

"You have chips, coffee and soda. That's not food." At his raised brows, she shrugged. "You think I walked into a stranger's motor home without checking everything first? My dad… My *step*dad raised us to be careful."

Conner acknowledged her street smarts with a nod.

"And given that I can't get a seat belt around my dress, I won't be able to squeeze into the little commode cabinet back there."

There was that, too.

"We'll gas up at the next truck stop." They'd have food and clothes. And a map of rest stops near Las Vegas.

She agreed.

Half an hour later they rolled into a large truck stop, one of those grungy places that never seemed completely clean. It was busy. There were vehicles at nearly every gas pump. The diner looked pretty full. The small store had a line at the cash register and the soda fountain.

Conner inched past Lily's skirt and stood. "You need help?"

"Ya think?" She held out her hands.

They were smooth, warm and well-manicured. They fit in his calloused ones like a broken-in pair of leather work gloves. He tugged her to her feet. The skirt had a mind of its own. It shoved her away from the seat and pushed him back onto the couch. She tumbled on top of him, smelling of flowers.

CONNER WAS REMINDED of the pleasant feeling of a woman filling his arms and the languid heat of slow kisses on a cold night.

"Sorry." Lily set her hands on his shoulders and pushed herself up, shoving aside thoughts of kisses in the process. "You must think I'm out of control."

"No, ma'am." She was too elegant to lose control. When they were both standing, Conner helped her down the motor-home steps and into the hot desert air. "I've got a Blackwell Ranch credit card. We can get whatever you need inside."

"From a fine selection of T-shirts and tube socks, I'm sure." She trotted toward the store, skirt bouncing up and down with each step. "So much for pride."

A man opened the door for them. "Vegas bound or returning?"

"Bound." Conner nodded his thanks. "Can't get hitched without a slushie and a hot dog first."

Lily huffed but didn't turn around. She stopped at a display of T-shirts proclaiming the dominance of Mack trucks, chose one quickly, grabbed a pair of sweats and showed them to the salesclerk before hurrying toward the restrooms in the back.

Lily stopped at the door to the ladies' room and turned. She had the most piercing stare. It probed and apologized all at the same time. "I need you to do something for me."

"What?" Cowboy kidnappers had to be careful what they promised to do.

"I need you to help me get out of this dress." Her cheeks bloomed with color.

"Whoa." Conner took a step back, giving her and the troublesome dress some room. Having eloped at eighteen, he hadn't had to deal with frills on his wedding day.

"It took all my sisters to get me into this." Lily stared at her hands before returning her gaze to him. "There are about a hundred little buttons on the back that hide a zipper."

"But…" He was a divorced man who hadn't dated in what seemed like forever, a simple cowboy who'd been told to safely transport a Blackwell to Montana. His fingers itched to touch while his head warned him not to. "Big E would not approve." There. He'd found a boundary to prevent him from crossing into dangerous territory. Conner skirted around Lily and leaned in the open doorway of the ladies' room. "Hello? Woman in need of assistance."

His words echoed and went unanswered.

He circled back around and surveyed the convenience store. Men. Men. Men. At the coffee station. At the gas pumps. Even the clerk was a male. *Really?*

"Calm down, cowboy." Gently smiling, Lily shrugged. "I'm not going to seduce you."

"I knew that." Hadn't stopped his imagination, though. His cheeks flamed with heat. And they kept on flaming when she turned her back for him to begin the disrobing.

I should never have left Montana.

"Are you Big E's foreman or right-hand man or something?"

Small talk. That was exactly what he needed. He laid tentative hands on those tiny buttons. "I hate to disappoint you but I'm just a ranch hand." One more used to girth straps and headstall buckles than delicate pearl fasteners on a wedding dress.

She sighed and her slender shoulders drooped. "I suppose I have relatives in Montana."

"Some." His fingers reached the buttons at the small of her back and he hesitated. Surely, she could move the zipper to her slim hips and wiggle out of this thing. "But…uh… Big E wanted to break the news to them himself. About you being family?" He drew a breath before tackling the pearls draping over the danger zone.

"What?" She sent him a concerned look over her shoulder. "So what am I supposed to tell the Blackwells when I show up on their doorstep?"

"You'll check in as a guest." Would the trail of buttons never end? "The Blackwell Ranch is a working cattle ranch but also has a guest ranch."

"Do you have a horse and everything?"

"I have a horse and everything." He reached the buttons at the gentle curve of her derriere and froze. "That's enough." He prayed that was enough.

Her hands came around, checking his progress. "Now the zipper," she instructed, as cool as a rodeo queen leading her entourage in the Fourth of July parade.

Conner choked on a gulp of air. "Can't you get it?"

"No, I can't." Her head lowered. "I had an accident when I was a kid. A sharp crack to my head and..." She gave a weak attempt at a laugh. "My fine motor skills aren't what they should be."

An image of her clumsily jabbing her finger at his cell phone came to mind. But this time it came with context, a ripple effect of sorrow and empathy for whatever had happened to her and the struggles she must have gone through since.

Conner glanced back into the convenience store. Again, finding only men, he rubbed his palms over his jeans, procrastinating touching her once more. The zipper would reveal skin and underthings.

Lily glanced over her shoulder, a glint of mischief in her blue eyes. "It's a hardship, I know. And as a family member of your employer, it might even be considered inappropriate for me to ask. But I can assure you this is a heroic act."

Conner had never met a woman like Lily, delicate and determined, strong yet vulnerable, gracious when faced with a challenge but handling it with a sharp sense of humor. He liked her, which made him feel guilty about his need to deliver her to Montana over any doubts or regrets.

She sighed. "I bet this day isn't going the way either of us planned."

Conner took the plunge and eased the zipper lower. "You got that right."

"WHAT'S ALL THIS?" Conner stepped next to Lily at the cash register. He'd given her a wide berth since releasing her from her wedding dress and leaving her unaccompanied to shop in the truck stop.

"This is my travel bag." Lily arranged her purchases on the truck stop's counter and drew a big, corset-free breath, which did nothing to dispel the awareness she had for the rawboned cowboy. "Makeup remover. Deodorant. Razor. Toothbrush." The razor handle was bulky and easy to grip. The toothbrush was also bulky and battery powered. Both compensated for her lack of reliable fingers, if she could get the items out of their packaging. But she had a cowboy for that.

"You hungry?" Conner had hung her wedding dress over his forearm, enfolding the broad skirt against his side. The largest hoop nearly touched the ground. He added a can of almonds and some protein bars to her purchases. "You want to eat at the coffee shop next door?"

"Oh, yes. Please." She hadn't eaten since a light breakfast and it was late in the afternoon.

Conner smiled a little. He looked like he never smiled a lot. He gestured toward the items on the counter. "After I pay for this, I'll put your dress and these things in the rig. Why don't you go get us a table?"

"Sure." She walked out of the store with him and then through a set of doors into the attached diner, which had views of the busy gas pumps and the air of hard use. She sank into a booth with duct-taped seats. Now that the wedding dress was off, there was no going back and she wondered how her family's afternoon had gone.

Dad—she had to remember to call him Rudy—would have had the most volatile reaction to her escape.

After an intense argument with Big E, Rudy would have stood on the altar and told the wedding guests the day's events were postponed. He wouldn't say "canceled." *Canceled* equaled defeat, a condition the career naval officer would never accept.

Peyton would have no such qualms about rescheduling. Ever pragmatic, she'd give back any gifts or cards attendees had deposited upon entering the church and promise to return other gifts guests had bought and delivered beforehand.

Fiona and Amanda would man the exit, handing out gracious apologies and helping Lily's elderly guests down the church steps.

Georgie would attend the groom's family in case anyone passed out or suffered an attack of high blood pressure.

Lily hoped her family had stuck around

to enjoy the chicken luncheon and chocolate wedding cake in the church hall. Regardless, Peyton or Amanda would arrange the rest of the food to be donated to a local homeless shelter.

And her groom? Danny would have retreated to the hotel they'd reserved for their wedding night, the one with the prepaid honeymoon suite. He'd be drinking and toasting bullets dodged, having canceled their trip to Hawaii. He'd insisted on buying trip insurance, after all.

Should she worry about Danny when he hadn't wanted to marry her in the first place?

My cold feet make his look frozen in comparison.

Still, a feeling of remorse was building inside her, like cotton in her throat. She'd taken the dishonorable way out. Her family and Danny deserved more from her.

I shouldn't have run away.

But she shouldn't have married him, either.

"Your wedding dress is in the rear storage compartment." Conner slid into a seat across from her, interrupting her thoughts. "It was either that or the bunk above the driver's seat, and I'm afraid I'll be needing you to sleep there tomorrow night. Tonight the bedroom is all yours."

"What you did with my dress… That's okay." Lily wouldn't be wearing it again. She held out her hand. "Can I see your phone again?"

"Why?" He pulled it from his back pocket and handed it over.

Lily opened the phone and checked his call record. *What?* She glanced up at Conner. "It's empty. You didn't call Big E?" Not while she was changing or when he went out to the RV? "And he didn't call you?"

Conner stiffened. "I'm a grown man doing a job. What kind of a man calls his boss every two seconds? Or needs him to call every three? A man like that… He'd be unemployed, that's what."

That spark she'd felt for him in the vestibule returned. He was passionately defending his character. A man like that would be passionate about other things. His home. His spare time. His bride.

"Sorry." Lily handed his phone back, impressed by his cowboy code. "Did you always want to be a cowboy?"

Did you always have this big honorable streak?

Did all cowboys? Did Big E? Did Thomas? Was Thomas even a cowboy? Was he alive?

So many questions. She rubbed the back of her neck. It was stiff from having to hold her head up all this time.

"I was raised on a ranch," Conner said, as if that explained everything.

"Following in your father's footsteps, no doubt." Lily nodded. Conner was probably a tenth-generation cowboy, as was Big E, she supposed.

"I never knew my father. He took off the day my mother told him she was pregnant." A shadow passed over Conner's angular face. "The ranch is my mother's. Or it was. I took over the paper on it when I turned eighteen because she'd been in a car accident."

Goose bumps rose on her skin at the word *accident*. "But she's okay? She called you yesterday." According to his phone's call log.

"Like you, she'd say she's fine." But the shadow remained over his features.

The rest of his words sank in, the ones about his father. "Was your dad's name on your birth certificate?" She backpedaled when confronted with his stone-faced stare. "I apologize. It's none of my business. I'm not normally so rude." She didn't usually tease men about their underwear preferences, either.

Rudy wouldn't approve of anything she was doing today.

Conner rubbed his jaw as if rubbing away the hurt and stigma of being fatherless. "I suppose it's understandable, given the day you've had."

Yes, it'd been quite a day. Hearing that Danny didn't want to marry her. Hearing that Rudy had forced him into it. Meeting a grandfather she'd never known existed. Walking out on her wedding. And heading to meet a new family in Montana.

Mayhem *should have been my middle name.*

Tears filled her eyes.

Conner sat back in his seat, a look of horror on his face.

"I'm sorry." She wiped away a tear. "I'm not usually weepy, either."

The approaching waitress paused midstep, staring at Lily's face. She spun away.

Conner cleared his throat, probably wishing he could bolt from Lily's drama the way their server had. "What are you? Usually, I mean."

"I'm an adventure tour guide," she told him without preamble and with some pride.

"A-a what?"

"I have my own adventure tour company. I take people on unique outdoor excursions— high-altitude wilderness hikes, paddleboarding yoga, white-water rafting, kayaking with killer whales." She warmed to the topic, which was easier to discuss than her abandoned wedding or her newly found lineage. "I arrange tours several times a month through online book- ings. And I reserve one weekend a month for Danny and me to do something out of the or- dinary." Something that might be toned down a bit for her clientele and her physical capa- bilities.

Conner cleared his throat again. "Aren't you a little old to be a camp counselor?"

It was Lily's turn to stiffen. "You sound like my...like Rudy." Or that small inner voice she tried to squelch in her head, the one that had been increasingly cautioning her to keep both feet firmly on the ground when Danny proposed something new. "Don't cast stones. Didn't you say you worked on a *dude* ranch? Aren't you on a road trip to pick up *guests*?"

"Ouch." There was a hint of a twinkle in

his eye. "In my defense, I also contribute to Blackwell cattle ranching and help the ranch manager with the books sometimes."

A shiny black truck pulled up to the gas pump near their window. It was the same color, make and model as Danny's. A dark-haired man—a dead ringer for Danny—hopped out.

Lily's body flushed with adrenaline. She turned in her seat, ready to run for the back door. But then common sense—something she'd been missing earlier—prevailed.

Danny isn't coming after me. Why would he? He doesn't want to marry me.

Conner stared at her, twinkle-less. He saw too much with those deep brown eyes.

Lily faced front, waving the waitress over, eager to put more miles between them and San Diego.

What had they been talking about? Ah, yes. Job choices. "In my defense, my business is thriving and I can't type worth a darn, so most office jobs are out." She smiled up at their waitress. "I'd like a chocolate milkshake and French fries. It's been that kind of day."

"Same," Conner said, completely surprising her. "But put a double cheeseburger on the side of both orders." He waved a hand in

Lily's direction. "We camp counselors need to stick together and you need more than protein bars and nuts."

"Apparently, I need a whole new life." Lily nodded, staring down at the truck logo emblazoned across her chest. The sweats were too big around the waist and severely short for her tall frame. Her clothes clashed with her sophisticated hairstyle and sparkly white sneakers. "Can we stop at a mall or something before we pick up those other guests of yours? My appearance says my life is at an all-time low." It was, but that didn't mean she had to let the world know it.

"You've discovered you've got some pride left?"

"I have indeed."

CHAPTER FOUR

NORMALLY, WHEN CONNER was on a road trip, he slept out under the stars, roughing it.

Since he'd left Falcon Creek, Conner had been sleeping on the convertible bed that was the motor home's dining table. It wasn't luxurious. He didn't fit. He slept diagonally and his feet hung out over the edge.

On the trip out west, he'd been lulled to sleep by Big E's snoring, which was like listening to waves regularly crashing on a beach. Loud waves that covered the noise semitrucks made when they pulled in and out of the rest stops where he and Big E parked each night. Tonight the sounds coming out of the motor home's bedroom weren't regular or soothing.

This Blackwell wasn't snoring. She was crying.

Using the meager light shining through the windows, Conner got up and opened a couple of kitchen cupboards. A few short steps later and he stood at the bedroom threshold.

"Lily?" He rapped on the door. "Are you awake?"

"Yes." The motor home shifted as she got up. The door swung open.

Her hair tumbled down in stiff loops. Because of her finger limitations, he'd helped her remove the hairpins and pearl strands earlier, but she was in need of a shower and a shampoo. The truck stop T-shirt hung loosely from her shoulders and the sweats bagged at her hips. She was a wreck.

A beautiful disaster.

Like me, without the beautiful part.

Not to mention Lily had more swagger than he did. She was in the risk business, whereas he was now risk averse. As a business owner, she was undoubtedly smart and tough. As a runaway bride, she was in need of a stiff drink.

He could use one himself.

Conner handed Lily a glass tumbler with a shot of whiskey in it. "To help you sleep."

Without a word, she took the glass in both hands and knocked the alcohol back. And then she bent over, coughing. "I'm wide-awake now. And done crying."

Fatigue pounded at Conner's temples as he poured a drink for himself. His strategy to get some peace and quiet was backfiring. A shift in tactics was necessary. "You can see the stars from the front seat." And maybe if she was quiet, he could crawl back in his short bed and fall asleep.

"I love looking at the stars." Lily asked him to pour her another shot of whiskey and made her way past him to the passenger seat, again carrying her drink with both hands as if she was afraid of dropping it. She set her glass carefully on the center console and peered out.

He sat next to her just as his cell phone rang. It had been charging next to her drink.

Lily lunged for the phone, fumbling to get it open. "Hello? Big E?" There was a plea in her voice. "Oh. No. You've reached Conner's phone. I was just—"

Conner set his whiskey on the center console and extended his hand. "It's for me." He hadn't called home this evening.

"My name is Lily. I'm..." Lily turned wide eyes Conner's way. "I'm road-tripping with Conner." She gasped. "No. Nothing like that."

Conner took possession of his phone, a feat easier than he'd expected since Lily's grip was loose. "Mom? What's wrong? Couldn't you sleep?"

"Couldn't *I* sleep? Let me turn that around. Did I interrupt something?" His mother sounded as if she had and was happy about it, too. "You should call before you enter the uninterruptible, get-busy time zone."

Whoa, Nelly. "Things were a little hectic today, Mom. I meant to call and then I realized it was too late."

"Too hectic? I want to meet the woman who made things too hectic." His mother chuckled.

"How are things at home?" Conner braced himself for bad news. It was always bad news. The Rocking H was like an old jalopy, kept running with a rubber band and a tube of Krazy Glue.

"Well, that stallion of yours made his way into the barn pasture again." She harrumphed. "You should have sold him to one of those fancy stables back east. He's a jumper, all right."

Conner's back tensed.

"And there are signs a fox is trying to get into my henhouse." Anger shook her words. His mother made small change selling fresh eggs. And those hens? They were dear to her.

"Same old, same old." Conner embraced

the concept of bad luck at the Rocking H. He embraced it so hard, his back spasmed.

"It wouldn't be that way if you came back to the Rocking H full-time." She was tapping something. A pencil most likely. She enjoyed her crossword puzzle books.

"We've talked about this." It wasn't happening.

"We'll talk about it until you come to your senses. You belong here." Such finality. Even the tapping stopped.

"With chickens and stubborn stallions?" Conner's gaze drifted to Lily. She belonged to the Blackwell Ranch. To pedigreed cattle and luxury accommodations.

"Yes to all of it." His mother huffed. "Are you still planning to be home in Falcon Creek by Wednesday?"

"Yes, ma'am. If not sooner."

"Good. Then I'll let you get back to your fast-paced lifestyle. Make good choices, son." She hung up.

Conner closed his phone and drained his drink.

"This is eye-opening. You call your mom every night?" Lily sipped her whiskey, holding the tumbler with both hands. "You accompany an old man cross-country. You pick up Blackwell relatives for road trips. You're a nice guy, Conner."

He wasn't feeling nice. His sleep deprivation was letting attraction to Lily slip in. Her long legs, the graceful arch of her neck and the mess of curls covering her shoulders were mesmerizing. Her pluck and sharp wit were intriguing. He wondered what she'd feel like in his arms, how she'd react to his kiss.

Conner rubbed a hand over his face. He needed that bonus money more than he needed to satisfy his curiosity about Lily. "Make good choices." He scoffed.

"Always good advice." Lily sipped her drink and stared out the windshield. "Everything okay at home?"

The darkness. The intimacy. The whiskey.

Tidbits of his life pressed at the back of his throat, pushing for a share. He tightened his lips together. Cowboys like him didn't spill the details of their lives. They weathered storms and didn't break.

Minutes passed.

Lily propped her bare feet on the dashboard and sighed. Her toenails were painted a soft pink. Today she'd worn tennis shoes instead of heels. She drank whiskey and took people on adventures, not trail rides or shopping trips like he did. He wanted to know more about her. Montana was a long stretch away. There was plenty of time to learn more about her. But in the grand scheme of things, he should need to know less.

Alcohol burned the back of his throat and spread heat through his chest.

"My mom thinks we're hooking up," he admitted, completely without meaning to. "I'm an only child, and since my marriage failed, she's been pushing for grandchildren."

"And you don't like her to get ideas. I can apologize to her now or when you call her tomorrow. Although I've been thinking…" Lily sounded distant, detached. "You should drop me off in Vegas tomorrow. I'll find a way to contact my family and get back home."

A low growl filled his throat. He claimed her drink and swallowed the rest. "You're going back to *him*?" Conner didn't know why that should bother him. They were strangers.

Other than the fact that I practically undressed her.

He should be thinking of his double bonus, which he wouldn't receive if Lily didn't set foot in Montana in a few days.

"My family will be—"

"Big E is—"

They both stopped, having talked over each other.

"I'm feeling a little overwhelmed," Lily said in that quiet voice that he hated, the one that implied in tone that she was insignificant. "The world is a scary place when you have a weakness."

"If you're talking about those fingers of yours, you don't need a husband to pick up that slack."

She scoffed. "Tell that to Rudy." Spoken like she was ready to turn around and head back to a deal with the devil.

Anger and frustration released a sharp memory...

Mom having fallen in the living room. Him running to her aid, only to be pushed away.

"I love you, son," she'd said staunchly. "But coddling won't do me any good. I need to claw my way back to independence."

He'd watched while she pulled herself up from the floor. She'd been rejecting his help and forcing him to watch her struggle ever since. Which partially explained his willingness to work for the Blackwells. And partially explained the anger and frustration he felt when a woman like Lily let her self-image be dictated by someone else. His mother would never let that happen.

Conner decided then and there to do everything in his power to support Lily to keep her from feeling insignificant.

Starting with keeping her on the road to Montana.

He winced. He had the best of intentions and the worst of motives.

"Lily, your dad isn't totally to blame, is he? You knew you didn't want to marry that guy when he proposed," Conner accused, emboldened by the shadows, the old memory and the whiskey. "And you've been back in that bedroom reliving and rewriting every moment of the past couple months as if you could have avoided this disaster."

"How did you…?" Lily wrapped her arms around her waist.

"You're not the only person who's ever made mistakes and harbored regrets." Something had come over him. Something that wanted to lash out, that refused to settle behind proper manners and respect for things that weren't any of his business. "But that's completely separate from whatever limitations you have in your fingers. Just get on with it."

"I am." There. She sounded like she'd rediscovered her inner strength.

"Good. Because it'd be a shame to take you back to your unappreciative groom." Harsh words indeed, ones that made her gasp. What was happening to him? Why did she elicit such an intense response from him?

Because I know what it's like to turn right when your family wants you to turn left.

He'd learned his limitations where running the Rocking H and training horses were concerned.

Regardless, he needed to tread carefully so that he didn't back Lily into a corner.

Kudos to her. She didn't crumple when facing confrontation. "You think I'm wishy-washy." Not a question. "Maybe I need to get out of my head and talk this through before I can move forward." Her arms unfurled and her words turned defensive. "I'm sorry if you were the only one around to hear me."

Hear her cry, she meant.

She was hurting. Conner drew a calming breath. "Your family wants you to get married. You may be feeling overwhelmed, but the worst thing you could do is go back right now and marry someone you don't love."

I'm becoming a good liar.

"There's no valid reason for me to go to Montana," she countered evasively. "Big E doesn't want my Blackwell family to know who I am. The worst thing I could do is go to a place I'm not wanted." Lily wiggled her bare toes. "I'd like to know about my father, and Big E never met him. I won't find any answers in Montana."

"You'll find more than if you hunker down in California." Conner ran his finger around the rim of her whiskey glass. "There's a lot of history around Falcon Creek and the Black-well Ranch. You might not get to know your father there, but you'll learn more about your family roots."

"By talking to people who don't know I'm a relation?"

He scowled. "By walking the land of your ancestors. By realizing they planted the trees that give you shade. By acknowledging the sacrifices they made to buy every acre of land. By knowing they wanted to create something real and lasting." His scowl deep-ened, not because Lily was arguing with him but because he hadn't thought about his heri-tage in those terms before. His chest burned with more than alcohol. Regret had a bitter sting. "At the Rocking H, we still have my great-great granddad's buckboard wagon. I heard tell he brought his bride home with it. And the family's branding irons still hang in our barn. Some are over a hundred years old. And our barn itself... It's seen a lot of memorable horses, including some used in the Pony Express. Some of my horses have made their mark in the world, too."

"How so?"

Too late, he realized he'd been sharing tidbits. "Cutting horses I've trained. Mustangs, mostly." Misfits like himself, if truth be told.

I won't be telling her that.

Lily angled toward him in her seat, hugging her knees. "You train horses *and* work full-time for Big E?"

"Not anymore." The recollection of a rattling metal paddock rail against his back and sweaty horseflesh crushing his chest had him fighting off a cringe, the memory of pain and a real stab of fear. He thought he'd beaten that fear a long time ago. He thought he'd chalked it up to an amateur horse trainer's mistake.

She waited to hear more. He left her waiting.

"I should go to bed," she said finally, returning to that flat, small voice. "And tomorrow—"

"We could look up some of your family's

phone numbers when we get to Vegas." Pepper was bound to have skills in that department. She'd just graduated college and, being young, likely had a fancy phone. Those things came in handy sometimes, like when it came to saving bonuses. "You might feel better if you touch base with someone, like a sympathetic sister."

Even if one of her siblings was sympathetic, there'd most likely be an argument, one which hopefully strengthened Lily's resolve to continue to Montana.

Lily unfurled those long legs. "Face-to-face. Phone. Email." She shook her head. "No matter the method, I know whoever I get in touch with, I'm not going to get a word in edgewise."

And they'd want her back in the safety of the family fold. There had to be some way to reach out without letting them influence her. This was bad. Conner could feel the bonus money slipping through his fingers.

And then inspiration struck. "What about the good old US mail?"

She stared at him blankly.

"We could pick up a postcard. You remember your home address, don't you?"

"Yes, but…"

Help me out here. "Instead of changing directions every few minutes, why don't you stick to the road ahead?"

"It's tempting, but if I stay with you, I'll only cause trouble." She held her head high, but that didn't mean she did so with confidence. "I'm good at causing trouble."

"I can take a little trouble." Conner hoped that was true.

THE DAY AFTER she was supposed to be married, Lily sneaked a peek at Conner from behind her new pair of sunglasses, trying to figure out why he struck her as attractive.

It's the hat.

Or that straight posture.

Or the way his smiles are slow to build.

Lily had spent the morning trying to figure it out. It was coming up on noon and the August sun was already heating Vegas to the extreme.

She'd showered in the motor home at first light and they'd driven the rest of the way to Las Vegas, arriving just past 9:00 a.m. They'd ordered breakfast sandwiches and black coffee from a fast-food place. And then Conner had taken her shopping at an outlet mall. She'd filled a small suitcase with clothing, items without buttons or zippers. They'd found a postcard during their shopping trip—a picture of the Welcome to Las Vegas sign. She'd scribbled a brief note: *Tell Danny he doesn't have to watch out for me anymore.* And Conner had stamped it and dropped it in a mailbox.

When they'd left the mall, the back of her T-shirt had been damp before they'd reached the motor home. Now she had two vents blowing on her and it was barely enough to keep her cool. It didn't help that Commando Cowboy was her driver.

Maybe I'm attracted to the way he blushes—when I joked about his drawers, when I asked him to undress me, when I went into the underwear section of that store this morning.

The enigma of Conner kept her mind off the sting of being a runaway bride. Mostly...

She imagined Conner and her former fiancé standing together. Danny was handsome in that Southern California, military way. Great posture, tons of confidence, thick black hair. But he'd never made Lily's heart stutter.

Conner did that with one long, slow look. He wasn't conventionally handsome. Some might have considered him too lean. Others might have said his face was too long. But when she looked at him, something fluttered in her chest. When she talked to him, something sparked in her veins. When he spoke, his deep voice soothed something within. And when he got angry on her behalf, as he'd done last night when she'd implied her fingers were an accepted liability by Rudy and Danny, that intensity took her breath.

That was a lot of somethings. And added together they made her wonder: *How would I feel if I kissed him?*

Which was completely inappropriate for a woman who'd been planning to get married to someone else twenty-four hours ago.

"You're awfully quiet this morning," Conner noted. "Regrets?"

"Of course." Although each mile away from San Diego allowed her to breathe easier.

He gave her a quick once-over. "Those regrets aren't as bad as they were yesterday."

"Remind me not to play poker with you."

Conner chuckled. He turned into the parking lot of an apartment complex. A trio of those beige stucco places that blended into the landscape, be it desert or the suburbs.

"I've forgotten. Which Blackwell are we picking up?" Had he told her? If he had, she'd been too distraught to remember.

Conner brought the motor home to a halt in front of the last building and tooted the horn. "We're taking Dorothy's stepgranddaughter and her best friend to the Blackwell Ranch."

Lily unbuckled her seat belt. "Who's Dorothy?"

"Big E's wife. His first wife. They were divorced for a long time before they remarried and there were a couple of marriages in between." Conner put the motor home in Park, leaving the air conditioner on, and got out.

Immediately, a gust of warm air embraced Lily as she followed him down the steps. Truth be told, her questions about her Blackwell family had been cast aside, given the fallout from her canceled wedding. "The reason for me being incognito becomes clear." Dorothy might be sensitive about Big E's sowing of wild oats. Gone was the relief that time and distance from her wedding had given her. "It'll be awkward when Big E's family finds out who I am."

"Yes, ma'am." That was Conner, man of few words. He took a slip of paper from his pocket, checked the address and then stared at the apartment complex.

"I should go back to California." Her life was complicated enough without tap-dancing around Blackwell territory. Let Peyton unravel the secret of Thomas Blackwell. She enjoyed mysteries.

"What happened to getting on with it?" Conner challenged her without even turning to look at her. "Don't lose your nerve. I have a plan for you once we get to Montana."

Be still, my heart.

If only I was in a space to be looking for a relationship.

Duly chastised, she said, "Well, don't keep it to yourself, cowboy. But please, don't tell me your plan is to keep me far away from the family."

"Why, yes, ma'am. You're a good guesser."

"That's a totally sucky plan." And it annoyed her that he called her *ma'am.* "Why did I agree to come?"

"To give you time to reevaluate marriage without the pressure to get hitched?" He continued to study the apartment building. "To save you the embarrassment of facing all your wedding guests?"

"I thought I was getting in touch with my roots." Lily twisted her long hair over one shoulder. "Blackwells, buckboards and branding irons."

Conner rocked on his heels, causing his

boots to creak. "That's my ranch. Minus the Blackwells."

"Right." It was upsetting to realize she was more interested in seeing the Rocking H than the Blackwell Ranch. Conner's property seemed to have more cowboy street cred, while the Blackwell Ranch and its dude ranchiness sounded like an amusement park experience. She'd never take her clients there.

A blonde and a brunette in dresses and sandals appeared on a high outdoor stairwell, giggling and wheeling large suitcases. Even three floors up, the amount of hair product and makeup was noticeable. Their poshness was intimidating to a woman like Lily, who didn't normally wear makeup and had forgotten to purchase hair product at the truck stop. Her hair was as limp as a spent tulip.

"Hello, Conner." The brunette waved at them before heading down, luggage clattering. "Where's Big E?"

"He sends his regrets." Conner walked over to meet them at the landing. "Never fear. We're sticking to your itinerary. I have my orders."

The two women arrived and turned their luggage over to Conner, strolling toward the RV with the confident sway of the high-heel initiated. The brunette was compact. Her hair was long and thick, and fell to her shoulder blades with a soft wave. The blonde's hair was thinner and curlier, which added dimension to her slight frame. Despite their heels, Lily towered over them both.

"I'm Pepper." The brunette practically wiggled with happiness as she approached Lily. *"The bride."*

Lily's mouth went dry. Conner hadn't warned her about this.

Here was her deal breaker. A reason to return home.

"And this is Natalie, my maid of honor." Pepper eyed Lily and then squealed, throwing her arms around her. "Oh, my gosh! You must be Ken's cousin." She drew back to get a good look at Lily. "Ken said you might cancel and Big E promised he'd be at the airport when your plane landed today just in case. But…" She curled her shoulders inward and gave Lily the sweetest of smiles. "I'm blanking on your name. This is horrible. You're my fiancé's cousin and I… Can you forgive me?"

"Yes," Lily murmured, not daring to look at Conner. "I'm Lily."

"This is going to be so much fun." Pepper

hugged Lily a second time as if she was her long-lost cousin.

Which in a way, I am.

"A week with my bestie and my new cousin," Pepper gushed. "I'm so glad we'll get a chance to get to know each other before the rest of the wedding party shows up at the ranch on Thursday."

"Woop-woop," Natalie chimed in, snapping her gum.

Here was Lily's chance to correct Pepper's assumption. Conner knew it, as well. He stared at Lily, arching a brow.

"You're going to love my grandma Dot," Pepper went on, climbing into the motor home. "She's the best."

Grandma Dot. Dorothy. Big E's wife.

This was Lily's ticket into the Blackwell inner circle. "I can't wait to meet her. And, gosh, wouldn't it be cool to surprise Ken in Montana?" As in, don't tell Ken his nonexistent cousin Lily was along for the ride.

Pepper clapped her hands. "Ken loves surprises!"

"Gosh, Lily." Conner went big on the sarcasm as he took Lily's arm and drew her away from the motor home, boots creaking. "This is one of those leap-before-you-look moments.

Best come up with a different cover story before any damage is done."

"You could have told me there'd be another bride on this trip." Lily tugged her arm free. "Or what the itinerary was. I'll make you a deal. If you come clean about whatever else you're keeping from me, I'll come clean with Pepper. Or at least tell her whatever lie you'd like me to use."

Conner scowled. Oh, he had secrets, all right. Juicy secrets, by the look of him.

When he didn't tell her what they were, Lily hurried up the motor-home steps, evading the Vegas heat and Conner.

Pepper and Natalie sat at the dining room table, cell phones out. True best friends, their phone cases matched—rose gold with big chunks of glitter.

"Did Ken fill you in on the details of our girls' trip and the wedding?" Pepper wriggled like a puppy awaiting a treat. "We're going full-on Western. Today we're going to get outfitted like cowgirls and then we're going to a shooting range that rents guns of the Old West. On the way to Montana, we're stopping at an outdoor concert, a spa and a honky-tonk." Pepper high-fived her maid of honor.

"Woop-woop." Natalie made duck lips and took a selfie.

"It sounds like tons of fun." Lily took her place in the passenger seat, turning sideways to face them. "What made you choose the Blackwell Ranch for your wedding? Does it have special significance for you?"

Conner swooped past her to take the driver's seat, whispering darkly, "Why don't you just read Pepper her rights and shine a light in her face during your interrogation?"

Lily shushed him, pressing her hand over his mouth and drawing it back just as quickly. Her fingers tingled from the touch.

Conner faced the windshield, cheeks turning red.

"Oh, my goodness." Pepper flung herself into the conversation the way she seemed to fling herself at everything. "The Blackwell Ranch? It's *the* wedding destination in the upper western states. I'm lucky Grandma Dot lives there because it has a two-year waiting list, even though it's out in the sticks of Montana. I've dreamed of a Western-themed ceremony since I was eleven. And guess what? My bridesmaids and I are going to ride down the aisle! Isn't that fabulous?"

"Woop-woop," Natalie said, but with less

enthusiasm than before. She was preoccupied editing her selfie.

"You're going to ride in your wedding dress?" Now, that would be something to see.

Pepper assured her that riding sidesaddle was as easy as pie. She'd apparently hired a riding coach for herself and her bridesmaids.

"Our first stop is the Painted Pony Western Warehouse," Conner announced with what sounded like false cheer. "Cowgirl duds for everyone, compliments of Big E, including you, Ken's cousin."

Lily refused to be baited.

"Can't wait." Pepper's attention was caught by her phone. "You totally rock that blouse, Nat. Which filter is that? It makes your skin glow."

"Wow, Conner." Lily couldn't resist a poke at her escort now that the wedding party was distracted. "This is the second time you'll have taken a woman clothes shopping in one day. What a hardship this job must be for you."

"Cowboys are trained to withstand the most trying conditions." Still speaking in a testy tone of voice, Conner settled his cowboy hat more firmly on his head before putting the motor home into gear.

"I think you meant the hot weather is try-ing," Lily teased. "Women are never trying."

Pepper and Natalie's high-pitched laughter filled the motor home.

He came to a stop at the exit and gave Lily one of those deliberate looks that made her blood race. "*Trying* is being a chauffeur for the next three days, a tour guide for brides and—"

"Point taken," Lily said before he could ref-erence runaway brides, raising a hand as if to cover his mouth once more.

His eyes widened but he didn't move an inch.

What am I doing?

Her hand fell to her side, but she couldn't let go of the impression of his warm lips or endearing blush.

Nearly two hours later, when Pepper and Natalie had finally found matching boots, jeans and Western tops, and Lily had given in to peer pressure and selected a pair of plain brown boots, Conner turned the motor home north, while Pepper and Natalie napped on Big E's bed, worn out by shopping.

"They're just babies." Lily shifted sideways in her seat, which allowed her a better view of Conner. "Pepper is younger than my sister Fiona. And she's only been engaged since May, pursuant to her carefully constructed life plan." Which involved being married to a mature man before she started dental school.

"You're going to fault her for being in love?" Oh, there was sarcasm in Conner's voice, all right.

"With the right guy? No." But Pepper's life plan felt more methodical than passion-driven. "You mentioned you were married?"

"Guilty."

"And divorced?"

"Also guilty." His jaw set.

"And that you took over the Rocking H when you were eighteen." Holy smokes, that was young. "You married your high school sweetheart."

He flashed her a grimace that confirmed her theory.

On a roll, Lily grinned. She did enjoy pushing his buttons. "You married your high school sweetie. That's almost as cheesy as me marrying my childhood BFF."

"No, ma'am." He waggled a finger her way. "I wasn't coerced to the altar."

They'd had enough conversations about her situation. She wanted to know more about Conner. "You used to train horses on your

ranch and now you work for the Blackwells."
Curiosity had her leaning forward, ready to
hang on every word. "What happened?"

"Nothing happened." Conner's lips pursed.

"I don't believe that. Did your ex leave and
take your prize horse with her?"

"No, ma'am."

Ma'am. The term was beginning to rankle.
"Come on. You know practically everything
about me."

He scoffed. "No, ma'am."

She drew herself up regally. "My name is
Lily."

"Yes, ma—"

"Lily," she reiterated. "Now, back to you—
Conner Hannah, horse trainer and ranch
owner. You can't just be Big E's motor-home
driver, ranch hand and... I've forgotten what
else it is you do there." It had been a long list.

"Why can't I?" He cocked a brow. "It's an
honest living."

"Because you're too smart." Too sexy. Too
much of a mystery. She suspected there was
much more to him hidden beneath all that
stoic exterior.

"I'm not. I just happen to be a good judge
of character—both human and equine."

"Smart," Lily said again. "Admit it. There's

more to you than meets the eye." And a story, too, she'd bet.

"Not all smart people control their destinies." He pointed a finger at Lily. "Not everyone is cut out to be Elias Blackwell."

"Oh? Why is that?"

Conner shook his head.

If Lily wanted details on the Blackwells before they reached their destination, she was going to have to get them out of Pepper.

CHAPTER FIVE

BIG E HAD suggested Clark's OK Corral in Elko for Pepper's Western experience because they offered historic gun rentals, specifically six-shooters. He'd thought Pepper's Western-themed wedding needed a real dose of Western.

Personally, Conner didn't think the college-age young ladies had a strong yen for shooting. They were on a quest for photos that were shareable on their social media accounts. And they recorded everything—cars broken down on the side of the highway, shopping trips, conversations, Conner driving. Stuff no one but the duo cared about.

When did I become so jaded?

Sadly, he knew the exact date and time to answer that question. Fifteen years ago last June.

His mother's car accident had gutted him. A semitruck had plowed into her out by the interstate. Her body was swollen from what the doctors had called *trauma*. And both her legs were broken, reconstructed with metal rods. She had more tubing coming out of her than a newfangled truck engine.

Overnight he'd aged twice his eighteen years.

"I need to see Joe Thompson," his mama had told Conner from her hospital bed after lifesaving surgery.

Conner shook his head. Joe was the only attorney in town. "You're not dying." He clutched his girlfriend Tanya's hand all the same, grateful that she'd come with him, because only the presence of an audience kept him from falling apart. "You don't need a will, Mom."

"That's right," she rasped, throat dry since they'd just removed her breathing tube. Even with her swollen features, Conner recognized the determined glint in her eye. "I won't need a will if I give the ranch to you outright. You're the last Hannah. It'll be yours some-day anyway."

"I don't want it." He'd just graduated from high school two days ago. He'd spent the night of graduation drinking with his buddies out by Falcon Creek, happy to be free of text-books and tests. His future had seemed limitless, awaiting his decision. "You're going to bounce back. We don't need Mr. Thompson."

"I won't be able to run the ranch for months." She'd drawn a wheezy breath, one that sent the machines hooked up to her beeping like crazy.

A nurse poked her head in the door. "Don't upset her or you'll have to leave."

"Yes, ma'am," he'd said to both the nurse and his mother, accepting his childhood was over. "I'll get Mr. Thompson up here." And when he and Tanya walked out of the hospital later, he'd turned to her and said, "Wanna get married?" Because he'd always known he'd run the ranch someday, have a wife and settle down. Might just as well start now.

And as simple as that, it was done.

If only running the Rocking H was that simple.

As soon as Conner parked the motor home in Elko, Pepper and Natalie skipped down the steps and headed for the shooting range, the exterior of which was painted to look like a Wild West saloon. They paused out in front for some selfies, calling to Lily to join them.

Conner offered Lily a hand down. "Have you ever shot a gun before?"

"No. And I've never had the inclination to, either." She exited at a snail's pace, walking carefully in her new cowboy boots. She wore leggings, not jeans, and a red pullover tunic, not a button-down.

"Be careful." He was slow letting her go.

"Come on, Lily." Pepper called from the front door. When Lily joined her, Pepper linked their arms as if they were the closest friends. "Every year since I was eleven, Grandma Dot took me to a local shooting range for my birthday. She used to tell me stories about her Western wedding and life on the ranch. She's a cowgirl even though she lived in the Las Vegas suburbs until she remarried Big E. I wish I were marrying a cowboy like she did, but Ken is an insurance salesman. It's a growth industry because everybody needs insurance."

Conner supposed there was truth to that.

"Did Dorothy ride down the aisle?" Lily asked.

"Oh, yes. She's the inspiration of my life plan. I want to be just like her."

Natalie drew her imaginary guns for the next photo. "She's a dentist?"

"I said inspiration, not a blueprint." Pepper had a way of giving a set-down without losing that bubbly smile of hers.

The women posed for a few more photos.

Lily had a nice smile. She seemed genuinely fond of Pepper, laughing at her enthusiastic observations and seemingly not at all bothered by her own deception.

Not for the first time since the misunderstanding of Lily's relationship to the groom, Conner wondered how Big E would want him to play the situation. Someone was going to get offended when they learned they'd been duped, and he could guarantee Lily would receive blowback by pretending to be Ken's cousin. But what could he do? He hadn't corrected Pepper's impression. Now he was just as guilty as Lily was. Because her deception was good for him. It kept her on the ride to Montana.

"Hurry up, Conner." Pepper led the women inside. "You're paying."

He certainly was. He only hoped he didn't pay later, too.

The interior of the shooting range continued the Old West theme. The walls were covered in barn wood. A player piano filled the room with music. It was plain corny. Except for the requisite slot machines, which were plain tacky.

"Grandma Dot always says a woman has to know more about the world than her man if she's gonna defend her heart." Pepper practically skipped to the counter, Natalie in her wake. "Grandma Dot's a Renaissance woman. Big E told me he can't put anything over on her."

Lily's steps slowed.

"Second thoughts?" Conner asked, catching up to her.

"Nope." Lily shook her head. "Thirds."

The women were given sound-canceling headphones, safety glasses, a box with bullets and an unloaded six-shooter, and then assigned a shooting lane. They received instruction on gun safety, and then were shown how to load, aim and fire.

"You're not shooting?" Lily asked Conner.

"No, ma'am. I'm just the help." For the first time in two years, his position annoyed him. It looked like fun. Conner took his place against the back wall.

Almost immediately, Pepper and Natalie began shooting.

Lily hemmed and hawed. Finally, she flagged down the gun trainer and shouted something Conner didn't catch. The man nodded and pressed a button so her target—a Wild West gunslinger—slid along the pulley to her. He returned a moment later with a replacement target—a traditional series of concentric circles.

"I couldn't kill a fly," Lily shouted to Conner by way of explanation.

She made him want to forget that he was someone else's employee. She made him want to remember what it was like to walk tall as the owner of a ranch in Falcon Creek. She made him want things he hadn't dreamed of in years.

His other two charges were striking poses and shooting their guns without hitting their targets. What they lacked in accuracy, they made up for with enthusiasm.

Lily fidgeted. Shifting her feet, spinning the empty chamber. She picked up a bullet and just as quickly dropped it. She bent to retrieve it and lost her balance in those stiff new boots. She banged into the wall of the shooting station headfirst.

"I got you." Conner rushed forward to help her up, grabbing the stray bullet in the process.

"Wow!" Lily shouted. "What a kick."

For a moment he thought she meant the impact of being in his arms. But that was just a small-town cowboy's imagination. Most likely Lily was commenting on hitting her head. She gingerly touched her temple.

He made sure she was steady before dropping the bullet into her box and stepping back, sliding his hands into his back pockets. Lily Harrison was off-limits. He was just a broke cowboy doing a job.

Lily frowned at her gun.

He returned to her side and tapped her shoulder so she could see him speak. "You don't have to do this."

"Good." She placed her gun back in the plastic box, looking relieved.

Conner led her away from the stations and out to a table near the player piano. He bought a couple of sodas and bags of chips. She didn't reach for either, looking as down as she'd been yesterday.

He opened both sodas and chip bags, letting her choose what she wanted while he returned to the counter. He came back with a borrowed pen and a black-and-white picture postcard of a woman wearing a buckskin outfit and holding a shotgun.

"I'm not sure I have anything more to say to my family." Lily smiled weakly at the postcard. "What just happened is the reason my dad pushed Danny to marry me."

"Because you can't load a gun?" Conner deadpanned. She was looking like her finger dexterity was the end of the world.

She lifted her chin. "So much in the world today requires small, deliberate finger movements."

"You've blown this all out of proportion." Or perhaps that was her dad and that groom of hers.

"Normally, I'm fine." Lily curled her fingers. "Toss me a ball and I'll catch it. Give me an oar and I'll row. But there are times when I want to do something—tie a shoe, braid my hair, pull a rip cord on a parachute—and it's like a communication failure between my brain and my fingers."

"I don't see—"

"I'm an adventure tour guide," she said, as if this explained everything, using the same tone of voice his mother had employed in the hospital when she'd asked for her lawyer over a decade ago.

Conner switched tracks from argument to tease. "I thought we agreed you and I are more like camp counselors." He'd downgrade himself from ranch hand if she'd go easy on herself.

"I take people into the wilderness and on

the water." Lily raised her voice, staring at the ceiling instead of him. "My dad—*Rudy*—is deathly afraid that my disability—"

"Now, that's taking it a little too far." It was Conner curling his fingers now. "You aren't disabled."

"That my disability—" she repeated, shaking her head "—will end up with me hurt or someone else...worse off."

"Poppycock." That was one of Big E's polite conversational swear words. "Take a look in the rearview mirror. Look at all you've accomplished."

"I'm quite good at self-reflection, thank you very much." Lily held out her arms. "I can tell you exactly who I am. I've always been the sister who can't sit still. The one who can't refuse a dare or a challenge. I don't like being inside watching TV. I can't bear the thought of working in a cubicle. And when someone tells me I have to live my life with kid gloves, it's like pressing my go button." Her hands dropped to her sides, bringing her shoulders down with them. "But Rudy has a point. I could be endangering my clients."

Rudy was going about this all wrong. Lily needed the space to fly, not a cage for her so-called safety. Wings clipped, she'd wither. A part of her already had.

"And do you know what the worst of it is?" she continued. "His opinion makes me doubt my ability to be a mom."

Conner didn't know where the anger came from, but it filled him quicker than a rattler's strike injected venom. "You dropped a bullet, Lily. A small bullet. You didn't drop a baby."

She studied the ceiling as if reading a script. "I can carry a baby. They're not small like a pen or tweezers. But what about things a baby needs? Doses of medicine. Feeding with those small spoons. Releasing tiny child-proof buckles on car seats."

The anger morphed into concern. "Are you pregnant?" Because she had some valid concerns.

Let me do it myself. His mother's voice slipped into his head.

"I'm not pregnant." Lily shifted. "But Rudy's right. I can't be relied on to perform one hundred percent of anything." She spoke in that tight, small voice. "I wish I could make him proud of me. I wish he'd be happy for the life I've chosen without feeling the need to arrange for someone to care for me."

"This isn't only about your wanting parental approval. You're questioning the boundaries that define your life." The same as he did on those days when Blackwell guests were annoying and he longed for a time when he'd been his own boss. "Why are you ruling out parenthood? It's not like you need someone to help you get through daily life." Said the man who was keeping an eye on her for the next few days. "Since my mom's accident, she can't walk unassisted. She has forearm crutches and a walker. She adjusted to life, the same way you have. The same way you'll do if you have a baby. You haven't let your fingers stop you from running your own business. Don't let them stop you from starting a family when the time is right."

The irony of his words wasn't lost on him. He didn't apply them to his own life. He'd let his failures define him. He'd retooled his life to keep his mother safe.

"Thank you, Conner. Your opinion means a lot to me." Lily splayed her fingers on the tabletop, staring at her hands as if they caused her no end of disappointment. "I didn't ask Danny if he wanted kids. I was too afraid of what I might hear."

Anger returned. That guy was a selfish jerk.

"Since my mom died, Rudy has been trying to tie up all the loose ends, including me, as if he's scared he'll get hit by a bus or something and the five of us will be lost. He hasn't been the same since we lost her."

"He's worried about the wrong things." Conner was certain of it.

"Maybe. Maybe not. The day before Mom's funeral, he just wouldn't let up." Lily kept her focus on something across the room, but in a way that had Conner doubting she saw anything. "Danny was going skydiving and he asked me to go."

A chill swept over Conner, brought on by something she'd said earlier. "This is the part where you wanted to pull the parachute cord and—"

"Couldn't," she rasped before swallowing. "Luckily, Danny knows about my…lapses. He waited to pull his cord until I had. And when I didn't, he dove into me to do the honors." She rolled her shoulder and smiled ruefully. "Midair collisions tend to leave a mark. Danny broke my arm. But I can't complain. He saved my life."

"He very nearly killed you." Conner wanted to howl that fact to the heavens. "He knew it, too." Conner held up a fist, much the way he'd seen Lily do yesterday whenever she referred to her physical challenges. "And your father should have known his extreme protectiveness had the opposite effect on you."

"It's not like that." But her retort lacked energy.

"It is and you know it. The more I learn about you, Lily, the more I'm glad Big E asked me to be sure you get safely to Montana. But where does that leave you? What are you going to say to your stepfather to defend your choices?"

"I don't know," she admitted, using her "I'm insignificant" voice. She palmed the postcard, got up and went outside.

In that moment Big E didn't have to pay Conner double to take Lily to Montana. He didn't have to pay him at all. Lily deserved a chance to make a life of her own without being challenged by others, and that included the man who'd raised her. More than anything, Conner wanted to wipe that defeated expression from Lily's face.

For good.

WHAT ARE YOU going to say to your stepfather to defend your choices?

Conner's questions echoed in Lily's head as she walked the perimeter of the parking lot. Despite the dry air and the merciless afternoon sun, she couldn't get rid of the cold prickle along her skin, even when she noticed Conner periodically poking his head out the door to check on her.

What made her skittish? Tugged at her fears? She'd escaped a loveless marriage. The worst was over. She could go back at any time…if she was brave enough to face her family.

This trip to Montana was just a respite. Reality would intrude soon enough. Little would change. Lily would still have her business. Rudy would still pressure her to find another line of work and a man to take care of her. Her sisters would still worry about her heart being broken or her suffering some embarrassment because of her misfiring fingers. Danny probably wouldn't talk to her anymore. He probably wouldn't miss taking care of her, either.

Shouldn't her canceled wedding result in a life-changing revelation? At the very least, she'd like to be able to say "I don't need anyone" and be able to convince her family it was true.

She completed her parking lot circuit just as Pepper and Natalie burst through the doors.

"That was so fun!" Pepper flounced into Lily's arms, shouting as if she still wore the sound-canceling headphones. "Conner said he'd be right out. He's tipping the staff."

Natalie stepped into the sunshine and slid on a pair of fashionable dark glasses. "He gave me the keys." She shouted, too, and hurried to the RV, blond curls fluttering in the hot wind.

"Conner is so nice." Pepper towed Lily toward the motor home. "He picked me up at the airport in Montana last time I visited Grandma Dot."

"He's responsible, all right." Everyone relied on him—Big E, Conner's mother, Lily. The urge to live up to Conner's high standards vibrated up from her toes. The time had come to tell the truth. "Pepper, I—"

"I'm starving." Natalie unlocked the door and charged inside, tossing the keys on the dinette and grabbing a bag of chips from the counter. They'd made a munchie run along the way to Elko. "What are we wearing to the concert tonight?"

"Before you get lost in appearance minutiae, you should hydrate and eat something meaningful." Lily took the keys and started the RV to get the air conditioner blasting.

And then she tossed the postcard Conner had given her on the center console before moving to the kitchen area. Lily had yet to see the pair of young women drink any water or eat anything with redeeming qualities.

"You sound like my mother." Pepper grinned. It was an expression that asked for forgiveness of all sin and promised to love forevermore. She must have gotten away with murder in school. She probably still did. She accepted the bottle of water Lily gave her.

"Mothers know everything." Lily's throat threatened to close as she plucked the potato chip bag from Natalie's hands and tried to hand her a wide can of plain, unsalted nuts, but her grip slipped. Luckily, Natalie caught it. "Where is this concert and what are we wearing?"

"Such a no-brainer." Pepper swigged some water, fluffing her swooping brown bangs. "Outdoor concert. Backstage passes. We're wearing boots and very little else."

"Woop-woop," Natalie said around a mouthful of almonds. "Are you coming with us?"

"Oh…" Pepper capped her water, managing to look cute as a button and sheepish at the same time. "Big E only gave us two backstage passes. Are you okay with staying behind, Lily?"

"Oh, yeah. Sure." She was, after all, not part of Pepper's inner circle.

Pepper and Natalie took their places at the dinette, predictably losing themselves in their cell phones.

Lily sank into the passenger seat and picked up the postcard Conner had purchased, balancing the edges in her palms. She stared at the woman in the photograph who held a shotgun like she knew which was the business end and who needed it pointed in their direction. She looked capable in her buckskin breeches and frizzy braids. And the upward tilt to her chin... Here was a woman who challenged the world to bring it on. The caption on the back read: *Taking names. Kicking butt. Clark's OK Corral.*

Lily took the pen in the console cubby, slowly and carefully addressing the back. And then she wrote: *I did the right thing.* The woman on the flip side would approve. She tucked the postcard into the cubby with the pen.

"You and Conner are so sweet together." Pepper's fingers danced across her cell phone screen.

"Oh, we're not together."

Pepper would hear none of it. "He adores you. I can see it in his eyes."

Irresponsibly, Lily's heart beat faster.

"Woop-woop," Natalie chimed in, fingers moving just as swiftly as her friend's.

"Let's not do this," Lily cautioned to anyone who would listen.

Not that anyone listened.

"You'll see. Tonight." Pepper winked at Lily so hard her false eyelash went cockeyed. She tried to press it back on her eyelid without success. "You'll get to know Conner better while we're at the concert."

"Don't." Lily was too old for matchmaking games. "I just got out of a serious relationship. I'm not looking for love." Lily was surprised at how steady her voice sounded, at how there was no threat of tears, no shame pressing on her chest. She had indeed done the right thing. "You know who I'd like to get to know better? I'd like to learn more about you and the Blackwells." Before Conner returned. That seemed a safer topic than her commando cowboy.

"I don't really know the Blackwells other than Grandma Dot and Big E." Pepper peeled off the false eyelash, scooted out of the dinette and headed toward the bedroom in back. "I mean, I know their son and his wife died, and that Big E raised his five grandsons after he and Dot divorced, but this will only be my second time in Falcon Creek." She dug in her suitcase, tugging a large travel case free and examining the contents.

Pepper doesn't know the Blackwells?

The ruse of being a cousin of the groom suddenly seemed pointless. Lily opened her mouth to set the record straight when Pepper cut her off.

"Did Ken tell you nothing about me?" The young bride's rummaging produced a new eyelash and a small tube of adhesive. "I'm a whiz at math and I just finished my first four years at UNLV. I'm going to be a dentist. Do you know dentists make their own hours? Best career ever."

"You want to put your fingers in someone else's mouth on the daily?" Natalie shivered. "I'll stick to interior design."

"I have two words for you, Nat—*lucrative freedom*." Pepper gave her friend a one-eyelash scowl. "And I won't have to be on call, like real doctors."

"Dentists are real doctors," Natalie said before Lily could.

"Whatever." Pepper opened the door to the bathroom and disappeared inside. "I'm so glad you came, Lily. Aren't you? *Family* has a loose definition nowadays, but I knew from the moment I saw you that we'd be close."

The urge to set the record straight drove Lily to her feet. "About that…"

"Lots of miles to cover, ladies." Conner climbed in and shut the door behind him. "Giddyap."

"Give me thirty seconds to put my lash back on." Pepper bumped into the lavatory's wall. "It's impossible to put one on in a moving vehicle."

"Lashes aren't her forte," Natalie explained with a private grin accented by two firmly placed false eyelashes. *Blink-blink.*

"Natalie, time her." Conner got behind the wheel. "Thirty seconds."

"On it." Natalie tapped an instruction into her phone.

"Don't rush me or I'll glue my eyelid shut." Pepper didn't gush. Not even a little. This eyelash thing was super important to her.

"Tick-tock." Conner managed to look at Lily like a mischievous eight-year-old without so much as a smile. "You okay?"

Lily nodded automatically, even if it wasn't

quite true. The moment to do the right thing with Pepper had passed. She couldn't embrace independence without her family's blessing. And Grandma Dot was going to hate her.

She took her seat and slid on her sunglasses.

Pepper shrieked. "I dropped it. Restart the timer."

"There are no do-overs." Conner drummed his fingers on the dash.

Natalie scooted out of her seat. "Can I take your picture, Pep?"

"No!" Pepper wailed and shut the bathroom door.

"Everyone has a breaking point." Conner stopped his finger drumming. "I was wondering where hers was."

"She's not a bridezilla." Lily realized Conner had been out of sight for nearly twenty minutes and he was chipper…for Conner anyway. She held out her hand for his phone, which he gave up without a qualm. She opened it and methodically navigated the menu. "Nothing?"

"Nada," he said, as if there would never be anything.

"Then why are you so happy?"

He leaned across the space between them to whisper, "Those girls fired a hundred rounds and never hit the target once." The twinkle was back in his eyes. "Correction. They did hit a target. One of them hit your bull's-eye."

"Woop-woop," Lily murmured, earning Conner's slow smile.

CHAPTER SIX

"LADIES, WE'RE ALMOST THERE." Conner drove the motor home down a dirt road with an hour to spare before the outdoor concert began, thinking he was ready for some fresh air.

There were thousands of people heading toward the remote field and makeshift stage in the middle of the barren high plains. The going was slow but faster than the conversation in the RV.

Pepper and Natalie were in Big E's bedroom changing clothes. Their reply to Conner was muffled. Lily had her arms crossed and her stocking feet on the dash. Her new cowboy boots were on the floorboards. She'd been quiet for much of the afternoon's drive. Was she thinking about the future? Or the past?

It was her recent past that should have been his only concern. And her immediate future—staying with him on the road to Montana. The more he learned about Lily, the more he wanted to take her under his wing, although not financially. He couldn't afford to do so, even temporarily.

"How long have those two been back there?" he asked Lily. "It only took you five minutes to get ready this morning after your shower."

"I'm low-maintenance. No makeup. No fancy hairstyle." Her brow furrowed, revealing her dissatisfaction with that fact. "I mean, toddlers can scribble better on a page than I can on my face. Why bother?"

"Good thing you have a pretty face." She didn't need makeup, not with those classic cheekbones and big, bright blue eyes.

Lily's feet dropped to the floorboards, along with that furrow. "Thank you?"

"You're welcome." He'd shocked the city girl. Conner felt like smiling. But more important, her reaction told him that her fiancé had been stingy with the compliments.

Conner slowed for another concert checkpoint, grabbing the VIP parking pass and showing it to security before taking a more direct route to the makeshift stage ahead. They ended up in an area where motor homes were parked like wagons. There were several such circles, and tent cities had sprouted around them.

Conner opened his window and flagged down a man standing near a vacant spot in a motor-home caravan, a space marked off with orange cones. "Can we park there?"

The middle-aged man sauntered closer, gesturing to their rig with his can of beer. "You must pass muster. I'm Bert. Who goes there?"

"Um..." Conner flashed Lily a questioning look before facing the parking attendant once more. "Conner and Lily. We come in peace?"

Bert nodded, smoothing his bright red Hawaiian shirt over his gut. "And peace shall get you this spot. There'll be no partying after the concert. This here's a mellow circle. We've all got security's phone number on speed dial."

"We'll be no trouble," Conner assured him.

"That's the secret phrase. You may pass." Bert moseyed over to collect the cones.

"Jeez." Lily picked up the postcard from the OK Corral and flipped it over and back. "We've had to pass through more layers of security than the time I went to Burning Man."

Conner pulled into the open spot and shut the motor home off. "Ladies, we're here."

Squealing, his two young charges burst out of the bedroom wearing flouncy blouses, denim skirts and boots. Their hair was teased higher than a brand-new bolero. And their makeup... Somewhere there was a raccoon missing the black around its eyes.

"Chance Blackwell!" Pepper boogied toward the door. "He's extra man. He's extra everything."

"Woop-woop." Natalie followed her.

"Make good choices," Lily called after them, grinning at Conner as she reiterated his mother's advice.

He snorted. "Or at the very least, don't fall prey to country-music stars with extra everything." Or Big E would have his hide.

"Wait. Chance Blackwell?" She put her hands over her ears and then made a sound like an explosion, floating her hands outward. *"I'm* related to Chance Blackwell, the famous country singer?"

"Yes. Come on, Lily. Don't get starstruck. There's work to do." He got out and began setting up the motor home's outdoor space. He spread a green outdoor rug and extended the tan awning.

"Why are you arranging all this out here?" Lily sat on the bottom step of the motor home and put on a lightweight jacket. They were in the high plains now and the temperature was dropping.

On the other side of their circle, crowds of people passed, heading for the concert proper.

"Sometimes guests come back from events early." He'd learned to be prepared. "You can chip in anytime."

She got to her feet. "I thought I was a guest."

He was on to her. She thought she couldn't help, given those fine motor skills she angsted over. "Blackwells always pitch in." He nodded to a storage locker in front of the rear wheel well. "Dig out some tables and chairs from storage, will you?"

It took her a few tries, but she unlatched the cargo hold and took out two folding chairs. "We're not going to the concert? It could be *super fun*." The way she said those last two words was odd, like they meant something else and he should have understood.

"This won't be your last opportunity to see Chance sing. He and his wife, Katie, have a house on the ranch. Besides, we'll be able to hear things just fine from here." He assembled the portable firepit. "Taking in the show from a safe distance away. No one to crowd your space or spill their beer on you."

"You sound like Rudy." Lily slid two side tables from the storage compartment.

"As if you wouldn't turn down a pair of

earplugs if you sat up close." He tsked. "We're old enough to know those concerts destroy our hearing and young enough to want to protect it for the future."

"Did you just call me old? I'm not even thirty." Lily put her hands on her hips. If she was going for an offended vibe, she failed. A smile tugged at the corners of her mouth.

"Do you really want to go?" He could probably slip a note to Chance's people through security and get her in.

"No, I…" She sat down in a chair. "Concerts lost their appeal to me a long time ago."

That wasn't surprising. Lily may call herself an adventure tour guide, but she was down-to-earth. Settled, even. He'd thought about it on the drive. Even though Lily made her living from outdoor excursions, she didn't act like a thrill seeker. They'd driven on the highway near the Las Vegas Strip. Lily hadn't said a word about wanting to experience the skyscraper rides. She had no interest in firing guns. Concerts weren't her thing.

The sun was setting slowly behind the Sierras, painting the clouds pink against the deepening purple sky. Conner sat, enjoying the view, one that included Lily. Gone was the furrow, the worry, the regret over her choice to flee her own wedding. She wasn't going back.

He drew a deep breath, feeling his own tension about his duties and his double bonus slip away.

A small airplane buzzed the venue, circling. It landed to the west, kicking up clouds of dust.

Lily shaded her eyes to watch. "The true VIPs have arrived."

"Planes always bring trouble." Bert sat in a fancy chaise longue next door, drinking beer. "That's why I've vetted every motor home here. You let me know if anyone makes a fuss. My wife and her friends will return exhausted. No one disturbs my honey's beauty sleep."

Lily thanked Bert for watching out for them, sliding Conner a sly grin.

"Come on." Conner locked up the motor home. "Unless you want barbecued potato chips for dinner, we need to pick up food. I saw a few catering trucks when we came in and I need sustenance for tonight's long haul."

"Hey." She caught his eye. "Aren't we staying the night?"

"Yes, but concerts like this are tame until

the after-party. I'll be sitting outside later with Bert."

"Guarding the castle." Lily chuckled.

"Exactly." They waded upstream through the excited concertgoers. Conner grabbed her hand. "Stay close."

A few minutes later Lily dug in her heels, stopping to stare at a bungee trampoline. A teenage girl wore a harness in the contraption. The operator pulled her down low, stretching the bungee straps, and then released her, shooting her into the air. The teen shrieked and laughed and rebounded.

"Those are so much fun," Lily said wistfully, poking holes in Conner's theory about her maturing past being a thrill seeker. "I love to fly."

"You want to take a turn?" Conner asked, hoping she'd say no.

"It's such a rush." She spoke as if she didn't hear him.

Conner realized he still held her hand. He couldn't just let go in the midst of a conversation. And he couldn't give it a censorious shake.

"But now I know better." She gazed up at him in a way that stole his breath. "I can get a safe rush from roller coasters, waterslides and river rapids."

"River rapids are safe?"

"Relatively." She nudged him with her shoulder, a gentle admonishment not to worry. "I don't need the adrenaline rush of skydiving or bungee jumping from a bridge. Been there. Done that."

"Thank heavens." He wouldn't have been able to have kept up.

"Big E implied the Blackwells were adventurous."

Conner smirked. "Can't say as I've ever seen a Blackwell bungee jump off a bridge."

Lily made to pull her hand away.

Tightening his grip, Conner rushed to put her mind at case. "They're cowboys, not thrill seekers. When I think of the Blackwells, I think of a family that faces whatever life brings, head-on."

"They don't back down," Lily said slowly.

"That's right." He tugged her toward food.

They reached a circle of catering trucks as the small plane took off again.

Conner purchased a brisket, mashed potatoes and coleslaw at one food truck. At another he bought an assortment of cookies.

The only thing Lily asked for was plain tortillas from a taco truck.

"I hope Pepper isn't dieting to get in her wedding dress." Lily smiled ruefully. "Me? I was so nervous, I don't think I ate all week. Do we have to wait for them to get back to have dinner? I'm famished."

"I'm not waiting." That wasn't quite true. When they got back, he put off eating until he'd started a fire in the portable firepit.

Lily dug into her food as if making up for the past week of fasting. She shoveled brisket, potatoes and slaw into tortillas, messy in her execution. She ate three. Conner couldn't stop smiling. He did so appreciate a woman who didn't hide her appetite.

"You continue to prove the nice-guy adage." Lily sat back, breaking off pieces of cookie and eating them. "I saw you eyeing that blueberry pie."

The one she'd struggle to eat without spillage. "Who needs pie when you can have chocolate?"

Lily dropped a piece of chocolate chip cookie on the outdoor carpet.

Conner swept it up and tossed the crumbs on his plate.

"Again with the niceness." She chuckled.

"If you were going for tall, dark and danger-ous, you should have chosen a black hat, not squeaky black boots."

The concert began with a twang of an elec-tric guitar and the roar of the crowd, negating the need for him to comment on her opinion of him as nice.

Supposedly the kiss of death to a man's ego.

It was a good thing Conner's ego was al-ready battered.

His phone rang.

Lily extended a hand as if expecting him to hand the phone over. "What?" She blinked too-innocent eyes. "If it's Big E, I want to talk to him."

Conner glanced at the display. "It's my mom."

Lily made a give-me gesture. "I like your mom."

Conner hesitated. "She'll think something's going on between us." And why wouldn't she if Lily answered his phone two nights in a row?

Lily rolled her eyes and took possession of the phone, balancing it near her ear with both hands. "Hello, Conner's mom. It's me again. Lily." She listened to whatever Conner's mother had to say, chuckling softly. "He's been a true gentleman. In fact, I was just telling him how nice he was."

More maternal chatter while Lily listened.

"I meant it as a compliment." Lily sounded apologetic. "Did he tell you we're escorting a bride and her maid of honor to the Blackwell Ranch?" Lily smirked at Conner. "Yes, Big E couldn't very well leave him to do this alone. These women may be drinking age, but they're just so…so…young." She paused, listening. And then she gave Conner a sly look. "I think the maid of honor is single."

Conner confiscated his phone. "Mom, don't get any ideas. Natalie is not my type."

"Woop-woop," Lily murmured, grinning.

His mother huffed. "When you get to be my age and don't have grandchildren, you always have ideas. They don't stop. But Lily sounds lovely. Is she?"

"Mom," Conner warned.

Lily leaned closer, trying to hear.

"You haven't dated since your accident. What's the harm in a little workplace romance?"

"That's how people get fired."

"You young people." His mama tsked before falling silent. She was rarely silent.

"What's wrong?" Conner sat up so fast, he nearly spilled the remains of his dinner.

Lily took his plate, using her palms rather than her fingers, and set it on a side table, before leaning close again. She laid a hand on his arm.

Her touch was nice. *She* was nice. *This* was nice. But it couldn't go as far as the Blackwell Ranch or he'd be fired.

No one was talking. "Mom, you're too quiet."

"It's nothing." Mom coughed. "At least, nothing I can't handle."

"Did the fox get into the henhouse?" Conner should be home. His mother wasn't equipped to run the ranch for long periods, or even the small part she had taken on. Like Lily, she rarely complained about her limited mobility, but being with Lily these past few days had made him realize his mother might be acting brave for his benefit. Conner laced his fingers with Lily's and waited for his mother to answer.

"I wasn't going to tell you, but the fox broke in last night." His mother sounded defeated. "There were chicken feathers all over the ranch yard. I think he took Bessie. She was such a sweet thing, too."

"Ah, Mom."

The crowd roared as Chance Blackwell sang the first line of "Butterfly Blue." Lily inched closer, her cheek nearly touching his. If he turned his head, he could kiss her. If he kissed her and his boss found out, Big E would have his hide and his double bonus.

Conner didn't move. "I might be able to get Ethan or Tyler over there tomorrow." If the Blackwells weren't too busy.

Who was he kidding? The Blackwells were always busy.

"Don't you worry about me."

Like he had a choice. "It's my job to worry."

She made a noise like a muffled curse.

"Is there something else you're not telling me? Do you need Doc?" Conner ran through a list of folks she could call to take her into town for treatment. "Ben and Rachel Blackwell promised to look in on you while I was gone." They were on the next spread over, the Double T.

"I'm fine. I just kicked the bucket." She paused and then laughed. "You know what I mean."

"The rain bucket? Is the roof leaking again?" Now it was Conner swallowing a curse. The

Rocking H was a dilapidated money pit, in desperate need of his double bonus.

"It only leaks when it rains. The storm's already moving across the valley."

A leak. Conner's temples throbbed. He should rush home, but if he left now, he'd lose out on any extra income.

"Don't you worry about me and my chickens."

"But, Mom—"

"No buts. I'll see you Wednesday, as planned."

"Only if you're sure."

"I'm sure, honey."

"Well, then. Good night, Mom." He'd pray for no more rain and for satiated foxes.

"Good night, Mrs. Hannah," Lily called. She settled back in her seat, taking her hand with her. "You know, I can drive this to Montana if your mom needs you."

Conner shook his head. "I'll give it another day." Take Mom at her word. "She's tough, like you."

That got a smile out of Lily, but only a flicker of one. "What's this about an accident your mom mentioned?"

"It's nothing."

"It's something." She rubbed a hand over her collarbone where a pendant might have hung if she'd been wearing a necklace. "Some-things mean something. Here. Inside." She tapped that spot over her heart. "Sounds silly, but my mom used to say that."

"My accident..." Conner grimaced. "It's nothing. I was training a horse and was thrown against a fence." Things might have been different if he'd landed in the dirt. Instead...

The shocking bolt of pain. The horror of his legs collapsing beneath him. Of watching his mother rage over her inability to do more than call for help.

"Ouch. I bet you got right back on." She leaned forward to watch a group in gorilla suits ride past on a golf cart.

Conner stilled. "I...uh... Not at first. At first, I couldn't feel my legs." The words came out slow and thick.

Lily jerked around in her seat and gaped at him, a question in her eyes.

He nodded. He'd been terrified that he'd never walk again. And once he regained the use of his legs, he'd been terrified anew. Who would take care of his mother if he had an-other, more serious horse-training accident? He was self-taught and he'd had some suc-cess. But the accident proved his accomplish-ments were based on luck. Telling him he should leave horse training to the professionals. "They say I defied the odds."

"That's why your mother wants to talk to you every night." She placed a hand on his knee, her warmth permeating his denim. "She wants to make sure you're okay. My mom did the same thing, even though my accident happened twenty years ago. I'd get these texts from her." She choked up a little, swallowing back her tears. "*Good night, little chick.* And I'd reply back, *Good night, mama hen.*"

Conner was reminded her mother had died within the past year. He vowed to show a little more patience with his mama.

"But eventually, you got back on a horse, right?" Lily studied his face.

"Yes. Just not that one." That stallion disregarded fences and had the run of the Rocking H. Conner crossed his arms over his chest, thought better of it and shoved his hands in his jacket pockets. "I don't break mustangs anymore."

"That's smart." Her gaze dropped to his hands. "As long as you don't miss it."

He needed to tell her he didn't miss a thing— not the challenge, not the bond he developed with the horse, not the pride and satisfaction of helping an animal find a place in the world and lead a productive life. He'd fallen into horse training as a way to make more cash than cattle provided. He wasn't a professional. He needed to explain all that. And he would have if his throat hadn't been bone-dry.

"You miss it," Lily said without accusation or judgment.

Conner swallowed past the lump in his throat. "Maybe a little."

"I understand." Her hand covered his. "When I was younger, I had a mindset of immortality. Rudy would never admit it, but I've been more careful the past few years. And yet there's a part of me that misses those big-time rushes."

"It's the wisdom of age," he said softly, unable to tear his eyes away from their joined hands.

"I feel the need to point out—*again*—that I'm not old and I'm not going to live in a bubble. Why should you?"

"I don't live in a bubble." Lo and behold, his ego made a surprise appearance. Terribly unjustified, but an appearance nonetheless. "But I have responsibilities."

She shook her head. "You gave up something you love. You modified the way you live. Call it whatever you like. I'll call it a bubble."

She's right.

He'd gotten back in the saddle, but not back in the groove of his life.

For good reason.

"How can we thrive inside if we turn our backs on our passion completely?" Lily stared in the direction of the bungee trampoline. "How do you find the balance that makes you feel good about yourself without giving up a part of you that once seemed integral to your very soul?"

He didn't know. He didn't know so much, like why he hadn't been able to put into words the tension he felt inside himself because he'd stepped away from horse training and the Rocking H. Lily had summed it up simply and succinctly. He hadn't realized her internal struggle was his internal struggle.

He wanted to train mustangs again, but there was the question about his skill level and, more important, he wasn't willing to risk his ability to earn money to support his mother. Just like he wasn't willing to risk his double bonus and kiss Lily. Sacrifices had to be made to uphold the status quo, even if said status quo didn't make you happy.

They sat holding hands in silence in front of the fire, listening to the music from the concert and the occasional roar of the crowd. And when the bridal party returned, a little tipsy and a whole lotta tired, they put them to bed, like an old married couple.

Just without the married part.

LONG AFTER THE fire had gone out, the after-parties had died down and the concert equipment trucks were packed up and headed for the highway, Conner sat outside, occasionally staring at Lily's Old West postcard, which he'd swiped from the motor home's center console when she went to bed.

I did the right thing.

That was what she'd written. Was the right thing taking Lily to Montana? His wallet still voted yes. And his heart. His heart wanted her to stay on the road with him. But was it the right thing for Lily? Would she be better off with her sisters? Or her grieving, over-protective father? He set the postcard on a side table.

A chilly breeze pushed past, nearly sending the postcard off the table. In his lurch to stop it, movement caught his eye.

A shadow of a man stumbled between two

motor homes across the circle. The intruder made his way through the carpeted outdoor space of one RV, pausing to poke around possessions left outside on their makeshift patio. He continued on. He had a method as he worked his way around the circle—poking at possessions, listening at doors—making his way closer to Conner, who was slouched in a webbed chair, and Bert, who reclined in his fancy folding lounger. On his present course, he'd reach Bert first.

Conner had the generator running and the heat on in the motor home. His charges were snug and locked up tight. Other generators hummed in the circle, covering the noise of the shadow man's approach, covering the noise of most any confrontation.

The man reached the campsite on the other side of Bert. He picked up a woman's jean jacket and smelled it before putting it back on a chair.

That's creepy.

Conner's hands fisted inside his coat pockets. This was the reason he'd stayed up, to protect his charges.

The creep reached the edge of Bert's outdoor carpet and paused, perhaps noticing a body in that outdoor recliner.

As quietly as possible, Conner set his cowboy hat on a side table and leaned forward, ready to run to Bert's rescue whether he had security on speed dial or not.

"You heathen. Who do you think I am?" Bert rocketed out of his recliner like a big rock from a loose slingshot. "An easy mark?" He danced around his outdoor rug like a boxer, one with a little too much weave, a product of all the beer he'd drunk and the rising breeze.

Conner made it to Bert's side in time to support him. "I think you should leave, friend."

"You." The dark-haired man stepped into the light of the banked coals in Bert's firepit. "I've been looking for you." He glared at Conner and raised his fists, steady as a rock compared to Bert.

"You're the groom." Conner felt sucker punched. He nearly let go of Bert. What was his name?

Lily's former fiancé growled. "Where's Lily?"

A series of beeps danced over the menace in the air.

"Security? It's Bert. I've got a cat burglar here." He belched and dropped his phone. "Oops."

Conner tightened his grip on Bert's beefy arm. "How did you find us?" What was this guy? CIA? A foreign spy? He couldn't be just another adventure tour guide.

"I overheard Big E reassure someone he'd arranged for a Chance Blackwell concert experience today."

"Smart." Supersmart. But also extremely villainous. The guy's fists were still raised, ready to strike. "Listen, I don't want to fight and you don't want to marry Lily." At the jilted groom's raised brows, Conner added, "If you want a conversation to be private, you shouldn't have it in a church hallway."

Two could play the eavesdrop game.

Bert belched again. "Do you know this fella?"

"No, sir." That was no lie. Conner couldn't remember his name.

"I need to talk to Lily. I have a duty to the Harrisons."

"And a financial interest?" Why else would the cold-footed groom follow them? "Your duty ended in San Diego. Lily's a Blackwell, not a Harrison." Conner would have thought Big E had made that point clear.

The jilted groom made another growling noise. He was a thickheaded, mean cuss.

On the far side of the motor-home circle, a golf cart with a flashing light cut between two RVs.

Conner had grown up around livestock, most of it nondomesticated—mustangs, bulls and the like. Sometimes it was better to let an animal show its true colors so you knew what you were up against. Sometimes it took a little goading to get that show. "Lily heard every word you said to Rudy in the church, too. She doesn't want to marry you. In fact, she never wants to see you again." That was a lie. Conner never wanted this guy to see Lily again. He didn't care that she claimed they were best buds or that he'd saved her life. "If you knew she might not be able to pull a rip cord, why did you push her to skydive?"

His adversary snorted, shifting his stance and tightening his fists until his knuckles cracked.

The golf cart reached center circle.

"Why risk her life?" Conner got ready to deliver the telling blow. "Did you need to prove her weak to make yourself feel more like a man?"

Lily's former fiancé charged Bert and Conner in full view of approaching security.

Conner thrust Bert out of harm's way, but

he hadn't factored in Bert's inebriation. The older man tripped and sprawled across his outdoor carpet at Conner's feet.

The cold-footed groom stumbled on top of Bert, grabbing for Conner as he fell, even as Conner stepped out of range.

"Cat burglar!" Conner cried, pointing at his adversary.

Two beefy security guards tumbled out of the golf cart, Tasers drawn.

"Help." Bert flopped, throwing the groom on top of him off balance and to the ground. "He's trying to kill me."

Conner almost wished Lily was around to see her former fiancé get tased.

But he had no time to waste. He packed up the tables and chairs, retracted the awning and rolled up the carpet.

He was headed down the dirt road toward the highway before security got things sorted out.

CHAPTER SEVEN

"HEY!" LILY BOUNCED awake in her bunk above the driver's seat, arms flung against the motor home's ceiling. She inched to the edge of the bed and hung her head over the side so she could see Conner.

"Sorry." In the driver's seat, Conner raised a travel mug. "I was sipping coffee and missed seeing that pothole until it was too late."

The sun was rising but the world outside was still gray.

She got a gander at her upside-down self in the rearview mirror. Her dark blond hair was a messy tangle. And then her gaze collided with Conner's dark-rimmed eyes. Concern, and perhaps the blood rushing to her head, made her dizzy. "Is everything okay? What time did you get up? I didn't hear a thing." It had been the first night in weeks she'd slept peacefully for more than an hour or two at a time.

"Haven't been to bed yet." Conner pushed

up his sunglasses and pulled down the brim of his cowboy hat.

He's not telling me something.

Lily swung down from the bunk and stumbled into the passenger seat, finger-combing her hair and straightening the T-shirt and sweats from the truck stop. "This isn't the dirt road we took to the concert."

"No, ma'am."

They were back to that? Lily drew a deep breath. Last night had been wonderful. She'd felt the bond between them grow. And it had felt right, that connection. And now? He was more like the nervous, kidnapping cowboy. "What happened last night?" Lily asked, not sure if she was asking for his perspective between them or what had made him pull up stakes and leave during the night.

"Nothing much happened after you went to bed. I had somewhere to be this morning is all." Conner didn't sound convincing. Plus, he hit another pothole and he hadn't even been drinking coffee.

Muffled protests from Pepper and Natalie drifted from the bedroom, complaints about road conditions and respect for their beauty sleep.

"Don't worry," Conner said. "I've got this."

Right.

Conner was keeping her on a need-to-know basis, just like her family and Danny used to do. An uneasy feeling spun through her stomach.

"We'll make sure your wedding is special," Amanda would say whenever she asked about logistics.

"I'll take care of everything," Danny would say whenever they went on one of his adventures.

"Let me sort through the details," Rudy would say whenever it came to important choices, like medical or car insurance, or automobile purchases.

She'd allowed herself to be directed through her life because she'd told herself it allowed more time to devote to her business, or time away with Danny. And they offered to do it because...

Lily slouched in her seat, staring at her hands. Her numb, tingling hands.

It was one thing for Lily to harbor doubts about her physical limitations and how that impacted her life. It was another for those who loved her to think her injury meant she was incapable of caring for herself or making decisions about her life. Their voices built in volume and echoed in her head.

I'll get that...

Don't worry about...

I signed for you...

She covered her ears. This was worse than Rudy wanting her to marry Danny. Her family didn't think she was capable of living independently. And she'd enabled them in that opinion. She was a businesswoman. An entrepreneur. She was capable of so much.

Except...

She developed her tours with Danny. He came up with the ideas. They tested them together. They talked about how to modify them so she could lead the tour on her own. Danny helped fill tour spots. He went with her on the tour's maiden voyage.

It's not my business at all.

Lily rolled down the window and leaned out to get some air.

"You okay?" Conner touched her shoulder.

Lily's hands returned to her lap. "I need to make some changes in my life." More than just backing out of a marriage. "Take the reins, so to speak." Could she run the tour company by herself? Would anyone book a tour?

"I thought that's why you were going to

Montana." Trust a cowboy to oversimplify when there was so much more to be considered.

Which reminded her. "You should have told me we were headed out early today." Her jaw clenched. She needed full disclosure, now more than ever.

"I didn't want to wake you."

Lily unclenched her jaw and said evenly, "I meant, you should have told me last night what was on the agenda today."

"I didn't want to—"

"Worry me with the details?" Lily's head began to pound. Even Conner was coddling her. She stared at the road ahead. A large brown cloud hovered over the next rise. "Are we going to that?" Whatever *that* was.

"Yes, ma'am." Conner set his coffee in his cup holder.

Ma'am? "Why?" she asked through gritted teeth.

"It's a wild-horse auction." Conner wrapped both forearms over the steering wheel. He leaned so far forward, his chin nearly touched his hands. "Big E and I were going to pick out some stock. Now it's just me."

"Are you going to train them?" Was he reconsidering the choice he'd made after his accident? That might explain his hesitation in telling her their destination.

"No, ma'am."

"Conner, if you call me *ma'am* one more time before I've had coffee, I might have to butt dial your mother." Which was impossible, given he had a flip phone.

Lily swiped his coffee mug from the center console, noticing her Old West postcard was missing. She glanced around the floorboards but didn't see it. She sipped Conner's strong coffee. Black. Why couldn't he drink lattes?

"Sorry about the ma'am-ing," Conner said. "I get polite when I haven't had any sleep… *Lily.*"

Conner could be a pain in the butt or utterly adorable. That statement was adorable. And yet… "I don't understand. Why are you picking out horses you aren't going to train?"

"I'm a representative of the Blackwell Ranch."

"Let me get this straight." Lily placed the mug in the cup holder on her side. "You own a ranch that you barely run, and you don't train horses anymore, although you loved it. You're a camp counselor to wedding parties and drive a motor home around the country for the Blackwells. Are you a cowboy or a corporate man?"

Conner opened his mouth to respond, but

nothing came out. He looked so perplexed that she reached across the divide and rubbed his shoulder.

They made it to the rise. The prairie spread out before them, divided into huge pastures filled with horses. Trucks and trailers rimmed the nearest fences. A few cowboys milled about. There were easily a thousand horses in all those enclosures. Dirt hovered over the area like a cloud, kicked up by incoming vehicles and the horses themselves.

"So many pretty horses." Pepper knelt at the center console wearing a cute pair of pajamas, pink with big red hearts. Her hair had been combed and fell in a thick sheet down her back. She'd brushed her teeth. All her put-togetherness totally put Lily to shame. "Is Big E starting a breeding program?"

"No." Conner frowned. "The Bureau of Land Management rounds up wild horses every year and puts them up for adoption through a sale. It's a great way to get good stock if you have access to a good mustang trainer."

"Which Big E does," Lily murmured before being struck by a thought. "There are more horses out here than cowboys. How can they all be sold?"

"They won't be," Conner said softly. "Some will live out their lives in this dust bowl."

Lily shivered.

"Grandma Dot said you'd train a horse for me." The reason for Pepper joining them in the front became clear. "I see some white ones. My life plan is to ride down the aisle on a white steed, like in a fairy tale."

"If you're looking for a white horse to ride down the aisle, it won't be a horse you find here. These will take months of work before they're ready for that task. You have to establish trust and work them with a gentle hand." Despite his cautionary words, there was longing in his eyes.

Why didn't Conner realize he should be schooling horses, not chauffeuring wedding guests? Forget her family sheltering her. Lily hadn't let her accident stop her from doing what she loved. Why should Conner?

"You're raining on my life plan, Conner." Pepper returned to the bedroom, stomping in a way that indicated the conversation wasn't over.

Lily waited until she'd closed the door to ask, "What does it take to become a horse trainer?"

"Are you considering a career change?"

There was no ma'am-ing in that question. But he'd delivered it with some disbelief.

"Would you discourage me if I was?" She sat on her hands.

Conner drew a deep breath. "If you had a passion for working with horses, I'd encourage you. But if you were drawn to the danger, I'd tell you it wouldn't replace the void left by that best friend of a groom of yours."

"What has gotten into you today?" Lily tugged at the seat belt, which suddenly seemed too restrictive. "Danny may be reckless, but he'd be happy for me if I pursued something that made me, well…happy."

"Danny," Conner muttered, slowing the motor home down and turning toward a spare patch of dirt. "You think he'd be happy if you found a new life in Montana? He and your stepdad couldn't keep tabs on you."

He was right. "I can't let them control me anymore." Didn't mean it was going to be easy.

"I need to know." Conner brought the motor home to a stop and turned to her. "Do you want to sit down and talk to this *Danny* person about what happened? Mend fences?"

Did she? Lily hesitated. And then she shook her head. "Everyone I left behind deserves a chance to say their piece to me. But I seriously doubt Danny will want to have anything to do with me."

Conner scoffed. "He was a fool not to see what he had all those years. A fool to have doubts. He'd be a fool to let you go."

"You think he wants me back?" *You wouldn't have let me go?*

Before he could answer, Pepper flung open the bedroom door. She wore her new cowboy outfit and a cross-body black leather purse. "I'm ready to go horse shopping."

"Grant me patience," Conner murmured before mustering a strained smile. "Sure. Let me register first."

Pepper paced while Natalie and Lily got ready. "I have a life plan. Mature love. Western theme. White horse. Lucrative freedom." She repeated those words like a mantra, even when pouring Lily a mug of coffee.

"Are you happy, Pepper?" Unable to suppress her concern, Lily tugged on her cowboy boots, the taste of black coffee in her mouth. "Life isn't a fairy tale. It doesn't always follow a set plan."

"Woop-woop," Natalie said, raising her hands like she was raising the roof.

"You sound like Ken." Pepper's countenance leaned more toward a frown than anything else. "I have to be true to myself. You don't know what it was like growing up…" She mustered a smile, but it was missing her trademark gush. "Dreams are important."

"But dreams change over time." Especially when those dreams had been made at age eleven, as Pepper's had. Or had been shaped at age seven, as Lily's had. Maybe Lily needed more than a break from her family. Maybe she should consider horse training as a career, more than just a charitable challenge. She could come to Montana not for a bit of breathing time, but for a completely fresh start.

They exited the motor home into the cold morning air.

"So long, hot desert." Lily shrugged deeper into her thin jean jacket.

Conner wove his way through several parked trucks to reach them. He moved with eye-catching confidence. That hat. Those shoulders. All that body-hugging denim. He was as much a breathtaking view as the mountain peaks surrounding them.

He folded a bunch of papers and stuffed them in his back pocket. "Come along. I'm cleared to buy." He veered toward the main pasture, but his attention seemed to be on the parking lot, as if he was looking for some-one. Big E?

Lily hurried to keep up.

A pair of cowboys on horseback whooped and cracked whips in the pasture, trying to separate a white horse from the herd.

Pepper and Natalie got sidetracked, stop-ping near the slew of cowboys hanging around the main gates. Lily and Conner walked on.

"How many horses are you going to buy?" Lily breathed in dust and the smell of manure.

He glanced over his shoulder, not toward her, but at the parking lot. "I've got permis-sion to purchase ten."

"That's depressing." Lily paused to watch a small group of horses thunder past. "Ten won't make a dent in the number here." Not even if every cowboy she'd seen bought ten. "Can't you purchase ten for your ranch?"

"No." That was a hard no.

"I'll buy ten if you agree to train them. You can float me the money. I'm good for it." If she didn't pay Rudy back for the wedding. She had to pay him back. But she could save some horses first. "How much are they? Can you spot me? I don't have my checkbook or a credit card."

"Don't go there." Conner was a brick wall

standing in the way of her admittedly early-stage plan to reshape her life.

A small burro ambled by, pausing to sniff in the direction of Lily, stretching its nose between the barbed wire.

"I like the burro." She reached for its nose. "Nothing seems to rattle her."

"Like you," Conner said absently, pulling her hand back. "Donkeys are stubborn. And a few are biters. Be careful."

Was there a compliment hidden in there somewhere?

"What about that brown one?" Lily pointed to a large horse grazing nearby.

Conner tipped his hat back and gave the animal more consideration. "He'd be a good trail or pack horse for a cowboy."

"That's so sexist." Lily plucked a clump of grass from the ground and held it toward the burro.

The little thing took the offering gently, without a sign of animosity. Lily reached out to pet it.

"Okay. Fine. I meant good for someone who has experience with difficult horses." Conner heaved a weary sigh, guiding her back a safe distance. "Look how big and muscular that horse is. You're not going to break him with soft words and carrots. That's a professional's job."

"Sounds good to me." In fact, it sounded like a challenge to her.

"It's a physically demanding task." His gaze drifted to her hands. "And before you fall in love with that burro, consider this. A burro serves no purpose on a ranch." He turned at the sound of an approaching truck.

"Other than companionship and overall cuteness, which lowers stress levels. The cuteness, not the companionship." She tapped his shoulder. "Are you expecting Big E?"

"No."

Lily didn't believe him. She shaded her eyes and perused the parking lot.

"This isn't productive," he muttered, staring at Lily with an inscrutable expression.

Just once, she wanted to make him smile the way she imagined he must have at least once as a boy, with pure joy. "What isn't productive? Checking every truck that pulls in or being here with me at the horse sale?"

He drew in a breath the way Rudy did before launching into a lecture he didn't want to give. "I have a job to do. I need to keep that in mind." And with that, he spun on his heel and walked toward the fence.

The burro ambled toward the brown horse. Both their coats were blanketed with dust and fringed with mud. The air above them was a dirt-filled blue-brown.

"I don't understand what you're looking for." Lily glanced around. The number of horses was overwhelming. "What criteria are you using to select horses?"

"Good confirmation. Bright eyes." Conner strode briskly near the fence line. "Character."

A dapple-gray horse charged toward them, baring its teeth.

Lily ducked behind Conner, who hadn't so much as flinched.

"Is lack of killer instinct on your list?" Lily peeked around him.

"It's a consideration." Conner watched the territorial beast trot away. "But not a deal breaker." He considered her, eyes full of questions. "Are you still interested in training mustangs?"

"If you put it like that, yes." She never could resist a challenge.

He shook his head. "Big E won't like that."

"Nobody will like that. But it's time I chose a life for myself."

He made a noncommittal noise and returned to the task at hand. They traipsed through the low, sparse grass, moving farther and farther away from the gates.

Conner stopped without warning and pointed toward a reddish-brown horse with white markings on its legs. "That one looks good."

"One?" They'd walked close to the length of the fence on this side of the road and he'd only found one horse he liked? Lily's heart ached for the rest.

A white horse raced past, followed by eight brown horses, and a couple of cowboys with lariats twirling.

Lily stopped to watch the chase. "Pepper's going to be disappointed if someone else gets that white horse."

"She shouldn't be. That mare would gallop down the aisle and jump over the fence on the other side of the altar." Conner rolled his shoulders back. "And that's even if she postponed her wedding six months."

"How can you tell?" Lily admired the white horse as it continued to evade her pursuers.

"That mare's alpha. See how she nips at the others, keeping some away from her little band and herding others to join her even with cowboys chasing her?"

"I thought only stallions did that."

"Mostly. But that mare… She's not going to want to join a human herd."

"I want her," Pepper announced, having caught up to them with Natalie in tow.

"You shouldn't." Conner turned, scowling. "You're starting dental school. You don't have time for a mustang, much less a retired trail horse. These animals require commitment, patience and love."

"I've got all of that." The young bride tossed her thick brown hair defiantly.

"I should have added courage and maturity to the list of things a mustang needs," Conner mumbled to Lily.

"I want her," Pepper said in a previously-unheard-of tone, one that rang with stubbornness. "And I'm going to have her." She waved a paper in the air. "I bought her."

"You what?" Conner's jaw dropped. And then his voice turned as hard as Pepper's. "I told you not to. Come on. We're going back to take care of this."

"No." Pepper trembled, not the way she'd done previously when she was excited, but a deep shaking that conveyed upset. "I told you a white horse was important to my life plan."

"Oh, get real!" Conner jabbed a finger to

the pasture and the white mare that galloped by. "She's not some puppy in a store window. That mare is a dangerous animal who could hurt you. This isn't like me taking you clothes shopping with Big E's charge card. Big E won't just go along with this."

"I know." Pepper's voice trembled now, too. "I bought her with my own money."

"Why?" Conner demanded, flinging his hands into the air. "How could you possibly justify buying her? Was she on sale? Marked down? Or is it just that she completes your wedding outfit?" Every question he tossed made Pepper flinch. "Unbelievable."

"Conner," Lily said softly, moving to put her arm around the young bride's waist. There was something going on that ran deeper than a white horse to complement a bridal dress.

"Conner," Natalie said more firmly, putting her arm around Pepper's shoulders.

"You're on her side?" He took a step back, staring at them all in continued disbelief. "Are you kidding me?"

"Do you see what they're doing out there?" Pepper nodded toward the pasture. "Cracking whips? Chasing them around? Shouting? Those horses didn't ask to be bullied. They don't understand what's going on. They have no place to hide, no way to escape to safety. They can't run to a bedroom and bury themselves underneath the covers, hoping everything will be all right in the morning."

Lily sucked in a breath as the meaning of the younger woman's words sank in. Pepper's carefully constructed dreams, her life plan, her desire for lucrative freedom. Could it be possible that Pepper hadn't been frivolously wishing upon a star? That she'd been wanting to create a life she, and she alone, controlled?

"I know I won't be riding that white mare on my wedding day. But I can save this one horse. I *will* save this one horse. Don't you dare try to stop me."

Conner stared at her for a moment, and then nodded and walked away.

CHAPTER EIGHT

OF ALL THE idiotic reasons to buy a horse.

Of all the brilliant reasons to save a horse. *Poor kid.*

Conner's heart went out to Pepper. It was clear she'd felt helpless and scared at some point in her life. Still, he couldn't give in. He'd have to see the government money man and null Pepper's purchase.

"What am I gonna tell Big E?" Conner stomped across the dirt road to another pasture. That white horse was going to be nothing but trouble. And with his luck, everyone at the Blackwell Ranch would expect him to train her. His charges were mad at him. They didn't understand the financial realities of ranching. This wasn't like rescuing a cat. Horses were a bigger monetary burden. When it came to fiscal responsibility versus sentiment, Conner chose responsibility every time.

"I'm not just another of your obligations," Tanya had shouted at Conner as she climbed into her truck, intent upon leaving him. "I was your wife!"

Was? Conner had stood in the ranch yard watching his soon-to-be ex-wife leave and wondering why he'd felt so much relief and so little heartache. He loved her. But if she wasn't happy here, then she should be one less obstacle to keeping the ranch in the possession of the Hannahs.

Love didn't come easy or cheap. And when survival was at stake, it was best to avoid love.

"I'll tell Big E." Pepper dogged Conner across the road.

Natalie trailed behind them, snapping a selfie.

"You won't." Frustration built inside Conner, so much so that he didn't even glance back at the sound of a truck approaching to see if it was Danny, he of the killer tracking skills. "If you're serious about keeping that horse, you'll tell your grandma Dot first and soften the blow."

"Is it wrong to do the right thing?" Pepper's voice welled with unshed tears.

"Training doesn't come cheap." His forehead pounded from the effort it took to frown. He marched ahead, not looking back. "When you run a ranch, it's all about resource management. A trainer's wages get sunk into the value of a horse, not absorbed into the overhead of a ranch." If only Conner had known that when he'd first begun running the Rocking H. He'd undercut the value of his services often enough to dance with bankruptcy.

"I'm serious about this," Pepper said from behind him. "She will be safe."

Natalie and Lily were silent.

They reached the last pasture. Conner was so annoyed he couldn't remember which horses he'd seen that had promise. Granted, that might have been because he hadn't slept in twenty-four hours, and guilt over not telling Lily about her former fiancé showing up at the concert was pinching the base of his neck.

Transporting three passengers to Montana was supposed to be easy bonus money. What a crock. He felt meaner than a hive of hot bees.

"She doesn't have to be trained." Pepper stood near Conner, sniffing. "Royal can run free on the Blackwell Ranch."

She'd named the mare? That would only make Conner's job more difficult.

"Big E won't allow a wild mustang free range." The only nonworking animals on the ranch were in the petting zoo for guests, and that mare wasn't a tame Shetland pony. She'd rile stock no matter where you put her. "Being an adult means you have to make adult decisions, Pepper. You have to think about the repercussions of this."

Pepper might have been thinking. At the very least, she was silent.

Natalie reached down to pluck an undersized dandelion near his feet. She blew the fronds into the wind. "Is Big E going to fire you over this?"

Big E had fired cowhands for less. For a moment uncertainty did a barrel roll in his gut. He'd be in a heap of trouble if he got fired.

Conner tipped back his hat and tamped down the doubt. "I suppose Big E's reaction depends on how much of a headache that mare and Pepper are going to cause the Blackwell Ranch."

"Can you help me save her? Please." Pepper sniffed again. "I won't be any trouble the rest of the trip. And I'll make sure Royal isn't any trouble at the ranch."

"Me, too," Natalie chimed in.

Conner didn't put much stock into their words. He searched inside for some compassion, which seemed to be missing, chased off by debt, he supposed.

But that wasn't the only thing that had abandoned him.

He looked around. "Where's Lily?"

"I BOUGHT THE burro and the big brown horse." Lily crossed her arms over her chest and dared Conner to try to deny her purchases.

Pepper and Natalie flanked Lily with the same obstinate expressions.

Talk about going from bad to worse. Conner's resolve threatened to crumble. Big E was never going to trust him again. All Conner needed to cap the morning in failure was the appearance of Danny. And with the number of trucks trundling up to park, that wasn't beyond the realm of possibility.

Conner removed his hat and ran a hand through his hair. "I thought you didn't have any money, Lily. You asked me to spot you."

Her arms locked tighter over her chest. "I paid with my online account. I remembered my bank log-in and password."

"Of course you did." Conner smashed his hat back on his head. Everything was against him today, including technology. "And what are you going to do with a horse and a burro?"

"I haven't decided about the burro," Lily proclaimed, as regal as a queen. "But I thought we could train the horse together, you know, with soft words and carrots."

Her ladies-in-waiting nodded.

"I decline." He pulled his brim low. "You can't just train a mustang without any training yourself."

"Then I'll find someone to train *us*." Lily wasn't backing down. "Big E will know someone who can help me."

A jealous growl tried to work its way out of his throat.

"Excuse me, ma'am." The government employee handling sales approached Lily with a clipboard and a harried smile. "Where do you want your stock delivered?"

Lily arched her eyebrows. "Conner?"

He pressed his lips together, refusing to enable this irresponsible scheme of hers. Horse training took two strong hands, a stronger back and a robust knowledge of equine behavior. He was torn between canceling her sale and letting Big E sort it out back in Montana.

His runaway bride gave up on Conner and turned to the BLM employee. "I don't have the address, but my grandfather is—"

"Ship them to me," Conner blurted before she could say another word. "And the white horse that Ms. Pepper purchased, too." At the very least, Big E couldn't fault him for manning up to his mistakes, costly as it would be. It'd take a good chunk of that double bonus to feed their animals. He gave the man the address to the Rocking H. "They'll be transported with the Blackwell stock." The ones he'd picked out for Big E.

How much trouble could three city gals be? Conner gritted his teeth. Lots.

The trio of females bounced up and down, squealing with excitement. And then they swarmed him in a group hug, begging him to save more horses.

Lily kissed his cheek, an action more persuasive than any verbal argument.

She needed a hero.

Enter Conner Hannah, horse savior.

And soon-to-be unemployed ranch hand.

"You're a softy," Lily said to Conner after all the equine purchases and travel arrangements had been made.

It was totally out of character, but he couldn't deny it. He'd purchased twenty horses for Big E, ten more than he'd originally planned, including the big gray stallion that had lunged at them. "I'm going to have some explaining to do." About how he hadn't been able to say no, particularly to one unstoppable runaway bride.

What would Big E have to say about that? Or Dr. Ethan Blackwell, the ranch's veterinarian? More likely it'd be Katie Blackwell who'd have an opinion and give him a talking-to. Katie was in charge of ranching operations and had been before she'd married Chance. No single person could train twenty horses efficiently, and those mustangs were going to need daily work by a qualified cowboy. He'd committed to taking on two horses and a burro, although not to train them. He'd let them run the Rocking H with Parsnip.

Lily was smiling at him and repeating, "A softy. Commando Cowboy. Go figure."

I could get used to that smile.

And the teasing. And the company. And the softness of her hand in mine.

"This isn't funny. I'm not training any of them." His back seized up just thinking about it.

Lily didn't stop smiling.

"I'm not," he reiterated.

"You could." She walked backward toward the motor home, following the path taken by

Natalie and Pepper, who were already inside. "You could teach me to be your assistant trainer."

Conner's steps faltered. This was different from Lily saying she wanted to learn how to break mustangs in general terms. If he was to mentor her, she couldn't very well return to California, could she? "You're going to stay in Falcon Creek? You haven't even seen the town or the ranch. Or met the Blackwells." *Who'd love her. Let's be honest.* "And what about that business of yours?"

Lily stopped, those new cowboy boots of hers slipping on a tuft of grass. "Well, I… You don't want me to stay." Not a question. That smile gave way to an expression of hurt.

"I didn't say that." Conner opened his mouth to say more and abruptly closed it again. These feelings he had for Lily were complicated by Big E, his bonus and her persistent, jilted groom.

"You think I'll be a burden." She didn't look at her hands, but they were bundled into uneven fists at her sides.

"I didn't say that, either." He rubbed at the kink in his neck.

Lily needed help with some of the simple

things in daily life—opening a jar, pouring herself a cup of coffee. She probably couldn't mend a tear in a work shirt or measure the ingredients for a batch of cookies. Conner was already caring for his mother and the Rocking H, and not doing a great job at either. What right did he have to invite Lily Harrison Blackwell into his life? If she knew the straits he was in, she wouldn't want that invitation. She'd toss it right back at him.

Which she might do anyway when she learned Danny had tried to win her back. It was time to come clean about last night. "Lily, I…"

She laid her hands on his chest. "You were thinking it's too dangerous for me to train a horse or even that adorable little burro. I can see it in your eyes."

That wasn't what he'd been thinking at all.

Of their own accord, his hands came up to cover hers. "You can't just leap from one life into another." But a part of him wanted her to. It'd been a long time since anyone except his mother had put their complete faith in him. "You're leaping without looking." Slow and steady was the key to surviving in this world, sticking to your strengths, tucking your head in like a turtle to avoid pitfalls as you moved through life.

She shrugged. "Why can't I start over? People do it all the time." She inched closer, near enough that her breath warmed a spot on his checked shirt. "Do you know how many times I've had to pick myself up, trying to keep up with Danny?"

"I don't want to hear about Danny." Not ever again. The strength of his statement stiffened his entire body.

"You fall down. You get up." Lily paid Conner no mind. "You hit your head or bruise your back. You get up. You drop a glass of milk. A pencil slips from your hand. A rip cord doesn't get pulled." Her eyes were suddenly shining with tears. Her hands dropped to her sides, but she still didn't move away. Her breath continued to warm that spot over his heart. "You get up. You try something new until you find the right place, the right passion, the right person."

Me?

Conner was in trouble here. His hands came to rest on her shoulders.

He couldn't have Lily staying in Falcon Creek. He couldn't have her flashing that grin his way, giving him that look that seemed to know what he was thinking. He couldn't hold a Blackwell in his arms, because Big E would not approve of this. Not at all. He'd say Conner had taken advantage of Lily when she was vulnerable. He'd say Conner didn't have his act together, that he wasn't good enough for his granddaughter.

And he'd be right.

Despite all that going through his head, somehow...some way... Conner's arms had come around Lily, bringing her close. He breathed in her flowery scent. He noted the way her head fit under his chin.

We're made for each other.

Or maybe they would have been if he could still train horses and she wasn't going to be a Blackwell. Blackwells didn't marry broken-down ranchers with nearly nonexistent bank accounts.

"Sometimes," Conner said gruffly, setting her away from him, "when you get up you have to move in a new direction. And sometimes that direction is governed by logic." Not hearts. "I can take your horse and burro in, but that's all. I won't train anything." Not even his unruly heart, which threatened to break if he pushed her away any farther.

Lily paled.

She gave the briefest, the stiffest, of nods and turned away, walking not toward the motor home, but to the paddock where the burro she'd fallen in love with was waiting.

CHAPTER NINE

"ARE YOU READY to go?" Pepper came to stand next to Lily at the paddock where they were keeping animals that had been sold.

Lily shook her head. "Not until I've named them. It doesn't seem right to leave until they have names." Not to mention she needed time to collect herself before she climbed into that motor home again with Conner.

What a fool I've been.

Mooning over a cowboy. Suggesting she could move to Montana. He'd said everything right. It was Lily who'd been presumptuously wrong. She'd jilted her groom just a few days ago. That action alone said a lot about her judgment, her character, her heart.

Cowboys milled about, giving the women a wide berth as they waited for their horses to be transferred from one pasture to the next or dogged the purchase agent to settle their accounts.

"What are you considering?" Pepper cooed

over the burro, who seemed as tame as a kitten. "Maybe I can help."

"Since they seem like good friends, I was trying to go for classic pairs. Calvin and Hobbes. Cory and Topanga. Rudolph and Frosty."

Pepper gave her the side-eye. "Those are horrible names."

"Hence the reason I'm still standing here." Lily stepped out of the way of a large group of cowboys. "I did have one idea. My great-aunt Pru…" She'd have to start referring to her as Grandmother Pru. "She loved this strand of silver-colored Tahitian pearls. And the burro is the same soft gray."

"Clever." Pepper nodded. "I'm going to wear my mother's pearls on my wedding day."

"That's a lovely tradition." And made Lily think of traditions her mother had established. One of which was gifting a daughter with earrings for every major life event. Her sisters had planned to give her earrings before the ceremony. She supposed it was fitting she'd left before that happened.

"And what pairs with Pearl?" Pepper asked, bringing Lily back to her naming dilemma.

"This is where my pairing-name convention fails me." Lily stopped herself from squirming. "Because nothing pairs with pearls except diamonds, and that horse strikes me as a mouse." Not a gemstone.

Pepper took a moment to process this. "The big brown horse?"

"Yes. A mouse can be scary but not dangerous." It fit the big-boned creature.

Pepper studied Lily's face. "There's a lot more going on in your naming process than meets the eye. But if it works for you…"

Lily nodded. "Pearl and Mouse it is."

"I can't wait to hear you explain this to Conner." Pepper looped her arm with Lily's and steered her toward the motor home. "He's 'having a day,' as my grandma Dot would say."

They walked slowly toward the motor home.

Lily knew she shouldn't pry into Pepper's past, but there was very little room for privacy in the RV. "About what you said earlier… When you were telling Conner why it was important to save Royal…" Lily placed a hand over Pepper's. "I want to tell you how sorry I am that you went through whatever it was you went through to feel safe." She didn't need the details.

Pepper bit her lip, and then details were spilling out. "I was bullied in middle school."

"You don't need to tell me," Lily said softly.

"I'm challenged in the height department and I went through an awkward stage where I tripped over everything. Kids can be mean sometimes, you know? I didn't seem to fit in with my friends from the year before. And I just felt vulnerable to attack all the time. So, I decided I wasn't going to school anymore. I just burrowed under the covers and wouldn't get out of bed, even after my parents met with school officials. When Dot heard, she came to see me. She told me you can rise above the tide if you accept who you are and know where you're going. That's when we formed my life plan. With it, I know life is going to throw obstacles at me, but I have a place I'm working toward and I have to believe things will get better. And they do. They did."

Her determination to stick with her life plan began to make sense. "You know, it's not a betrayal of Dot to change that life plan of yours. She'd understand."

"I know. But I'm happy."

Lily nodded, but she was struck by how brittle Pepper sounded when she made that claim.

"How did you meet my son?" Conner's mother, Karen, had a cheerful voice and a playful attitude. She rarely let an opportunity to tease slip past.

It was just what Lily needed after an afternoon on the road, an afternoon where Pepper filled Conner's silence with chatter, gushing words that couldn't quite smooth over the various rebellions of his passengers.

Lily forced herself to smile, knowing that smile would come across in her words to Conner's mother. "Conner and I bumped into each other at a wedding."

"I hope you caught the bouquet and he caught the garter. That would be so romantic."

"But sadly, not true." Conner wasn't the type to vie for a garter. He was more the brooding wallflower who watched the party pass him by. "We're very different." And the distance between them seemed unbearable after he'd given her that tender embrace only to set her aside at the horse auction.

Lily knew she wasn't the kind of woman Conner and the Rocking H would most benefit from. He'd told her his ranch needed work and an infusion of capital. She couldn't provide either. He required proper motivation to return to the work he loved. She'd been unable to inspire him to try. He had a full plate of obligations. She'd proved over and over that she could use a hand with daily living.

Not that I can't live my life alone.

Conner was outside, setting up the outdoor living space in the fading light. They'd stopped for the night in the Warm River Campground. He knew Lily was talking to his mother on the phone, but he hadn't come inside.

"You two aren't different, Lily." Pepper butted in from the dinette.

"Woop-woop." Natalie concurred.

Lily rolled her eyes at them.

"I heard that." Conner's mother chuckled. "Are you a horsewoman? I've been hoping a nice cowgirl would come along and get him back to training."

"I own a pair of boots, a bur—"

"Never mind," Karen said. "I don't want to judge as long as you make my son happy."

Lily didn't deny anything.

Conner hovered near the screen door, wearing a grim smile and a question in his eyes: *Is it my turn to talk?*

"Here's Conner." Lily tried to keep an equally grim smile in place. "He's smiling at me now. And for the record, we're just friends."

"I can fix that. Let me talk to him." It was easy to see where Conner got his commanding attitude. Karen's tone oozed with it.

"Perfect timing." Lily handed Conner the phone as he came up the motor-home stairs.

"How are things, Mom?" Conner took the phone and went back outside, walking toward the campground bathrooms. His words grew too faint to hear.

"Psst." Pepper set down her phone and grinned at Lily. "He's sweet on you. He didn't get half as mad at you for buying Pearl and Mouse as he did with me for getting Royal."

"It makes no difference." He hadn't agreed to help her train Mouse. "After this week I'll hardly see him." It sounded like the Blackwell Ranch was large and he'd be busy. Still, the realization knocked her back in her seat, longing pressing on her chest.

How can I want to be with a man I just met?

Amanda would worry if Lily admitted such a thing. Peyton would scoff. She welcomed their perspective.

It defied logic. Logic—and her family— would have said she and Danny were perfect for each other. But she'd had enough of other people guiding her decisions.

She wasn't ready to let Conner ride out of her life. She'd like to see where things between them might lead. But to do so meant braving scuttlebutt and flouting convention. Runaway brides didn't turn starry eyes to someone else so soon.

She stared up at the emerging stars, wishing she were strong enough to grab on to what she wanted in life and not let go.

"THAT POOR GIRL." Conner's mother sounded worn out upon hearing the true reason Lily was with him. "It takes guts to walk out on your wedding. I hope this trip cheers her up."

"Well, if it doesn't, it won't be for lack of trying." Conner walked the campground's main loop at a pace conducive to staring at other campers to make sure there weren't any jilted grooms in the vicinity. The smell of campfires and pine permeated the air.

"Lily is so sweet." His mother tsked. "Just don't fall for her if she's on the rebound, hon. Make sure this is real."

"Mom. That wasn't why I told you about her." Was it? When it came to anything about Lily, rational thought scattered to the wind.

"I'm just sayin'. You have your own set of problems separate from hers. And a runaway bride like that might not know her own mind."

That was sound advice. How Conner hated hearing it.

"I can tell when you're being stubborn. Let her go, hon."

"Mom, you can take a banana and accuse it of being a pineapple. But it's still a banana." She was seeing something where there was nothing.

His mother huffed. "You'd best listen to me. It's not as if you haven't had your share of hard knocks. Don't tempt fate." She hung up.

"Right." Conner didn't tempt fate anymore. He tucked the phone in his back pocket and continued his circuit. The occupants of the campground favored big rigs with bump-out rooms. Whatever happened to roughing it with a tent?

As he neared the motor home, Pepper and Natalie came out to meet him, blocking his path.

"Dude, you're in need of some serious love advice." Pepper was once more the bride without a care in the world. "You're breaking Lily's heart."

Natalie made the *woop-woop* gesture without saying a word.

"Pepper…" Conner couldn't bring himself to say she didn't know what she was talking about. "Butt out," he said instead.

She smirked at him, which inspired Natalie to do the same.

At the next campsite someone began playing a guitar. Beyond that, someone laughed. Everywhere around them, people were happy.

Roughing it in the lap of luxury.

That was not—and would never be—Conner. He'd forever be the guy scraping by.

"Just so you know, ladies…" Conner leaned forward as if he was going to share a secret. "I'm not that great of a catch. Lily can do better." And wasn't that the truth?

Pepper and Natalie stared at him, stared at each other and then burst out laughing.

"Conner." Pepper hadn't smiled that big since the concert last night. "You have no idea what kind of men are out there. The fact that Big E put me in your care says a lot about who you are inside."

"And trust me." Natalie sized Conner up in a way that made him uncomfortable. "We can appreciate what kind of man you are on the outside."

"Ladies, you flatter me." But Conner refused to be swayed. He tried to step around them.

Again, they blocked his path.

Pepper held out her hands in the universal stop position. "The way you close yourself off isn't healthy. Humans were meant to be social, to be loved."

Conner rubbed the back of his still-stiff neck, reminding himself he was an employee paid to provide Pepper a good time. If that meant occasionally listening to her romantic notions, so be it.

"Do you know what happens to bachelors who stop dating?" Pepper didn't tease. The future dentist was serious about dispensing advice. "Do you?"

"They live happily ever after?" Was there any other answer to give?

Pepper scoffed. "They become lonely, crotchety old men."

"Word," Natalie echoed, crossing her arms over her chest.

Patience. Conner rubbed his neck again, eyeing the motor home a mere forty feet away.

"They eat frozen dinners and watch too many hours of reality TV." Pepper nodded sagely. "They have holes in their socks and nothing to do on a Saturday night. In a word, they're unhappy."

Conner tamped down his pride in favor of his need to humor Blackwell guests. "I'm perfectly content, ladies, holey socks, reality TV–filled Saturday nights and all."

"Are you?" Pepper's expression turned sly. "There are dark circles under your eyes, and you drank so much coffee today you're not going to be able to sleep tonight. What's been keeping you awake?"

Jilted grooms.

"It's Lily," Natalie answered for him, her short blond hair ruffling in the evening breeze. "You're going to toss and turn with Lily mere feet away, wondering how you can pass up this opportunity at a fun and fulfilling life."

Conner stifled a groan.

The girls flanked him, each taking hold of one arm and marching him toward their motor home.

"Now, if you had friends to take care of you," Natalie said, "they'd have made you take notice how much caffeine you were taking in."

"Nag, you mean." He had his mother for that.

"Nurture," Pepper corrected. "Relationships are symbiotic."

"And here I thought they were romantic." Conner tsked.

"Sweeping gestures are romantic," Pepper corrected. "Love is… It's that safe, comfortable place you always wanted but didn't think you could find."

They reached the edge of the outdoor carpet and stopped. The motor home was dark inside, Lily's silhouette visible in the front seat.

"Go on." Pepper released him.

"She's waiting." Natalie did the same.

Conner didn't move. If any man was heading down the solitary path they described, it was him. He didn't have the time or financial resources to court a woman, much less a Blackwell.

He stifled a sigh.

"You're a tough one," Pepper said, as if her pep talks usually motivated folks to go out there and win their one true love.

Natalie sniffed. "He probably likes old recliners and stale sandwiches."

"Beer in cans and beef jerky instead of wine and beef bourguignonne," Pepper agreed.

"I'll tell you what I do like." Deciding he was spending another night outside, Conner moved to a storage cabinet, taking out a small bundle of firewood. "I like a warm fire and quiet time to reflect upon tomorrow."

He didn't allow himself to think beyond that.

"A PENNY FOR your thoughts." Conner brought Lily a cup of coffee the next morning.

She accepted the mug with both hands.

"I was thinking it was a brand-new day." A chance for new beginnings. Lily sat outside the motor home watching the sunrise. She'd gotten up as soon as she heard Conner moving around outside. She'd just returned from the bathroom, where she'd showered and dressed for the day in leggings and a sweater. "I was wondering how to approach it."

How to approach him.

"That sounds heavy." He sat next to her, a slow smile building on the face she found so endearing. "I should have laced your coffee with whiskey."

"That would've been good." Just knowing he was giving her that smile made Lily's insides warm.

"I'm assuming you're wrestling with issues regarding the wedding last weekend." Conner sipped his coffee, making her wait for his reply. "Is it time to move forward without looking back?"

"I don't know. Is it too soon?" Lily set her coffee down and leaned forward, ready to hang on his reply.

"If you're the strong sort, it's not too soon." Conner sipped his coffee and then leaned toward her. Anyone walking by would see a couple bridging the gap between them. "Maybe the answers you seek are yet to be found on this road trip of ours. Ask me what's on the itinerary today." There was a playful glint in his eyes. And then he sat back in his chair, glint disappearing as if he'd just remembered there should be no bridge between them. "The ladies are going to have a spa day," he said, not waiting for her guess.

"They'll be in heaven." Lily tried to hide her disappointment in Conner's guard going up behind a smile.

"They won't be the only ones. You're going, too. We'll have to drive an hour or so to get there." He sank deeper in his webbed seat, staring at the horizon. "But there's a mud bath in your future. And I heard something about goat yoga." He chuckled. "Sounds right up your alley."

Lily recognized his babbling for what it was—him trying to put another wedge between them. She was the sort to bounce back and she wanted to bounce in his sphere. That required a lot of resilience and a little subtlety. "You know what would be better than Pepper and Natalie doing goat yoga?"

He shook his head.

"The entourage's chaperone doing goat yoga." Lily waggled her fingers at him.

"No, thank you, ma'am." Conner reverted to his stoic cowboy expression. "I'll leave farm-animal meditation to the city folk."

Across the road, a man hopped out of his motor home and gathered his fishing gear.

"City folk. Really?" Lily picked up her coffee and cradled the warm mug to her chest. "Are you up for a small wager?"

Conner shook his head. "Never. I don't gamble."

"Oh, come on. Everyone accepts a dare now and then. I promise no money will exchange hands." She offered a sly grin. "You're curious about what I might wager, aren't you?"

He cleared his throat, staring at those black boots of his. "What did you have in mind?"

"If I can get the ladies up and moving in thirty minutes or less, you'll do goat yoga with us."

His eyes narrowed. "And if you can't?"

Lily propped her elbows on her knees. She hadn't anticipated he'd have terms. What could she put up against goat yoga and mud baths? Racking her brain, she watched the fisherman walk down the road. And then it came to her. "I'll tell Pepper the truth about who I am."

Conner chuckled. "This is too easy. Those two didn't get dressed yesterday in under an hour." He tipped his hat to her. "But I'll be kind. Tell me when you want me to start the clock."

"Now." Lily set her coffee on the little side table and bounded into the motor home. "Ladies, I just saw Chance Blackwell's tour bus drive toward the exit. And Conner heard they're headed for the nearest diner up the road. But he's determined we don't move until you're up and moving."

It was a gamble, possibly no enticement at all. Pepper was related to Chance and might see him when they reached the Blackwell Ranch. Why would she get excited over this?

Despite that, Pepper squealed. The motor home rocked from them leaping out of bed. There was a mad rush for suitcases and the bathroom.

"Tricky." Conner admitted defeat, folding his chair to stow away.

"I didn't work ten years as an adventure tour guide without learning how to make people move." Now, if only she could motivate Conner to see her as more than a flighty city girl. "It'll be a pleasure to observe your yoga technique later."

"I'M NOT A sideshow attraction," Conner grumbled at Lily. "And this is not relaxing."

"Yoga is about strength and looking inward, not relaxation." Lily spared him a half smile that made him forget Big E and repercussions from this trip.

They were on their hands and knees with goats balanced on top of their flat backs amid a group of people similarly posed and paired. Pepper and Natalie were taking this completely seriously, eyes closed and looking utterly Zen-like, cell phones filming. Conner and Lily had been unable to achieve inner peace.

"Admit it," Lily whispered. "You thought goat yoga was some silly stunt."

He had. But so far yoga in general had surprised him. First off, the positions weren't easy to hold, especially in blue jeans. And second, you often had to hold them while goats climbed on your back or your behind.

Marty, his goat, hopped off his back and army crawled beneath him, reaching up to nibble on the neck of his undershirt.

"Hey, hey! Stop that." While Conner tried to gently discourage his little friend, Lily's goat jumped onto his back. *"Oof."*

Lily rolled over and giggled, staring up at him as if he hung the moon for her.

I would, if I could afford the moon.

Their yoga instructor tried giving the goats quiet commands, but the animals ignored her.

"Quiet, please," Pepper whispered. "You're disturbing my inner peace."

"Ditto," Natalie said. Her goat was tucked up on her back like a cat waiting to see if someone was going to pour her some cream.

Lily rolled her eyes. Sprawled on her purple yoga mat, she was the happiest he'd ever seen her. He stared a little too long, committing the moment to memory.

Lily's goat nibbled the hair at his nape, right above that kink in his neck.

"Oh, no." He wasn't goat feed. Conner got to his knees, sending Lily's goat to the ground. Not that it stumbled. He pulled his T-shirt free from Marty and then stood, helping Lily to her bare feet. He didn't let go of her hand. "Come on. We're disrupting their session."

Lily allowed herself to be led away, whispering, "That was totally worth the bruises those tiny hooves are going to leave on my back."

"Ditto." Conner chuckled once more. Wait until he told his mother.

The spa walls were a soft blue. The hallway was edged with tropical plants and filled with soft music. If he'd had on his boots, they would have rung on the white marble, destroying everyone's Zen.

"Excuse me." The concierge flagged them down at the end of the hall. "You're a little early for your mud bath, but we have two openings."

"Sweet." Lily lunged ahead like this was a good thing.

"No." Conner shook his head, digging in his heels and trying to free his hand.

"Ignore Conner." For someone with grip issues, Lily wasn't letting go. "He's a mud-bath virgin. Nerves, you know."

"It's not nerves." Conner ignored the concierge laughing at his expense. "Cowboys don't do fancy mud baths. We sit in the river if we want to get dirty."

"You don't know what you're missing. Your skin is going to be as smooth as a baby's bottom." She clapped her other hand on his wrist and stared up at him with an inviting smile.

If it had been anyone but Big E's granddaughter and any invitation but to a mud bath...

Conner shook his head. "Cowboys aren't supposed to—"

"Shhh." Lily pressed her fingers against his lips.

They both stilled. Her touch was warm, just as inviting as that look she'd given him earlier. If things had been different... If the Rocking H was in better straits...

I'd be holding her right now, kissing her right now, thinking beyond tomorrow.

"Come this way," the concierge said.

Lily's hand dropped from his mouth.

Conner let her lead him to the mud room. The way she made him feel inside, darned if he wouldn't let her lead him anywhere.

The concierge took them to a room with two tubs of mud and a flimsy peach-colored curtain hanging in between. Floor-to-ceiling windows faced the mountains. Anyone who walked by on the grass outside could look in. Not that Conner noticed any foot traffic. But he wasn't a window display.

"There's a robe for each of you to put on after you change." Their attendant gestured toward a small alcove where two thin blue robes hung from hooks. "I'll knock in a few minutes with a female associate to help you into the bath." He left them alone.

Conner should have been focusing on Lily. But the room smelled like rotten eggs, and the tubs looked as if someone had stirred them with a baseball bat since the last person had sat in them and made mud pies.

"Is this sanitary?" Conner was having second thoughts, not about kissing Lily, but about their wager.

Lily went to the alcove and pulled another thin curtain across. "The woman who checked us in this morning said they add fresh mud and water from the mineral springs for every client."

"So you say." Conner turned his back because he could see her silhouette through the thin curtain. "I suppose we're all going to smell like this when we get back in the motor home."

"Cut to the chase, Conner."

He gulped. "I'm gonna assume they don't provide us with bathing suits for this bath."

"Correct." The sound of Lily disrobing from the other side of the curtain was alarming. In fact, it sounded the same alarms that had gone off the other day when he'd unbuttoned her wedding dress. "I'm going down to my—"

"Cowboys aren't cut out for spa days." Especially commando cowboys.

"You are such a coward," she teased. "My Coward Cowboy."

He preferred Commando Cowboy, not that he was going to tell her that. "This mud thing. It's overstepping personal boundaries."

She yanked the curtain aside, causing him to turn and look. She held her chin high as she tightened the sash of her robe. "You and I are way past most personal boundaries."

Conner smiled. She was right. Pretty, too. And so far above his pay grade.

"Go on." Walking toward him, Lily pointed a thumb toward the alcove. "Get in there and strip."

He couldn't have moved if his pants were on fire. Lily came to a stop in front of him. If she was wearing anything beneath that thin robe, he couldn't tell.

Lily tugged at the hem of his shirt. "They'll be here soon to help us in the tubs."

His hands had somehow managed to find her hips. His gaze couldn't be removed from hers. He didn't care about attendants. If they knocked, he'd tell them to go away. He'd tell them to never come back.

Conner bent to kiss Lily in a slow move designed to allow her plenty of time to stop him.

She didn't stop him. Her eyes drifted closed and she sighed.

This is trouble, son. You better git.

Conner tensed. Straightened. He let her go and ran a hand through his hair without ever touching his lips to hers.

How did Big E's voice get in my head?

Did it matter? Disaster avoided. No kiss had been made.

Conner mumbled an apology and escaped to the alcove, yanking the curtain across. The smart thing to do was to exit.

Conner had never been smart. He stripped down and put on the paper-thin blue robe.

The attendants knocked and entered just as he tied his sash.

Conner came out of the alcove and sneaked a glance at Lily. She hadn't said a word since he'd almost blown his double bonus. She stared out the windows, fingers tangled in the collar of her robe, dark blond hair spread across her shoulders.

The mud-bath personnel wrapped their hair in stretchy towels and applied mud to their faces. Then they gave them instructions regarding how to enter the bath without scalding themselves in the hot mud, standing nearby in case an assist was needed.

The key to successfully avoiding mud burns was to lower oneself inch by inch. Conner took his position on the other side of the curtain from Lily. He should have been worried about the voyeurs in the room. He was more concerned with Lily. This would probably be his last chance for a private conversation to explain why he couldn't kiss her before they all climbed back into the motor home.

"Wowzer." The sucking sounds from the other side of the curtain indicated Lily was taking the plunge. "These are some hot springs." She heaved a sigh. "Okay, cowboy, get in so we can peel back the curtain and have a discussion without a barrier between us."

Without barriers? He needed those barriers.

Conner lowered himself into the tub, sinking down and stretching his legs slowly. "Whew, doggy. You ain't kidding. That's hot."

An attendant drew the curtain that separated their tubs aside, and then they were left alone.

Their eyes met.

She was in the mud bath up to her neck. She had a twisty towel around her hair. Mud covered her slender neck and her face.

"You look hideous." And that summed up his technique with the ladies.

"Right back at you, cowboy." Lily tilted her head back and smiled. "Now, this is my path to inner peace. A nice hot bath and a gorgeous view."

Conner nodded. Much as he'd like to sit back and relax, he had to clear the air. "About what almost happened earlier..."

"If you apologize for something that didn't happen, I'm going to get out of this tub and leave you here."

Conner's mouth went dry.

"I'm guessing my runaway-bride status is why you didn't kiss me. I know I shouldn't feel anything for another man so soon," Lily continued quietly. "But I do, despite the fact that I was supposed to be married by now. And because of that, I feel like there should be penance and Hail Marys."

"Are you Catholic?"

"No." She turned her face toward him. "But they get all the good guilt resources."

He chuckled and then remembered he had little to laugh about. "I shouldn't admit that I like you, too, Lily. As a Blackwell employee, I can't cross that line." No matter how much he wished things were different.

"There's a right time for everything, I suppose," Lily said, voice filled with regret. He nodded solemnly.

"Change of subject. I'm proud of you for doing goat yoga and getting into the tub, Conner. What an adventure, right?"

She was the adventure, not that he could say that.

"City experiences. Go figure," he said instead. Just wait until he told Tyler Blackwell about how people paid to sit in mud. Ty was always looking for ways to make the guest ranch experience unique.

"And it's not over yet. When we're done here, we get to shower." The tease had returned to her voice.

"We?" How much was he going to be tested today? He tried to wiggle his toes, barely moving beneath the thick, hot mud.

"I'll shower first," Lily told him. "And alone

to save your tender sensibilities. Now enjoy the view."

How could he when all he could think of was Lily getting out of the tub...?

CHAPTER TEN

IDAHO WAS FULL of bad-decision bars.

But Pepper had done her homework when she and Big E had planned this trip. She wanted to go to Rustlers, which was the kind of place you entered at your own risk, especially if your vaccinations weren't up-to-date.

Rustlers had once been a place where Idaho Falls locals had come to belt out off-key karaoke and let their hair down. Now that the tourists had discovered Rustlers, it no longer lived up to its reputation as a place to show one's wilder side. But it was still talked about enough that there was cachet in putting it on a road trip.

Conner and Lily hadn't talked any more about the almost-kiss or the intimacy of taking mud baths together. Truth be told, despite Conner reinforcing the boundary between them, it felt like the line had been smudged. Maybe it was because Conner's neck was no longer kinked, and despite soaking in mud, his skin had never felt so clean. Rustlers was nothing like a spa—not as clean, not as open, not as quiet—which might have explained why he wasn't looking forward to their visit.

Lily edged toward Conner as they entered, looking anxious. "Have you been here before?"

"Once or twice. Back when there were nightly brawls." Those were the days when he hadn't known when to pick a fight and when to walk away.

Pepper and Natalie made their way to the bar. They were styled to attract attention, having spent hours getting ready for the evening's festivities.

"We should stay with them." Lily made to follow.

Conner steered her toward a booth on the side instead. It'd been built on a raised platform so diners could eat and look out over the dance floor, pool tables and bar. "We'll see them and all the action from here."

"We don't fit in here. We should go." Lily still looked nervous, but she also looked lovely. Pepper had brushed her hair and braided it from the base of her neck. The bride-to-be had also worked her makeup magic. Lily looked as sophisticated and polished as any city girl, although Conner preferred her natural beauty.

"Big E wanted me to let the ladies have their fun. We won't stay long." Conner ordered two bottles of beer, a basket of curly fries and a postcard from the waitress.

"Beer on tap is cheaper," Lily pointed out, ever the penny-pincher, practically shouting to be heard over the rising chorus of a classic rock anthem.

Conner nodded toward a large man in a leather vest a few feet away. "See that guy over there? He's got a lipstick stain on his beer glass." And Conner hadn't seen him with anyone, much less anyone wearing lipstick. The glasses weren't clean.

Lily shuddered. "Bottled beverages it is."

The dance floor was packed. Pepper and Natalie each held a canned hard seltzer and grooved together on the periphery of the dance floor like middle school wallflowers, which they'd never be. Several cowboys checked them out. Conner hoped they'd be intimidated by his young charges. A group of leather-vested men and women who looked like they belonged to a motorcycle gang overflowed from a table near the stage. Patrons on the dance floor shifted to give them some room.

Conner kept one eye on Pepper and Natalie, and one on Lily, wishing he could just concentrate on the woman sitting across from him. Their time together was coming to a close. Irrationally, he didn't want it to end. Tomorrow they'd be in Falcon Creek.

The music changed to a quieter slow song, making conversation more intimate and less of a shouting match.

Lily's gaze collided with Conner's and then fell away. "Pepper is such a sweetheart. I'm going to tell her the truth in the morning, regardless of what Big E wants."

"You can tell her in forty-five minutes when we're back in the motor home."

Lily frowned. "Admitting I lied needs the clear light of day."

"You're wrong. The sooner the truth comes out, the better." Not that Conner wanted Lily to know the truth about that double bonus he'd been promised. He got to his feet, stepped off the platform and held his hand out to Lily. "Come on. Slow dances were made for confessions, and confessions are good for the soul." Or at least, the souls of those who weren't in desperate need of cash. "You can practice what you're going to say on me."

Lily swiveled in her seat, set her feet on the

platform, but her hand hesitated above his. "I shouldn't be dancing. Or having fun. I just left a man at the altar."

"Technically, he never stood on the altar." Conner took Lily's small hand. When they were together, it was easy to forget all the reasons they shouldn't be. "Dance with me, Lily."

She didn't move, not back into the booth and not forward into his arms.

Conner drew her hand toward his chest and the ball of emotions spinning there, trying to break free. "Sometimes you have to go with your gut, even if others might raise their eyebrows. Even if what you choose to do goes against the norm." *Or your boss's wishes.* "Sometimes you have to honor your feelings because they don't fit into a polite box. But following those feelings makes you feel more like yourself."

His hold on her hand tightened, because being with Lily made Conner feel all kinds of emotions he'd kept locked away since his accident—guilt, tenderness, duty, joy. "Let's forget about social norms and what people might say. Let's dance, Lily. Just you and me." Because they'd be in Falcon Creek tomorrow and go their separate ways. He'd have to pretend he didn't want any excuse to talk to her, or to steady her when life threw her a curveball. He'd have to pack away his curiosity regarding what she wasn't wearing in a mud bath and how it would feel to kiss her, stuffing his feelings back inside his chest, where they belonged, because feelings got in the way of responsibilities. Always.

Blue eyes luminous, Lily got to her feet. "Is it wrong that you understand me so well?"

"No." Not until real life intruded. Conner led her to the dance floor, silently cursing the fact that the slow song was half-over. And then he was facing Lily and drawing her into his arms.

She came to him with tender certainty, as if she, too, knew this was a moment where time stood still and lines that shouldn't be crossed could be breached.

Bodies jostled them closer and toward the darkest corner of the dance floor, where shadows beckoned lovers. A stroke of a hand down a slender back. A gentle brush of cheek to cheek. A kiss that lingered. None of it would be seen if he crossed that blurred line in the shadows. Did he dare seize the moment and risk a kiss that could lead nowhere but to sleepless nights and endless what-might-have-beens? Fate had never been kind to him before.

He kissed her anyway.

Big E wouldn't be happy. This wasn't the old man's idea of delivering his granddaughter safely to the Blackwell Ranch while giving her time and space to air her concerns. He'd point out that Conner hadn't been thinking.

Her father wouldn't be happy. He'd claim there was a buffer period after a breakup, a time when hearts shouldn't find love anew. He'd point out that Lily hadn't been thinking.

There was no more thinking, though, because Lily was kissing him back.

There was just a slow country song and a couple deepening a kiss in the shadows.

His fingers tangled in her long, silky braid, loosening the loops. Lily's lips were soft, as soft as her skin. She smelled of the mineral massage lotion at the spa. And her kiss... It was like he imagined skydiving was. He was pumped from adrenaline, breathless from the rush, heart pounding with hope that this moment would go on forever.

But just as quickly as it had begun, the kiss ended.

Reality intruded. Someone jolted them apart.

Lily's eyes widened. Her lips trembled. "Oh… I…I'm sorry. I…I thought I could do this." She bolted.

"Wait!" He had no right to follow. He ran after her anyway.

"Hey." Their waitress grabbed Conner's arm with one hand, juggling a tray with their order and the tab. "Are you gonna pay for this?"

Conner thrust a couple of bills at her, grabbed the postcard and headed for the door. He forgot about babysitting Pepper and Natalie. He forgot about his obligation to Big E. He forgot about saving the Rocking H. Front and center in his head was the need to find Lily.

He burst out of Rustlers and scanned the parking lot. No Lily. Not even by the motor home. He started to sweat.

What if he couldn't find her? What if he couldn't apologize? Not that he regretted that kiss, but she surely did.

His phone rang.

Mom.

Conner didn't answer. But the world came crashing back into his head.

What if Lily decided she couldn't finish

the trip with Conner? He'd lose that double bonus.

What if Pepper and Natalie got into trouble while he was looking for Lily? He'd lose his job.

For the moment it didn't matter. Conner turned, heading toward the street, rounding the corner of the bar.

And there she was. *Safe.* Not sobbing. And she didn't run off upon seeing Conner. Relief coursed through him.

Lily sat on a curb at the end of the block. She didn't look at him as he approached; she just held up her hand in a universal gesture to stop. "I am the worst person on the planet."

What? "You're not." Ignoring her attempt to erect boundaries, Conner sat next to her, draping his arm across her shoulders.

"I sent mixed signals." Lily leaned away from Conner but didn't shrug him off. "We shouldn't have done that. Don't try to make me feel better."

"Okay."

She sneaked a sideways glance at him.

"I'll try and make myself feel better," Conner said. "I shouldn't have kissed you. It was too soon. It was too selfish and irresponsible. I'm supposed to be bringing you safe and sound to the Blackwell Ranch. That kiss was…" *Fantastic.* "It was…" *Awesome.* "Um…"

"It can't be anything," Lily said firmly. "Not yet. I have too many unanswered questions ahead of me about my future."

"About a horse and a burro?" Conner rubbed her shoulder as he teased. "Or about a father you need to stand up to?"

"By all means, let's not forget Rudy. He's a naval officer. There's a rule or regulation for everything. And in this case, I don't know how long the cool-down period is after ditching your wedding, but I do know that one exists to him." Lily rested her head on Conner's shoulder with a sigh. "It was a nice kiss. But right after, I was overwhelmed."

Me, too.

"Let's go back to the part about the kiss. It was just nice?" Conner should be offended at the label, but how could he be when Lily was tucked firmly beneath his arm? "It was more than nice."

Her palm rested on his knee. "You know what I mean."

He did indeed. Kisses like that… He hesitated to give it a label. "So we become simply the cowboy and the runaway bride again?"

"Can we?" She lifted her head to gaze into his eyes. "No pressure? No expectations?"

No.

Conner dismissed the need to fight her suggestion that they dial their attraction back to the friend zone. "Just the memory of nice." It was the honorable thing to do, not to mention it got him out of a bind with Big E.

"Agreed."

And there it was. Bullet dodged. Not to mention a question had been answered: *What would it feel like to kiss Lily Harrison Blackwell?*

Like heaven.

A taste of heaven could last an honorable, responsible cowboy a lifetime.

If I look away.

If I drop my arm.

If I can squelch the feeling that being with Lily is worth the price of financial ruin.

His phone rang. Without thinking, Conner looked away, dropped his arm and gave the phone to Lily.

"Is CONNER ALL RIGHT?" Conner's mother asked Lily. "Why do you always answer?"

"He's fine. He's right here next to me." Lily had expected him to be angry that she needed to slow down after that knock-her-socks-off kiss. Despite his treating her differently than her family or Danny… Despite her feeling more independent at his side than she had in years… Everything was happening too fast. "How are you, Karen?"

"I was just doing my word puzzles and making cookies."

"What kind?"

"Peanut butter." Karen sounded pleased that Lily had asked. "You'll have to stop by when you reach Falcon Creek and have some."

"I will." Lily bade her good-night and handed the phone to Conner.

The muted music from Rustlers drifted to them. A stiff breeze swirled down the empty street. But everything was so faint, so distant. It was as if she and Conner were in their own world, one where mistakes were forgiven, second chances offered and love dangled like a promise waiting to be made.

When I'm ready.

There were times with Conner when she felt more than ready.

"I agree, Mom. Lily is great." Conner inched farther away on the curb. "But she's not ready to date right now, so pump those brakes."

A clearer sign of speed bumps ahead could not have been made.

Exactly what I wanted.

Lily drew a deep breath.

Exactly what a runaway bride is supposed to want.

"I know." Conner spared Lily an eye roll. "What was I thinking the first time I got married? Running off to Reno without you? I should have cleared my plans with you. You're the top brass and... Uh-huh. Hey, I hear the timer for the cookies. Yeah. See you tomorrow, Mom." He snapped his phone closed and returned it to his pocket.

See you tomorrow, Mom.

Lily glanced up to the night sky, missing her mother. If she were still alive, Lily wouldn't have become engaged to Danny. She'd never have found out Rudy wasn't her father until later, perhaps from one of her sisters. But then she'd never have met Conner.

Good night, mother hen.

The crowd at Rustlers roared and then cheered. Catcalls and whistles arose. A woman *woop-wooped* into a microphone.

"You don't think…" Lily left the thought unfinished, turning to face Conner.

"I do." Conner got to his feet and pulled her to hers.

"Pepper and Natalie," they said at the same time.

Together, they ran back to the bar.

But Conner's two words echoed in her head. *I do.*

CHAPTER ELEVEN

ON STAGE AT RUSTLERS, Pepper had a microphone and stood in front of the karaoke machine. Natalie was in backup-singer position behind her with a microphone of her own. The pair had shed their tight-fitting jackets and were showing enough skin to give Big E a heart attack.

Conner pushed his way through the crowd on the dance floor, hanging on tight to Lily's hand.

Under a disco ball, Pepper belted out the chorus of Billy Idol's "White Wedding," complete with dance moves. It was a combination of punk and a cheer anthem. The audience was eating it up.

If Pepper planned to perform this at her wedding, Conner didn't think Dorothy Blackwell would approve. There was too much sneering and below-the-belt hip action. His provocative charges finished out the song by jumping in the air and landing on their heels like hard-rock guitarists. The resulting applause and shouted adulation was deafening.

"Do you want another?" Pepper cried, clearly ready to give them more.

The crowd roared their approval, pressing forward, calling out requests, not all of them song titles.

If anyone threatened the two young women in any way, Conner had no way to protect them. He navigated toward the stage with renewed purpose and caught Pepper's attention. "Hey, it's time to leave."

"But..." Pepper pointed at the karaoke machine. "We're about to do our next number."

"We've got to get to the campground soon, or they'll give away our spot." A lie, but it worked. He tossed jackets at his charges and then herded them toward the door, glaring at anyone who tried to stand in their way.

A lot of dudes tried to block their exit. It was a slow walk.

Pepper sulked her way out the door, tying her jacket around her waist. "We could have closed down the place."

"For sure," Natalie added.

Choosing not to argue, Conner set a brisk pace toward the motor home. He was too old for this job, unable to find any sympathy.

"I loved your choreography." Lily's tone was cajoling.

"We were in a dance troupe in high school." Pepper perked up at Lily's interest. "The wedding party is going to be performing that song at the reception."

Conner made a mental note to warn Dorothy.

"I can teach you the steps if you like." Pepper was back to her gushy self. She hooked her arms through Natalie's and Lily's. "I love it when wedding parties do production numbers."

"So fun," Natalie chorused.

"Thanks, but no." Lily was nothing if not gracious. "I have two left feet."

Conner got them into the motor home and was about to take the driver's seat when Pepper shrieked.

"We have to go back!" Pepper looked like she might cry. She tossed her jacket on the dinette table. "My cell phone is missing."

"No-no-no-no." Natalie dug in her pockets until she had her own sparkly device in hand. "Whew."

Conner dropped the keys on the center console and searched Pepper's jacket pockets. Nothing. "Stay here. I'll get it." There was no way Conner was letting those gals head back into that bar again. "Rose-gold case and rhinestones?"

"Yes. I think I left it on the stage. I'll go with you." Pepper was already hurrying down the steps.

"No. Stay here." Conner's words had no stopping power.

Pepper charged ahead.

"Let her go with you," Lily said from the passenger seat. "If someone found her phone, it might get awkward if you claim it as yours."

True. He and Pepper hurried back to the bar.

But it wasn't that simple. The phone wasn't on or around the stage, and no one had turned Pepper's phone in to the lost and found at the bar. Plus, a few persistent cowboys kept offering to buy Pepper a drink.

"Conner." Pepper clutched his arm. "That girl has my phone."

That girl hung out with the motorcycle gang. She was about Pepper's age but was wearing leathers and a dark expression. She held up the glittery phone and snapped a selfie with a duck-lip pout that wasn't as palatable as Natalie's.

Pepper reached the woman before he did.

"You found my phone. Thanks so much." She gushed; she smiled; she held out her hand.

It was as if the entire leather-vested, chain-wearing group growled at sweet Pepper.

She stiffened, but held her ground.

"Now isn't the time for heroics." At least, not by Pepper. Conner stepped between her and danger. "We don't want any trouble."

The growling became a thing, audible above the music.

"We just want the young lady's phone." Subtly, Conner planted his feet hip distance apart, his hands loose at his sides.

"Or we'll call the cops." Pepper poked her head around Conner, wearing an expression of schoolyard superiority, the one that said: *Na-na, I told Teacher what you did.*

This wasn't that type of negotiation.

Conner gently elbowed Pepper behind him and repeated himself. "We don't want any trouble." But that didn't mean he was shying away from it, either.

"We'll give it back." A grizzled, gray-bearded man got to his feet from a table filled with glasses of beer. He plucked the phone from the woman's hand. "We'll give it to her in exchange for a kiss."

"Keep the phone," Conner said without missing a beat. He turned and firmly nudged Pepper toward the door.

"But…" The bride-to-be dug in her heels. "My life is in there."

Just as Lily's had been in her phone, the one she'd left behind in San Diego. "You'll live."

Pepper darted around Conner, leaving him no choice but to reverse course.

The bearded biker chuckled and licked his lips. "I guess it's my lucky day."

Pepper took a slow step toward him. "Have you ever heard of the '#MeToo' movement?"

"This guy hasn't heard about personal hygiene," Conner whispered in Pepper's ear. "When I say the word, grab your phone and run." He came around in front of her again.

"You know what I've heard?" Scowling, Gray Beard hitched up his pants. "Finders keepers, losers weepers."

"Now!" Conner swiped a full beer mug off the table and tossed the contents at the biker.

Pepper snatched her phone from his beefy hand.

They both ran toward the door with what seemed like an entire biker clan hot on their heels.

He hadn't thought this through. There was

no security to bail him out as there had been at the concert the other night. There was no easy escape, either. Their best chance was to lock themselves in the motor home and hope none of the bikers had a gun or the desire to kick the RV's door in.

Conner and Pepper burst out of the bar just as Lily brought the motor home to a stop in front of them.

Natalie threw the door open. "Get in!"

Pepper ran up the steps, stopping at the top to take stock of the damage. "Gross. I'm soaked in beer." She smelled like it, too.

"Go-go-go!" Conner locked the door behind him. "No time to change."

Lily gunned it down the street as soon as the door clicked closed. "You were in there so long, we got worried."

"I've never seen anyone as brave as Conner." Pepper half hugged him, half fell into his arms as the motor home lurched ahead. "You saved me."

Behind them, motorcycle engines rumbled to life.

"I haven't saved you yet." Conner set Pepper aside and came to stand at Lily's shoulder, holding on to the upper bunk as they careened around a corner. "I should drive."

"I'm going to use my soft words and tell you to eat a carrot." Lily took another hard turn. Her hold on the steering wheel slipped a little and sent the motor home rocking before she tightened her grip. "I've got this."

Conner bent to look out the rear window. No one was behind them. "Do you know where you're going?"

"Not a clue." Lily turned again, bringing them onto a narrow, twisting country road. "I've always wanted to drive a getaway car, though."

"Maybe we should slow down." Conner knelt next to her. "I don't see anyone back there."

"One last turn, just to be sure." Lily braked hard and took a sharp left onto a dark country road.

"Slow down," Conner cautioned. "Sharp corner ahead."

"These brakes are mush." Lily pumped them, glancing down.

"Sharp corner ahead," Conner repeated over Pepper's and Natalie's panicked screams to brake.

"We're not making that turn." Lily kept going straight, sending the motor home barreling down a dirt road instead of turning.

"There's a gate," Conner said as calmly as he was able. Inside, a voice was shouting, *There's a gate. An iron gate. And we're not stopping!*

"I see it." Lily continued to pump the brakes. But they weren't slowing down.

Conner reached for the gearshift, dropping it to Low. But it was too late.

The motor home busted through the metal ranch gate with a cacophony of sound and came to a halt in a swirl of dust.

Lily frowned up at him. "Would you like to drive now?"

"It was all my fault," Pepper said for what must have been the tenth time. She'd changed out of her damp clothing into stylish sweatpants and a matching pink hoodie. "If I hadn't left my phone in the bar, none of this would have happened."

Lily shook her head, wrapped in a blanket and a thick layer of guilt as she stared at the damage she'd caused—the smashed fenders, the gate bent and hanging on one hinge. "It's my fault. I'm the one who missed the turn." And now they were stuck in the dark, heaven only knew where, with no sign of life anywhere nearby.

The darkness was vast. Not a light from a house or a street visible.

Claiming to fear wolves, Natalie couldn't be coerced to come outside.

Conner had the motor home's hood propped up. He stood on the crumpled bumper, shining a flashlight at the engine, also munched. "I'm going to call the Blackwell Ranch."

"Let's not make a fuss with an SOS." Lily wasn't even officially introduced to the family and she was already causing havoc. *Way to create a first impression.* "Why not just call a tow truck?"

"For one thing, this isn't a quick fix, like an oil change." Conner hopped down to the ground. "The radiator is punctured and the engine block looks cockeyed, which means the frame might be damaged. I could be wrong about that, though. And then there's the brakes."

"The brakes weren't my fault." But everything else was. Lily pulled the ends of the blanket tighter around her shoulders, pressing the fabric with her palms. "This sounds bad."

Conner nodded. "And Big E only trusts his mechanic to work on this. We're over two hundred miles from Falcon Creek. I think insurance only covers the first fifty miles, maybe one hundred. That's quite the tow premium."

"What are we going to do?" Much as Lily tried, she couldn't bring back the fluttery feeling his kiss had given her. She felt as bent inside as the ranch gate. Now both the Harrisons and the Blackwells would consider her a disappointment.

"The Blackwell Ranch has vehicles that can tow us to Big E's mechanic in Falcon Creek." From Conner's grave expression, Lily knew she should be more contrite. "Hopefully, we can apologize properly to the owner of this gate in the morning."

"Of course," Lily said. "I'll pay for all the damage." Her car insurance might cover most, if not all of it.

"I'll split it with you." Pepper clutched her cell phone as if afraid to let it go. "It's only right."

"Before any money passes hands, let's see how this shakes out first." Conner made the call, moving away and talking privately before returning. "Katie's sending Ben. But it's going to take him about four hours to get here. Best try and get some sleep." He shut the hood and dragged the ranch gate closed, fencing them on whoever's property this was, presumably to keep their livestock safe.

Pepper disappeared into the motor home. She and Natalie went into the bedroom and closed the door.

Lily waited at the door for Conner. "Tell me the truth. How much trouble am I in with Big E and the Blackwells?"

"I suppose that's relative." He smoothed her hair behind her ear, bringing warmth and forgiveness with his touch. "You're going to have some explaining to do concerning your so-called cousin Ken. You know that. I'd say Pepper and Dorothy will be the emotional barometer of how that's received. And then there's this old thing." He patted the motor home's exterior wall. "This is Big E's favorite mode of transportation."

"Great." Lily felt like she was sixteen again, having taken her mother's car without asking permission and misjudging the width of a parking space. But this was more than a scratch that could be buffed out.

"I'm not saying it can't be fixed," Conner was saying. "But it's not the best way to introduce yourself to the Blackwells."

"They're going to think I was drunk." She hadn't touched a drop of alcohol.

Conner shook his head. "More than likely, they'll never let you hear the end of putting Big E's ride out of commission. Those Blackwells have a sense of humor and long memories, especially Ben."

"I can take a little ribbing."

Conner scoffed, an indication that *little* might not describe the ribbing ahead. "If that's the case, if I were you, I'd straighten out things with Pepper sooner rather than later."

Lily nodded, not moving inside. She still had something to say to Conner. "Are we good?"

"You mean, am I mad at you for this?" He stared at her with that slow smile she loved so much. "We, Miss Lily, are more than good. We're okay. Now, get inside before I do something we agreed was too soon to be doing."

Kissing.

Lily was tempted to linger and null that agreement. But she was in enough trouble already.

She hurried inside and spent a long time in her bunk second-guessing her decision to slow things down with Conner, instead of worrying about how her apology to Pepper would be received and how her meeting a Blackwell cousin would go in the morning.

CHAPTER TWELVE

"RISE AND SHINE, ladies." Conner hurried outside to greet the driver of a large black semitruck in the gray light of dawn. "Our ride is here."

Our ride. A Blackwell.

Lily hopped out of the bunk and scurried into the small bathroom, needing to make herself look presentable for both her cousin and Conner. Teeth brushed, hair combed, she was just slipping into her cowboy boots when Conner opened the motor-home door.

"I'm not sure the front bumper will stay on if you use it to pull the motor home onto the flatbed." Conner's gaze collided with Lily's. There was no trace of past kisses or shared laughter in his expression. This cowboy was all business. This wasn't a relationship slow-down. This was a full-on stop.

Lily was unexpectedly gutted. She couldn't move, not even to draw a breath.

"I think the rear axle will work." The cowboy behind Conner had broad shoulders, dark hair and an assessing smile, so like Big E's that Lily was taken back to the moment her grandfather had walked into the bridal vestibule.

Past Conner.

Who'd looked much the same as he did today.

"Good morning," Ben said. "I've got room for you ladies in the truck."

Natalie checked him out. "Are you the married one?"

"Honey, all the Blackwell boys are married," Ben said, seemingly without taking offense. "But there are plenty of cowboys working the ranch if you're a sucker for Justins and Stetsons. How are you doing, coz?"

For a second Lily thought Ben knew who she was. But then he quite clearly tipped his cowboy hat to Pepper.

"I'll be fine, as long as we get to the ranch today." Pepper made her way down the steps with all the swagger she'd exhibited the day they'd picked her up in Vegas. She wore a darling red sweater, black leggings and suede booties. "Oh, and coffee. I'll be needing a latte."

"Ditto." Natalie followed her down, wearing a nearly identical outfit only with a beige sweater.

"So this is how Conner feels." Ben slapped Conner on the back. "A beck-and-call cowboy."

"Your sense of humor hasn't improved since kindergarten." Conner had no qualms about firing right back, but he caught Lily's eye as he did so, as if to say, *You can't give these Blackwells an inch.*

"I'm Lily." She came down the steps and hesitated in front of Ben, unsure whether she should shake his hand or hug him.

"She's the cousin of the groom," Pepper called back to them, dwarfed next to the semi Ben had brought.

"Right," Lily said in a small, flat voice.

"Let me expand upon my introduction." Ben gave Lily's hand a bone-breaking shake. "Ben Blackwell, attorney, happily married, soon-to-be father of two." He arched a brow at Conner's scoff. "What? Katie said this was a bachelorette party."

Conner gave Lily a significant look, which she ignored. Now wasn't the right time to explain who she really was.

At this rate, there might never be a right time.

"I'm the one who got us into this predicament." At least Lily was fessing up to something.

"Really?" Ben raised his eyebrows and glanced at Conner. "I thought you were driving."

"Big E doesn't like anyone to drive his motor home without prior approval," Conner clarified for Lily's sake.

"Peachy." She was doubling down on ways to disappoint her grandfather. "Again, I was driving. And I'll step up and pay for the damages."

"Wow. What a surprise. Conner let you drive?" Ben chuckled, tipping that cowboy hat back. "Conner doesn't like to go against the rules. Never has."

"Here it comes. There were extenuating circumstances, Ben," Conner grumbled. "It won't happen again."

Ben's humor dissipated. "It shouldn't. You should be your own boss. You were one of the best horse trainers around."

"I told him that, too," Lily blurted.

"Did you?" Ben gave her another assessing look. "Maybe together we can convince him."

Conner caught Lily's arm and tugged her toward the big truck. "Those conversations are best rebooted at the Silver Stake over a beer when the music is so loud I can't hear you Blackwells nag."

A blue pickup approached from the ranch proper.

"Here's the rancher whose driveway you're blocking." Ben settled his hat more firmly on his head. "Time to make offers of reparation."

"Tell him I'll pay for the damage," Lily called back to him over her shoulder. "Tell him there was no alcohol involved. Tell him—"

"Let the lawyer handle this." Conner helped her into the truck, which was running with the heater blasting. "If you want to talk, you should talk to Pepper."

"Right." *Wrong.* Lily leaned back toward Conner and said in a soft voice she hoped Pepper couldn't hear, "You won't think poorly of me if I hold off until later."

"You're running out of laters, Lily."

"Right." She climbed into the back seat with Pepper and Natalie, but couldn't think of a way to broach the topic.

Besides, the pair was engrossed in social media. She couldn't interrupt them.

"Stop!" Pepper cried as they drove into Falcon Creek. She pointed to a feed store. "There's Brewster's. Grandma Dot said I should pick up some boots there. And I need a new pair of jeans."

Lily knew that wasn't true. She'd seen the inside of Pepper's suitcase.

Ben slowed down. "You have plenty of time to shop before Saturday."

"I don't." Pepper used a bridezilla voice, one that raised concerns about the stress of the bride-to-be. "My days are filled between now and the wedding. We need to stop *now*." That tone… Gone was the gushing, happy-go-lucky bride who was checking off items on her life plan.

Natalie reached for Pepper's hand.

"We can drop the ladies off here," Conner told Ben. "They can shop while we take the motor home over to Charlie's."

Ben frowned, but pulled over so they could get out.

Conner dropped to the ground and helped them down. "Look out for Pepper, will you?" he said to Lily.

"Like she was my own," Lily assured him, wishing Ben wasn't watching so she could squeeze Conner's hand or kiss his cheek or tell him she had meant slow down, not stop. But Ben was watching, so she followed the two younger women up the steps to the loading dock and front door.

An old man sat in front of a chessboard near the feed store entrance. Natalie and Pepper breezed right past him. He waved Lily over. "Name's Pops. You look like a chess player."

"Actually..." She wasn't.

"Sit down and make a move." The old man was thin and neatly groomed, and wouldn't take no for an answer. He shuffled his boots on the wood planks. "I've been itching to start a new game this morning and no one's been by."

Lily perched on a wooden chair and moved a pawn forward with concentration and careful fingers. "I don't know much about chess, I'm afraid."

Pops mirrored her move with a black pawn. "I'm a chess master. Play every day. I'm always up for a friendly game."

Lily focused on how to move another pawn forward. "I don't think I can stay for the whole game."

Pops moved the horse to the middle of the board. "Heading out to the Blackwell Ranch?"

"Yes. Have you been there?"

The old man guffawed. "To one of the biggest and oldest spreads around? Yes, I have. They had quite the shindig out there when Big E turned eighty a few years back. Your move."

The biggest and oldest? She'd had an image in her head of a quaint ranch. It wasn't like the motor home was new. Were the Blackwells Montana royalty?

I'm not royalty.

Lily tried to grab a pawn, but her fingers fumbled and it spiraled around, knocking other pieces over. She apologized and tried setting the board to rights, but it was a lost cause. Her fingers weren't responding to her brain's orders. Pieces fell and scattered.

"I want to play chess." A cowgirl of about eight or nine ran up the steps, trailed by her mirror image, who was no less insistent on playing with Pops.

"Speakin' of Blackwells." Pops nodded toward the girls and a tall, lean cowboy who followed them. "Hello, Jon. Girls."

More Blackwells? Should I introduce myself?

Chickening out, Lily got to her feet. "I should get inside. My friends will be wondering where I am." Not to mention Pepper seemed to have a case of wedding jitters. "Thanks for the game."

Her place was quickly taken by the twin girls.

Lily entered the store with Jon Blackwell. They acknowledged each other with head nods.

This is going to be so awkward when we're formally introduced.

Lily veered toward Pepper and Natalie, who were rummaging through a table of blue jeans. Now was the time to come clean with Pepper about how she wasn't related to Ken before things got worse. "Pepper, remember the day we met?" She cleared her throat. Tried to look nonchalant. "Do you?"

Oh, jeez. Stop babbling.

"That was just a few days ago." Pepper did the giggly-gushing thing, but her words came out strained. "How could I not?"

Right. "I meant to tell you then—"

"Pepper?" Jon Blackwell walked over, tilting his hat back to reveal the same bone structure as his brother Ben. "Grandma Dot's Pepper?"

"That's me." Pepper rushed over to hug him. "Good to see you again, Jon." She introduced Natalie. "And this is my fiancé's cousin Lily."

Oh, boy.

Lily raised a hand. "Actually, about that—"

Jon interrupted her with a laugh. "The Lily who ran Big E's motor home off the road?" He was playing to the crowd—Pepper, Natalie, the middle-aged salesclerk—who responded with laughter. "Ben just texted me about your mishap from the repair shop. Wait until Big E finds out."

Oh, come on.

As one of five children, Lily knew this teasing could not pass without a defense or she'd be forever labeled as an easy mark. "Did Ben tell you we were being chased by a motorcycle gang who—"

"It was so dark," Pepper interrupted. "Super creepy."

"I was scared of wolves," Natalie added. "Conner said he didn't hear any, but I did. I swear I did."

"That doesn't really pertain to the actual motor-home incident." Lily tried to regain control of the conversation, but Jon would have none of it.

"Conner never lets guests get out of hand."

Jon gave them a once-over. "You three must really be a handful."

"Your order is ready, Jon." The woman behind the counter waved to him.

Pepper and Natalie drifted to the cashier behind Jon, asking about the boot selection.

"We're not a handful," Lily muttered, stomping back outside. "*I'm* not a handful."

"Check," one of the little cowgirls told Pops, who gaped at the board, wondering aloud how that could have happened.

"We had to start your game over," one cowgirl told Lily. "That board was a mess."

Lily nodded, owning up to the disarray she'd made of the chess pieces. Why would that be any different from the muddle she'd made of her life?

"Daddy always says he can't make sense of a mess." Her twin nodded.

"And it was a big mess," the first twin said, causing both girls—*both Blackwell girls*—to laugh.

On the bright side, the Blackwells seemed to have a good sense of humor. If only Lily wasn't the butt of their jokes!

A few minutes later Ben and Conner pulled into the parking lot just as Natalie and Pepper came out with their purchases. The motor home was no longer on the flatbed trailer. Conner helped them up, without smiles, slow or otherwise.

"Was the news at the mechanic's shop bad?" Lily asked.

"The jury is still out," Conner said flatly. "How was shopping?"

"Small-town news travels fast—about me and the accident, that is," Lily grumbled, fastening her seat belt.

Ben laughed. "I only texted my brothers and their wives. Of course, if they each tell two friends, and they each tell two friends—"

"Soon all the town will know." Lily frowned at her cousin. "Thanks for that." What a great start she was making as a Blackwell. She hunkered into her seat and refrained from saying anything else on the drive out of town.

"There it is!" Pepper squealed from her window seat. "The Blackwell Ranch."

Ben turned on a narrow lane that cut through two empty pastures. It was difficult for Lily to see around a pair of cowboy hats and two excited women leaning into her line of vision.

And then things came into view. The impressive arch that proclaimed this to be the Blackwell Ranch. A grand two-story home surrounded by lush gardens. Beyond that were barns, corrals, pastures filled with horses and cattle, small cabins and a quaint white farmhouse.

But the home… The mansion…

Lily gaped. "When you said the Blackwells had a guesthouse, I thought you meant they had a *guesthouse*. Not a hotel." Who were these people?

"My brother Tyler would tell you it's both a guesthouse and a hotel." Ben stopped in front of a welcome sign. "Large, yet intimate. This is the end of the line for the wedding party."

Lily got out with Pepper and Natalie. They each grabbed their bags from Conner, assuring him he was no longer needed. No one was more vocal about that than Lily. Nothing was going right today. She needed space.

Conner held Lily back when she would have followed them inside. She peered at him, searching for the man she'd felt such a connection to, but to no avail. The cowboy she'd assumed was Big E's bodyguard on her wedding day was back. All business.

"It's time to tell Pepper the truth," Conner said gravely. "You think her groom isn't going to show up and out you tomorrow?"

"I tried telling her at Brewster's." Lily eased her arm free. "I'll tell her tonight." She took a step toward the guesthouse, needing a room, a space of her own, a moment to accept the fact that she was alone and another to remind herself that that was okay.

"Good luck in there." Conner tipped his hat. "It's been a pleasure being your chauffeur."

Lily's feet stopped forward progress. She turned. "Am I...? Am I not going to see you anymore?" He'd given her all the signs, but she had to know.

"Yeah. I'll be around." But the way he said it implied he'd be keeping his distance. He shuffled his feet and then there it was—that slow smile. "I'm a camp counselor for the Blackwells, after all. Got rules to follow and everything."

Rules he broke for me. Rules he won't break anymore.

She couldn't let him go without a proper goodbye. He'd done so much for her, meant so much to her.

"You're not a camp counselor." Lily moved closer and reached up to rearrange his cowboy hat, tilting it at a jaunty angle. "You're a cowboy. And a horse trainer. And a fixer of broken brides." She pressed a kiss to his cheek. "Take care, Conner Hannah."

And then she walked off into the main house, head held high.

Just the way a Blackwell would do it.

CHAPTER THIRTEEN

"HEY, GUYS." KATIE BLACKWELL crossed the ranch yard to greet Ben and Conner after they'd parked the big truck. Her multicolored shaggy dog trotted at her heels.

"Can't stay, Katie." Ben tossed Conner the keys to the semi. "I've got court this afternoon and you know how Judge Myrna is about being prompt." He beelined for his brand-new SUV.

"Thanks for the rescue, Ben." Carrying his duffel, Conner turned to face Katie, torn. He wanted a check for that double bonus, but to get it, he'd have to produce receipts for his trip, come clean about the mustangs he'd purchased, and confess what Big E had promised and why. And then he'd have a lot of explaining to do.

"Where's Big E?" Katie stood with her hands resting on the swell of her pregnant belly. "He hasn't answered his phone for days for anyone except Dot, and even then, I understand he was cagey about his ETA."

"He's taking care of business in California." Conner didn't like to lie, but with Big E, you never knew who he'd told about what. It was best to be vague. He handed Katie the semitruck keys.

The midday sun beat on his shoulders, but nothing weighed as heavy on him as letting Lily go. The way she'd said goodbye had a finality to it. He needed to abide by that farewell, but he wasn't ready to feel happy about it.

"It's always something with Big E, isn't it?" Katie waved a hand as if she could erase her boss's mischief from the record. "Whatever. How did the stock auction go?"

"It went well." Conner tried to hedge but there was no point delaying the inevitable. "I let the gals sway me a bit."

"And…" Katie tapped her boot impatiently.

"I bought twenty."

Katie muttered something Conner didn't catch and then she pinned him with a cool stare. "Twenty horses. That's a lot." She knelt to pet her dog. "For the record, I wanted to send Ethan to the auction."

Conner braced himself for Katie's ire, for a

list of expenses associated per horse and then for the unpleasant moment when she multiplied that per-horse figure by twenty and began a lecture about ranch overhead.

"Did I hear my name?" Ethan Blackwell came out of a nearby barn, a stethoscope draped around his neck. He was a veterinarian who divided his time between a clinic in town for small animals and the barn, where he based his large-animal practice. When Katie explained what Conner had done, Ethan made light of it. "Conner can evaluate mustangs better than I can. If he bought more than we planned, you can rest assured we'll make more than we planned."

Suddenly, the weight on Conner's shoulders didn't seem so heavy.

"I'm sure they're all quality stock." Katie surveyed Conner darkly. "But that doesn't change the fact that they've all got to be trained before we can claim a profit and…" She blew out a breath. *"Twenty?"*

Conner nodded, grimacing.

"No problem." Ethan slapped Conner on the back. "Conner and I can handle them."

Conner rubbed a hand over the base of his spine and said nothing. But we—he and Ethan—wasn't a reality. Ethan was often on the road visiting patients on ranches and driving back and forth between his home bases. The handling would be laid at Conner's door.

What if I wanted to learn how to train horses? Lily's cool voice echoed in his head.

He rejected the idea. She knew nothing about horses or ranch life, the headaches, risks and worries.

Ethan headed back to the barn, leaving Conner with Katie.

"Tyler wanted some tame horses for guests to ride come spring." Katie sighed. "Will any of them fit the bill?"

"Yes. And the good news is that we can retire some of our working horses for use as guest stock." Freshly broken horses were best paired with experienced riders.

"Twenty." Katie shook her head again. It was going to take her a while to get over the figure. "You'll need to review the budget for training with me."

He'd become something of a jack-of-all-trades at the ranch since Katie had announced her pregnancy. Conner was worried the Blackwells were expecting him to step up and fill in for her while she was on maternity leave.

I'm not that guy.

Just check his track record running things at the Rocking H.

Conner took his trip receipts from an outer pocket on his duffel and handed them to Katie. It was time. There was nothing for it but to say, "Big E promised me a bonus for this trip."

Her eyes widened and then narrowed. "And he promised this because…"

Conner opened his mouth and promptly closed it again. He couldn't tell her he'd transported not one but two Blackwell family members.

Katie peered at him. "You look like you ate sour grapes. What's wrong?" She moved closer and lowered her voice. "Is Pepper a bridezilla?"

"No. Nothing like that. She's a sweetheart. It's just…" He mimicked the gesture she'd made earlier about Big E and hung his head.

She sighed. "We'll discuss the deal you made with Big E when he gets back. For now, you have about forty-five minutes to get cleaned up and make an appearance at the guest lodge for dinner."

"Why?" His head came up. Had Lily requested his presence?

"Dorothy thought a cowboy concierge would be appropriate for Pepper's cowboy-themed wedding." Katie chuckled softly. "I'm going to have to talk to her about that. I'll need you to work those mustangs when they arrive this week. Talk about time constraints. But for now, you've earned your place at the big table tonight. You can get cleaned up in Bunk House One."

Conner nodded.

A ranch hand hailed Katie. With a nod to Conner, she headed toward the next emergency. He didn't envy her the headaches of keeping the working ranch running so efficiently.

Conner hurried to Bunk House One, where he knew he could get a quick shower, a shave and a change of clothes. He almost felt like a new man.

When he entered the guest lodge later, Lily was coming down the stairs, biting her lip. Her dark blond hair tumbled over her shoulders. She wore a spaghetti strap green dress and a yellow shawl around her shoulders. She looked prettier than a field of wildflowers. When she saw him, her eyes lit up and then just as quickly became hooded. "Are you eating with us?"

"Apparently, I'm Pepper's cowboy concierge." He kept his tone, his expression and his body language neutral. "Unless you'd rather I didn't."

"I'd rather we'd shift things back into low gear rather than this full stop you've initiated." Lily hesitated and then closed the distance between them, claiming his arm. "But apparently, my opinion doesn't matter."

"Lily, I—"

"Humor me. I could use a friendly face. Pepper and Natalie said they'd be another few minutes, and I expect Dorothy at any time." Her brow clouded with worry. "I don't know what to say to her. I'm used to facing things with a slew of sisters at my side."

"Well, tonight you've got me." He owed her as much for that double bonus.

"Thank you," she whispered, leaning into him and staring as if she wouldn't mind another one of those kisses they'd sworn off.

Conner swallowed the urge to give her one.

Good thing, too.

The main door opened behind them, and Dorothy Blackwell entered.

"Hi, AND HELLO THERE." Grandma Dot was tall with silver hair and eyes that looked like they could flash sharply. She wore blue jeans and a burgundy button-down with fancy embroidery on it. Her boots were white leather. Overall, she looked like a woman who could handle a man like Big E. "You must be Lily."

"Yes." The truth about who she was pressed on the back of Lily's tongue. "Pepper's told me so much about you." She'd left out the fact that Grandma Dot was an intimidating presence.

"It's a pleasure to meet you." Upon reaching Lily, Dorothy didn't hesitate. She hugged her, hugged her tight, belying all that slightly terrifying veneer. "Welcome to the family." And then she held Lily at arm's length, much the way Big E had when they'd first met. "If you need anything, you let me know. My husband thinks he knows where everything is around here, but he's wrong." She slapped the back pocket of her jeans. "Come on. I hope you're a meat eater. Though we could fix you something else. The beef we're serving tonight comes from my grandson's cattle ranch. Jon has done a really good job of standing up on his own."

"I met Jon in town." Lily's smile felt strained. She'd botched that meeting completely.

Do the right thing.

The time had come to tell the truth.

But before she could begin, Conner said, "I've yet to find a food that any of these gals won't eat, ma'am."

Dorothy led them into a grand dining room that looked like it could accommodate all of Pepper's wedding guests. There were several long tables and dozens of chairs, but only one table had been set for dinner. Decorative gold charger plates waited at each setting.

"This place is lovely." Lily drank in the traditional, upscale furnishings. "When Pepper told me the wedding was going to be at a ranch, I had an entirely different impression."

"The ranch has been in the Blackwell family for generations, expanded by my husband, Big E." Dorothy's words were taut. "The guesthouse opened a little over two years ago and we added on last spring, including expanding the dining room. The idea for the guest ranch was originally Big E's ex-wife's idea."

One of her grandfather's exes? Lily looked to Conner for context and clues about potential pitfalls, but he gave her none. She smiled harder. "I met Ben on the drive in. I'm curious about your other grandsons."

"Ethan is a veterinarian and lives in town. Chance sings a little now and then." An understatement, but Grandma Dot seemed to appreciate the change in subject, smiling a little. "And Ty helps manage the guest ranch, among other things. We Blackwells are a stubborn lot, but we always seem to gravitate toward home eventually."

Lily glanced around the dining room. Although it was beautiful, it told her nothing about the Blackwells except that they had good taste. "I should tell you who I—"

"I know who you are, dear." Grandma Dot indicated Lily should sit down at the dining room table.

"Me, too." Pepper entered the dining room with Natalie in tow. "I can't believe you didn't tell me you're a Blackwell."

"When did you…? How…?" Lily floundered over what to say. "I'm sorry. I didn't mean to imply or lie about who I was. Given how I found out about the Blackwells, I'm not really sure who I am….*should be* in relation to the Blackwells."

"Oh, don't apologize. My husband is quite the orchestrator." Grandma Dot's smile grew. "Welcome to the Blackwell Ranch, granddaughter."

"I'm sorry," Lily said to Pepper again. "I've angsted over this for days. I tried to tell you a couple of times, but Big E wanted to tell Dorothy first and… I'm sorry. Truly."

"Don't be." Pepper gave Lily a hug. It seemed heartfelt. "The best news I got today was being told you really are my cousin."

"Who told you?" Conner asked, taking a seat next to Lily.

"Me." A deep voice had them all turning to the dining room doorway.

"Danny?" It was a good thing Lily was sitting down because shame and unease pressed down on her, weakening her knees.

Her former fiancé strode toward Lily with purpose, as if he was a knight sent to her rescue, a knight wearing khakis, a black polo and a strained smile. "Your father sent me."

"Rudy…" Shame fell away, like the shawl slipping from her shoulders, to be replaced by annoyance. Lily held up a hand to ward Danny off and thrust her chin in the air. "We're not getting married."

"This is juicy." Natalie took a seat across from Conner and raised her phone as if she was going to record the proceedings.

Pepper sat next to her bestie and tsked, raising her glittery phone the same way. "I was wondering why Danny said he was your fiancé when you said you'd recently ended a relationship."

"His excuse about Lily wanting privacy on the trip out did seem flimsy, Pepper." Grandma Dot's eyes narrowed on Danny.

And Danny, who was used to being trusted, respected—revered even, if one counted Lily—slowed his steps.

"I can fill in that information gap," Conner said in a voice edged with animosity. "This is the man Lily's stepdad convinced into proposing to her. She jilted him last weekend when she overheard him admit he'd asked her to marry him for all the wrong reasons. He had cold feet and she was right to leave."

"Props to Lily." Pepper aimed her phone at the jilted groom.

"That isn't the full story." Danny came to stand at Lily's right side, glaring over her head at Conner, who sat at her left.

"Blackwell rule." Grandma Dot took a seat at the head of the table and sent a stern look all around. "No fighting during dinner."

"I'm not here to fight." Danny extended his hand toward Lily without dropping the fierce glare at Conner.

For a moment Lily thought he might be inviting her to take his hand and leave. *That is so* not *happening.* But then she realized Danny was handing her… "My postcard." The one from the shooting range. She spun in her chair to face Conner. "The last time I saw this—"

"Was at the Chance Blackwell concert," Danny said in a hard voice.

Lily stared at Conner, waiting for an explanation, waiting for the myriad emotions—disappointment over Rudy, guilt over ending things poorly with Danny, confusion about the postcard—to coalesce into clarity and, hopefully, calm.

"Your father sent him," Conner said simply, getting to his feet, never taking his eyes off Danny. "They need to respect your wishes, Lily."

Danny scoffed. He and her family rarely respected Lily's wishes.

"This isn't up for negotiation." Conner spoke like he was a judge handing down a sentence.

Lily experienced a growing sense of wonder, a feeling that soothed, that settled, and made her want to wrap her arms around Conner. Because he was standing up for her. And Conner… His behavior all made sense now. *He* made sense. Driving all night. Sneering anytime she brought up Danny's name. The two men had talked the night of the concert, maybe even done more than talk if she was reading their body language right.

"You should have told me," Lily chastised Conner, but gently, softly.

Conner didn't answer. He was too busy glaring at Danny.

He's protecting me—not out of duty, but because he cares.

Wonder blossomed into excitement. Excitement raced from her head to her toes. This was what she should have felt for Danny. And if that was true… Lily stared up at her cowboy and breathed in deeply, carefully, trying to slow down and acknowledge what was happening. Only this love wasn't slow. It didn't amble. It shot off like a rocket. This feeling. This love.

I love Conner.

But there was no time to savor that revelation. Rudy had sent her to be collected, like a child who'd wandered off the playground. And Danny had obeyed her stepfather's wishes, rather than Lily's.

The two men towered over her shoulders, breathing like football players who'd just chased down the same ball and were preparing to pounce on it. Pepper and Natalie were a rapt audience, cell phones recording. Grandma Dot raised her brows at Lily but did nothing, said nothing.

And why would she? This is all my fault.

The postcard of the take-charge woman slipped from Lily's fingers. She told herself she'd dropped it on purpose as she turned on Danny. "Did you not read the back?" She'd written an affirmation of her decision *not* to marry him.

"I brought your cell phone." Danny placed the device on the table near Lily, and then reached into his pocket and produced a blue velvet ring box. "And our wedding rings. I love you, Lily."

He loves me? He chose now to tell her three little words he'd never spoken before? She shook her head. *He's not even looking at me.* He continued to glower at Conner.

"Did you hear me?" Danny asked impatiently. "I said—" He lunged forward, throwing a crude punch at Conner, who leaned sideways to avoid the contact and then stepped up to land his punch squarely on Danny's face, knocking him to the ground.

The room erupted. Lily jumped out of her seat and held Conner back, thin yellow shawl falling to the floor. Grandma Dot rushed to the dining room doorway and called for two bags of ice in a calm voice, as if she was used to physical outbursts. Natalie ran around the table and helped Danny to his feet while Pepper continued to film because Conner and Danny were angrily chirping and posturing at each other, threatening to brawl.

"Don't." Lily bunched the crisp cotton of Conner's shirt in her hand and pinned him with a stare.

"Lily…" His brown-eyed gaze softened a little but not enough to promise peace.

She captured Danny's gaze next. "Please, don't."

Grandma Dot returned to the table. "Why is it that you young folk find it so hard to obey my no-fighting rule?"

"I'm sorry. But…" Lily turned to face Danny, so angry at Rudy's continued interference, she could howl. "*You love me?* Danny, why didn't you tell me before? Why did you tell Rudy you didn't have to marry me to protect me?"

Danny's expression reflected anguish, visible past the red bruise rising on his cheek. "That was after I pointed out to your dad that

I thought you had cold feet. You must not have heard that part."

"You're saying that *you* didn't have... And that I felt..." Stomach churning, Lily gripped the back of a nearby chair.

Danny knew her inside and out. He knew her well enough to plunge out of an airplane and wait to make sure she pulled her chute before he pulled his. The fact that he cared for her had never been in doubt. But love...

"Don't believe him, Lily." Conner laid a hand over hers on the chair. "He said your father sent him."

There was that. But perhaps the two men had talked, and Danny had received Rudy's blessing to chase after her.

He loves me?

"You never told me." And now... Did it matter? *No.* It was too late. She loved Conner.

"Don't believe him, Lily," Conner said again.

"You." Danny glared at Conner and Lily's joined hands and trembled with apparent rage. He pointed at Conner. "The other night you said you didn't want to fight me. And now, with an audience, you pull this." He gestured to his rapidly swelling eye. "Don't imply I'm

trying to manipulate Lily when it's you and that Big E trying to pull the strings."

Lily's stomach didn't like the accusations flying about the room. They were asking her to choose sides.

"Conner's not that calculating." Pepper angled her phone for a close-up of her face. "He told it like it was, whereas Danny doesn't seem like a straight shooter. Look at what happened just now, throwing the first punch out of nowhere. That's not the way to win back your fiancée."

"Don't forget Danny never told Lily how he felt, either," Natalie said sagely. "That's some big overthinking. No, if anyone is manipulative—"

"Enough audience chatter," Danny snapped. "This is between the cowboy and me."

Lily frowned. "Shouldn't it be between you and me?"

"You think I was afraid of you?" Conner sneered, picking up her shawl and moving between Lily and Danny. "I didn't need to fight after the concert because security was coming with their Tasers."

"Security?" Pepper turned to Natalie.

"Tasers?" Natalie faced Pepper.

"We missed it!" they both cried.

"Ladies, not now," Grandma Dot said, employing a severe tone that should have deterred everyone at the table from more upset.

"You wily dog." Danny laughed. "You goaded me to charge you in full view of security. Well played, cowboy. Well played. But you're still the old man's puppet."

"Be careful, young man," Grandma Dot said, voice as hard as steel. "That's my husband you're talking about. It's not too late to ask you to leave."

Danny leaned to one side, gaze connecting with Lily's. "Notice the cowboy isn't denying his role as a puppet."

Lily drew a calming breath. "But, Danny, you said—"

"The way you're digging a grave, Danny, Conner doesn't need to say a thing." Pepper grinned.

"He just needs to watch you." Natalie made the I'm-watching-you gesture, pointing at her eyes with two fingers and then pointing those two fingers at Danny.

Of course Conner was watching Danny. He was paid to keep the Blackwell family and guests safe. So yeah, he needed to watch her ex. And yeah, his knowledge of horse behavior from being a trainer meant he knew how to judge character and evaluate threats. Wild mustangs were unpredictable. Men—especially upset, jilted grooms—could be unpredictable, too.

Lily should have felt reassured. But there was something about Danny's accusations that upset her stomach. If she hadn't been sure—gosh, not 100 percent, but close—that Conner wasn't a puppet trying to pull her strings, she'd be racing out of here.

Conner was a good man, a smart man. And Lily loved him. But she loved Danny, too, as a friend. And both were saying things with a ring of truth.

Rudy. Big E. She wasn't certain of the motives of either man. But she had more experience with Rudy pulling strings than Big E.

A woman rushed into the room and handed Grandma Dot two small bags of ice. Dorothy told her to hold dinner a few more minutes and gave a bag to each man. Neither put it where it would do the most good.

"I know this looks bad," Danny said to Lily, shaking the bag and rattling the ice. "I should have talked to you—not Rudy—about your feelings."

Grandma Dot scoffed. "It might be a little late for sensitivity, young man."

"Is it?" Danny's gaze captured Lily's. There was no anger. Not at her. "I'm not the one who hijacked a vulnerable bride or had me tased and detained. I haven't had a chance to talk to Lily or to let her speak her mind to me. I haven't had her locked in a motor home for days, feeding her lines to turn her against me."

There was truth in that. It spun and banged about inside Lily, trying to undermine her feelings—those sparks she'd felt for a just-met cowboy and hadn't felt for her best friend turned fiancé, that toe-curling kiss, that certainty of love. Could she be wrong? About everything?

Ice clattered on china as Conner dropped his bag on her charger plate. "I haven't brainwashed Lily. I've listened to what she's had to say." He glanced at Lily tenderly.

The way Lily felt when she was in Conner's arms returned. The warmth. The comfort. The magnetic spark. There was truth in that, too.

A woman wearing a white apron appeared in the doorway, frowning.

"Blackwell rule." Grandma Dot returned to her place at the table's head. "Never upset the cook. It's time to eat." She indicated everyone should take their seats. "Put those phones away and abide by my no-arguing rule or you'll be sent to your rooms." She arched a silver brow and gave each of them a scathing look. "And don't think I won't do it."

CHAPTER FOURTEEN

CONNER'S KNUCKLES THROBBED.

He handed his bag of ice to the server who set a plate in front of him.

Pain was good. It made him sharp. He knew what the alternative to pain was—that numb feeling inside. He'd take pain any day, anger, too, especially when it came to protecting Lily from that jerk Danny.

"Prime rib." Lily stared at her plate and the thick slab of steak. She hadn't picked up her knife and fork.

"It's fabulous." Pepper had already cut into hers and was chewing. "Isn't it, Nat?"

"It is." But Natalie stared at Danny, who sat across from her.

"Let me." Danny—the groom who refused to be jilted—slid Lily's plate nearer his own and began cutting her steak.

Conner should have known she'd need help. He should have been the first to come to her aid. He hacked at his prime rib, which was so tender he could have pulled it apart with a fork. He should have remembered Lily avoided food that required cutting or fork dexterity.

"Lily loves barbecue." Danny cut in a precise pattern, as if he cut her food all the time. "And spicy dishes. I've only been in town since yesterday, but it lacks the diverse cuisine we have in San Diego."

Dorothy gave him a cold stare, which was totally wasted since the man's attention was on preparing Lily's food as if she was a toddler.

"You don't have to dice her asparagus," Conner snapped. "Or separate her mashed potatoes into bite-size portions."

"I know what Lily likes." Danny centered Lily's plate in front of her, turning it just so.

Just enough to annoy Conner and embarrass Lily. There was color in her cheeks.

"Sure," Conner allowed. "You knew what she liked when she was a kid."

"Enough! Stop, the both of you. And, Danny… Don't. Ever. Do. That. Again." Lily glowered at her ex and then slowly picked up a fork. Slowly speared a bit of meat. Slowly brought it to her mouth.

"Pepper, I can't remember what your bridesmaids are wearing." Dorothy tossed the conversational ball in a safer direction. "Remind me."

While Pepper and Natalie prattled on about fabrics and specific hues of color, Conner leaned forward and glared at Danny. "We're fully booked this week. You'll need to leave in the morning." The wedding party was due to arrive tomorrow.

"I'll be moving to one of the bunk houses in the morning." Danny smirked. "It's all arranged."

Bunk House One, Conner bet, gritting his teeth.

"Lily, there's a mountain bike trail about thirty minutes away." To his credit, Danny had thought ahead, dangling treats Lily might find enticing. "A bike rental place, too. Want to go tomorrow?"

Danny didn't realize Lily had outgrown the desire for an adrenaline rush.

"The mustangs are being delivered tomorrow." Conner bared his teeth in a smile at his adversary. "If Lily's serious about horse training, she'll want to be there. But you go ahead."

"Not without Lily."

"You can go, Danny." Lily, very slowly, slid

her fork beneath a small mound of mashed potatoes. "I'm not your sidekick."

"Is the job open?" Natalie whispered loud enough for everyone to hear. It was clear she wouldn't mind an opportunity to get to know Danny better.

Conner would have been rooting for Natalie if Danny showed an ounce of interest. But she was about a decade too young in terms of life stage to catch the jilted groom's eye. Not to mention Danny wasn't honest. But Conner had arrived on scene at the church a good minute before Lily. He hadn't heard Danny make any references to Lily having doubts.

"You're not my sidekick," Danny snapped. "I care about you. You're my responsibility."

Lily blanched.

"How romantic." Conner scoffed. "What you really mean is she's the audience you need to make you feel more like a man."

Lily's potato-laden fork paused in front of her lips.

"I'm going to have to remind you of the house rules," Dorothy said firmly. "No arguing at the table. Last warning." She cleared her throat. "Pepper, I can't wait to meet Ken. You said he's coming tomorrow."

"I can't wait to see him." Pepper gave Danny

a put-upon look. "Ken is fabulous, mature and the love of my life. If I thought he had any doubts, I'd talk to him about it, not his father or my father."

Danny's mouth was set in a hard line. Nothing anyone said was going to change his opinion or his objective. He wasn't going to leave the Blackwell Ranch willingly, not without Lily.

And Conner was determined to thwart his every move.

"DOROTHY." CONNER LINGERED at the guest ranch after dinner, helping wash dishes as he waited for the opportunity to talk to Big E's wife. "Do you have a minute?"

"Of course." Dorothy was a tall, imposing figure, not to mention her personality was as large as Big E's. She led him out to the porch. "I'm guessing you want me to send Lily's fiancé away? You know, that's something only Lily can do."

"Actually, I was thinking he needs a little help remembering his feet were the ones with a chill." Conner cleared his throat before pressing on into dangerous territory. "He needs a worshipful audience. Let's give him one."

She studied him. "Pepper's friend Natalie might do the job. She's interested."

"Beg pardon, ma'am, but she's not the challenge a man like Danny falls for. There… uh…" He cleared his throat. "There used to be a woman here at the ranch. She's been banned from the property, but…"

"Conner." Dorothy scowled, looking as if she'd like to ban Conner from the property. "You can't be serious. You want to invite the *last* Mrs. Elias Blackwell here?"

He dared nod his head while the idea hung between them in the rapidly chilling evening air. Zoe Blackwell was in her thirties and combined a toxic mix of alluring beauty and unpredictable chaos. But there was no way Conner was going to jump into this further than he had already until Dorothy chewed on the idea a bit. And she'd only gnaw on it if she cared for Lily.

"Zoe has a way of upsetting the apple cart." Dorothy was mumbling now. "*My* apple cart, if truth be told."

"Zoe has a knack for picking up seasoned strays, ma'am. And worshipping them."

"I don't like this Danny character any more than you do." Dorothy's voice seemed distant. "That doesn't mean I'm going to invite

Big E's biggest mistake back in the Blackwell gates. She'll take a mile out of the inch we need her for and then keep showing up like a weed in my flower garden. If you want to protect Lily, why don't you—"

"Beg pardon, ma'am, but I don't look like Blackwell-marrying material." Conner leaned on the porch railing. The setting sun cast his shadow like a slim shard of tall grass across the front yard.

Dorothy considered him in silence for an uncomfortable bit. "You know, I talked to Big E about his long-lost son. Lily's not a Blackwell like my grandsons. She wasn't raised with generations of expectations and responsibility, nor do we expect her to come in here and uphold the family legacy."

"And yet she has a legacy to uphold." One she'd never live up to on the Rocking H.

"Save me from men who think they're undeserving of a good woman." Dorothy leaned her hip against the railing next to him. "Whether you consider yourself worthy of Lily is neither here nor there. It was Lily's choice to walk away from the marriage, and it'll be her choice as to whether she sticks with that decision or comes to her senses and sees the cowboy who's right in front of her. Trying to distract Danny with other women isn't what's needed here. You should pay attention to your own house before you try to redecorate someone else's. Now, I'm relieving you of your concierge duties for the wedding. We can't be known as the resort where staff gives guests black eyes."

"Yes, ma'am." Conner headed down the steps, Dorothy's rebuke stinging in his ears.

"Oh, and, Conner."

He turned.

Dorothy gave him that hard stare of hers, the one that made Big E nervous. "Don't ever ask me to invite one of Big E's ex-wives here again."

THE ROCKING II looked the same way it had when Conner had left over a week ago.

A few fence posts by the thinly graveled drive were cockeyed. A couple of boards swung loose on the side of the barn. Parsnip trotted along the fence line, keeping up with his truck. And everywhere Conner glanced, things seemed to be covered in a layer of grime and neglect.

Conner was familiar with guilt. It blossomed every time he returned from the Blackwell Ranch. He should reset those fence posts.

He should grab a hammer and nails and secure the loose barn boards. As for the stallion…

He'd somehow managed to jump a fence. He stood in the pasture nearest Conner and whinnied.

"Like you want to pick up where we left off," Conner told him, grabbing his bags from the back of the truck and heading for the door.

"'Bout time you got home." Mom stood in the doorway leaning on her forearm crutches. Her red sweatshirt had an appliqué of a chicken. Her jeans hung off her skinny frame. Her brown-gray hair was loose but neat. "Where's Lily?"

"She's staying at the Blackwell guest ranch." Conner's boots crunched across the gravel as he eyed the front porch steps. The foundation had shifted again. The steps were pulling away from the porch proper. It was becoming a safety hazard.

Mom backed into the house, banging against the front door and stepping around Ned, her orange tabby, as she did so. "I thought Lily would stay with us."

"Why?" Conner dropped his bags and hung his hat on a hook. He kept his boots on. He needed to go out later and check his mother's chickens. He breathed a sigh of… Not relief. Not exhaustion. Not regret.

Sadness. The Rocking H deserved better than him.

Mom stood in the middle of the living room on the worn brown carpet. "Why would I think Lily was staying with us? Because she sounded perfect for you."

Conner frowned. "I thought you said I shouldn't be her rebound man." Wise advice.

"Pishaw." His mother banged her crutches on the floor, sending poor Ned fleeing for cover. "I only said that because it seemed like you wanted to hear it. You always do the opposite of what I say. I thought you might rebel."

Conner's jaw dropped. "That is the worst logic ever." But he'd expected as much. He marched into the kitchen, taking stock of the clean, if worn, counters and comparing them to the luxury of the Blackwells' granite finishes. They didn't have a bucket beneath a leaky roof, either.

"Anytime you want to try being a parent and do better…"

"Save me the lecture. Please." Conner sat down at the kitchen table. The house was quiet. Lily wasn't sitting nearby slinging a quip, huffing about something or other, or beaming at him as if he hung the moon.

The only thing he hung was his hat on that lopsided hook in the foyer.

"Do you want to eat?" His mother's tone had changed from teasing to caring.

"No. I had dinner with the Blackwells." And afterward Lily had excused herself without so much as a thank-you for standing up to that ridiculous ex-groom of hers. In fact, he wondered if she'd been swayed by Danny's accusations.

She wouldn't like to hear about that double bonus.

His mother sat down next to him, resting her crutches on the arm of her chair. "Do you want to talk?"

Conner sighed.

"You want to talk." She took a moment to stand and adjust her grip on her crutches. "I'll get the cookies and milk. The cookies I made for Lily, by the way. She said she wanted to come over."

"That doesn't mean she should. Mom, please…"

The crutches banged on the floor again, her eyes flashing. "You're ashamed of being a Hannah."

"I'm not."

"Then you're ashamed of me."

"I'm not," Conner said through gritted teeth.

"So it's the ranch." His mother was so angry, she wobbled.

Conner didn't argue. He got up and steadied her.

"I never should have transferred ownership to you," she said with unusual bitterness.

"True. I brought us to the edge of ruin." A position they teetered on today.

"You didn't." She pounded her crutch on the floor as if stomping a foot. "I asked too much of you. You were eighteen and had never balanced a checking account. I should have figured out a way to stay the course while I recovered."

"Now, that's asking too much of you." She'd spent weeks in the hospital and then weeks at home in bed, relearning to walk.

"Big E would have helped me. Or the Taylors." She pounded the floor with her crutch once more.

"For the love of Mike, sit down before you ruin the last decent chunk of floor." Conner helped her into a kitchen chair. "You aren't supposed to have regrets. You chose to focus on getting well. I don't begrudge you giving me the reins so you could do that." She'd given him so much in life. Long after the Rocking H passed hands, they'd still have each other.

"You chose to focus on getting well after Parsnip sent you into that railing." His mother's breath was ragged, her cheeks mottled. "But then you turned your back on this place."

"Because the overhead is too high and the profit too low. That's a hard lesson for a man to learn." But it wasn't the reason he'd turned his back on his heritage.

"Yes, the overhead and profit weren't what either of us liked when you first began training cutting horses and had no reputation." She gripped his fingers, squeezing in a display of strength. "But now you have a reputation—"

"Had."

"And you can command good prices. The Rocking H could be great again. What's holding you back?"

Conner stood. He couldn't tell her the truth.

If he was injured again—or worse—there'd be no one to take care of her.

CHAPTER FIFTEEN

THE MORNING AFTER Danny told Lily he loved her, she stared at her phone's favorites list.

Dad. Peyton. Amanda. Georgie. Fiona.

It was time to call someone in the family, time to talk about what she would do next. The question was: *Who?*

Irrationally, she didn't want to talk to any of the Harrisons. She wanted to talk to Conner. She wanted to be reassured by his even voice and slow smile as she went through her options. She wanted to see his face when he told her he wasn't pulling her strings, the way Danny had accused him of.

Lily sat on a bench in the yard behind the guesthouse while Pepper and Natalie discussed decorating options with Hadley, a Blackwell by marriage. The three women took turns pointing, gesturing and otherwise spreading their arms as if indicating where something grand would go.

Grand. The Blackwell Ranch was that. But

it didn't seem to have much history. Most of what Lily had seen so far was new. She thought back to Conner's speech about looking for roots in the place of her ancestors. Lily had found none. Although a large oak tree in a nearby pasture looked promising. Had someone planted it? Or was it a volunteer, a tree sprouted from a seed dropped by a passing bird?

"Good morning." Danny sat on the bench next to her. "Great place for a wedding. We could get married out here. Who needs a church and hundreds of wedding guests?"

Although Lily's gut reaction was to deny-deny-deny, she took a moment to study Danny's face. The bruising near his eye had gotten worse. "Jeez, Danny. You should see a doctor."

"I've been icing it and taking something to reduce the swelling." He shrugged. "If I leave, someone might not let me back on the property."

"It's not like that." Although Conner's ferocious face and Grandma Dot's stern one came to mind.

The sun's rays had chased away the morning chill, promising a hot afternoon.

Danny nodded toward the mountains. "I

bet there's good skiing on those slopes in the winter and zip-lining in the summer. And surprise. It's summer." He gave her a half smile, an invitation to get out and do something wild.

"I'm not up for anything super fun." *Why couldn't I have fallen head over heels in love with Danny?* That would have been so easy. What she felt for Conner was risky, the future uncertain.

The bridal trio laughed, drawing Lily's attention, taking her back to a time when she'd believed love was easy.

It wasn't long after the rocket accident that the Harrison girls had been allowed to stay up until midnight on New Year's Eve.

Mom was a stickler about watching those network shows with musical performances, mostly because every time the music came on, Dad would shed his stiff military image and bring her to her feet to dance. That night Dad had cut a rug with all six of his girls— Mom and the Harrison sisters.

Stiff, formal Rudy Harrison had moves in their living room. He was wild when he boogied, dancing circles around the girls. It was the first time Lily was conscious of thinking something wild didn't always entail danger.

But the slow dances… The slow dances had been reserved for the parents.

"I love you down to my toes, Rudy," Mom would say during those slow songs. "Always have. Always will."

It was the first time Lily remembered thinking her parents were sappy romantics and had wished for a sappy marriage of her own someday. How had she forgotten that wish? Pepper's laughter filled the air.

Lily sighed. "You know, Pepper is thrilled to be getting married. I never felt like that about marrying you. Apologies if that sounds harsh."

"You're not like Pepper," Danny said evenly. "That woman's nonstop energy is exhausting. She probably gushes when she gets her oil changed."

"That's not very nice." But it was probably true.

"You don't gush, Lily." He turned to face her. "Don't judge your love for me by the high-pitched energy Pepper exhibits."

Lily touched his hand. Once. Briefly. Just to be sure there were no sparks, no rush of attraction making her heart pound.

Nothing.

Because he's not Conner.

"Look, I'm sorry I walked out on the wedding without talking to you. But it was for the best." That was what she would have written on the postcard from Rustlers, given the chance. "We're better friends than we would have been lovers."

"I want to spend the rest of my life with you, Lily." Danny stared at the hand she'd touched. "I'm sorry you heard me talking to your dad in the church. You know, a lot of people have cold feet and then go on to have wonderful marriages."

They'd been friends forever, talking about all kinds of subjects. But they'd never talked of love or the depth of their love. And Lily found she had no desire to. What she felt for Danny was different from what she felt for Conner.

"How old do you think that tree is over there?" Lily pointed toward the tall oak.

"I couldn't say." And it sounded like he wasn't interested in finding out.

"I wonder if my great-great-grandfather planted it."

"Who cares?" Danny inched closer until his leg nearly touched hers. "This is the first opportunity I've had to talk to you alone. I love you, Lily. And I know you love me, too.

We can get past this. I've loved you since the day I met you."

Lily found that hard to believe. "Has anyone ever told you that you're a good kisser? Any of those *many* women you dated even though you claim to have loved me for decades?" Despite her best efforts, bitterness crept into her tone.

"I was giving you the time you needed to spread your wings." Danny smirked. It was a superior smirk, the kind that preceded what he thought was going to be a win.

He was wrong. Just like he'd been wrong last night to cut and divide every bit of food on her plate until she felt small and helpless. Conner knew about her lack of finger dexterity, but he'd never embarrassed her with it. In hindsight, Danny did it all the time.

"Hang on. You like the way I kiss you?" Danny chuckled, missing the point completely.

Lily cleared her throat. "Your kissing technique doesn't make up for our lack of chemistry."

Her ex had a fierce expression made more intense by the bruising. "I followed you to the ends of the earth after you left me at the altar." He was practically shouting.

The three women turned to stare.

"Can we keep this civil?" Lily whispered. *Stay out of trouble. Do the right thing. Honor your word.*

"I know you and Rudy set me up in business," Lily told him. "You made me feel like I was in charge, and I suppose I should be grateful for that. But it was just a sham. *I'm* just a sham."

"That's not true." But his protest lacked conviction.

"I want to give you the business, if you want it." And just like that, Lily closed a door on her life in California. *Horse training, here I come.* "You could make the tours edgier. And who knows? It might do so well you could retire from the navy." Get out from under Rudy's thumb.

"But…it makes you happy." For once, Danny didn't tell her how to feel. "And you'll have nothing to do. Unless… Unless this means you want to get married so I can take care of you."

"No." When he would have protested, she hurried on. "I appreciate everything you've done for me, but I'll be okay on my own."

A young man wearing blue jeans and a blue-checked button-down, both with store creases, came around the corner, walking with the stilted steps of those uninitiated in the use of cowboy boots. "Pepper."

The bride-to-be turned, squealed and charged across the lawn, leaping into the man's arms. "Ken! I wasn't expecting you until later."

Ken was nothing like what Lily had expected. He was kind of a nerd.

Ken kissed Pepper like she was air he was in desperate need of, and then he drew back and stared into her eyes in silence, seemingly content to reacquaint himself with her face.

There was truth in that kiss, that stare, that connection. And there'd been nothing like that between her and Danny. Ever.

Lily stared at her hands. "You never looked at me like that." Much less kissed her like that.

That kiss was more like the one Conner had given her.

"Don't get so high and mighty." Danny stubbornly refused to back down. "Love like that is rare and doesn't last."

"That may be," Lily said. "But it doesn't mean we both shouldn't hold out for it."

"LILY?" AMANDA PICKED up after barely one ring. "Lily? Are you okay? I'm so mad at you right now. Lily? Can you hear me?"

"Yes. If you give me a chance to speak, you might hear me." After returning to her room, it had taken Lily only twenty minutes of staring at her contacts list to work up the nerve to call her sister. She stood at her bedroom window, staring at Ken and Pepper in the yard below. They held hands and walked the perimeter, looking utterly in love and causing an ache in Lily's chest.

Maybe I could get a love like that if I had a life plan like Pepper's.

"Thank heavens you're all right." Amanda sounded out of breath. "Good boy, Clancy. Water that tree. Maybe then you'll slow down. How can you just run away like that?"

"Are you talking to me or the dog?" Her sister was always rescuing strays.

"Don't joke, Lily. I was worried sick that you'd been kidnapped even though Dad said we had to give this Blackwell character the benefit of the doubt." She huffed the way she did when she didn't have faith in someone. "You shouldn't have run off and left us with that scribbled note."

"I'm sorry."

"Are you sure you weren't taken against your will? That would be easier to stomach than Dad not being our father. Clancy, don't eat grass!"

"No kidnapping. Just a cowboy chauffeur." They'd been together in close quarters for so long, Lily glanced around, expecting him to be nearby.

He wasn't.

She missed him.

Amanda ignored Lily's attempt at a joke. "So you're okay? What are you going to do about Danny?"

"Nothing." She told Amanda about overhearing Danny at the church and that he'd confessed to everyone how Rudy had sent him to Montana. "I'm not going to marry him." And she suspected they could no longer be friends. "My life is a joke. My father isn't *my* father—"

"Don't say that!"

"My business isn't *my* business. My ex-fiancé isn't my one true love. And I don't even like doing risky things."

"Hang on. That last one is a shocker. Am I really talking to Lily Harrison?" Amanda sighed. "And if it is you, are you getting enough to eat? You sound a bit peckish."

"Amanda." Lily stared at the ceiling. "What did Big E tell you about my birth certificate?"

"None of us spoke to the mysterious Mr. Blackwell, except Dad. Besides, I was too upset to listen. I left the church and drove to your apartment. My heart is pounding just thinking about it."

"But what did Dad say? Or Peyton?" The most levelheaded of the Harrisons.

"Lily, that birth certificate is a hoax. Clancy!" Amanda grunted. "Down, boy. Sorry, sir. He's a lover, not a fighter. Forget about this, Lily, and come home. I need to know you're okay."

"I told you I'm fine. What's this about a hoax?"

"Dad is our dad, Lily. We're Harrisons. If we weren't, someone would have told us long before now."

"Just because you don't want to believe it doesn't mean it isn't true." Bold words for a woman who was hiding in her luxury hotel room because she didn't feel like a Blackwell.

Amanda scoffed. "I'm taking a DNA test. You know me. I need proof. Until then, that birth certificate is a hoax, as far as I'm concerned." She let out an exclamation. "Clancy! Stop it with the inappropriate sniffing. No, I…I don't want a date. My dog is not Cupid. Ha ha." Amanda made a growling noise, lowering her voice. "I swear, this dog should have been a bloodhound. He has to smell everything and everyone."

"He has the right idea, Amanda. You haven't dated in forever."

"Thanks for reminding me." She huffed. "Are you remembering to brush your hair?"

"I'm not the little terror I used to be. I can get myself ready in the morning, you know."

"No, boy." Amanda gave Clancy another stern command. "Come home, Lily. You shouldn't be out in the wilds of Montana with strangers."

"I'm not with strangers. Don't forget Danny's here. He brought our wedding rings and everything." She wanted to ask Rudy why he'd sent her fiancé, but she was afraid she knew the answer. Her stepfather didn't think Lily could get along without him.

"Ew. Your wedding rings. That is kind of sad. You've just given me a whole new set of scenarios to worry about."

"I can handle it."

"I know you can. Just… Whatever happens, don't run away this time."

CHAPTER SIXTEEN

"Look, Conner. It's Christmas." Ethan waved Conner over to the ranch yard on Thursday morning as a large horse trailer rumbled to a stop.

A similar rig was coming up the road. The mustangs that Conner had purchased for Big E had arrived. He glanced toward the guest-house to see if Lily was coming out to greet them. No such luck. He should have known. He'd spent all morning working with Ethan to build several large portable corrals. Once the horses were inside, they'd move the sections of fencing until they formed ten-by-ten enclosures for each mustang.

But during the morning's activity, there'd been no sign of Lily. Conner had a feeling she was avoiding him. Or her ex had finally convinced her that Conner and Big E were up to no good. He gritted his teeth.

Ethan slung a bag containing his veterinary equipment over his shoulder, prepared to check the stock. "What's your plan for them training-wise?"

"My plan? Click my heels three times and have you and Katie make all the decisions." Despite his protests, excitement rushed through Conner's veins. He attributed it to the fact that Lily wanted to learn how to train horses. Not that she was staying long enough to get serious about it, but it was a chance for Conner to be with her. Early horse training wasn't as dangerous as the later stages.

Ethan gave Conner a gentle shove. "The guy who decided to overpurchase is the one who has to decide what to do with all that stock. With so many, you know we'll need two good horse trainers."

Conner shook his head, continuing to resist. "You know I don't—"

"You should." Ethan laid a hand on Conner's shoulder this time. "It's been long enough, don't you think?"

Gone was the adrenaline. Conner's chest was tight.

"Yes, Conner. Get back to training." Katie appeared at Conner's side, her dog at her heels. "I could work up a contract with the Rocking H. It'd be less of a drain on our personnel."

It was easier not to argue. It was easier to pretend great interest in the newly delivered horses.

Katie didn't take the hint. "I can get the Jamison boys to come in from town to cover for you. They enjoy hanging out at the ranch, and high school doesn't start for a few more weeks. It's not that hard to take folks on trail rides."

But it was hard to acknowledge that your mother depended upon your good health and strength to keep food on the table and a roof over her head. That tended to make a man think twice about unnecessary risks. "And what about the guests I pick up at the airport? Or the ones like Pepper, who don't want to be bothered with driving at all?"

Katie rolled her eyes. "Those duties are so much easier to find a replacement for than a legitimate wild-horse trainer."

"At least think about it, Conner." Ethan approached the first transport. "Now, let's see what you've got here."

Katie moved on to other ranch business. Conner and Ethan removed horses from the trailers one by one through a chute into the corrals. From there they worked another chute system to get them into smaller, individual pens. Ethan examined every horse as best he could by a quick visual inspection, making sure none of them showed signs of illness that might infect other stock.

"This fella's got parasites." Ethan stood near the gray horse that had lunged at Conner and Lily. He pointed to an unusual-looking pile of manure.

"Stomach upset." Conner nodded. "That explains his poor temper. Do you want him in the quarantine paddock?"

"Yes."

"They're here! They're here!" Pepper skipped toward the horse pen area like a little girl, followed by Natalie, Lily and a man Conner didn't know. "I want to see Royal."

"We're naming them now?" Ethan arched a brow at Conner.

Conner shrugged. "Royal's already been delivered to the Rocking H, along with Lily's two purchases." And given the parasite problem they'd found, he'd have to have Ethan come over and give them an exam.

"Morning," Lily said in that small voice of hers that he'd hoped never to hear again. She wore leggings and a T-shirt, city-girl clothes except for her boots.

"Morning." Conner smiled at Lily because

she had to know someone didn't find fault with her. "If you'd like to watch, there are benches over by the barn." Given how skittish the mustangs were, rail sitting was dangerous.

"This is so exciting." Pepper introduced her beloved Ken, insurance salesman and future saint.

Conner plucked a size sticker from the chest of the groom's shirt. He handed it to Pepper.

"Oh, Ken." She giggled. "I miss removing tags sometimes, too."

Conner bet not, but kept that sentiment to himself.

"I hear there's a new Blackwell in town." Ethan gave Lily a mischievous smile. "Just don't ask to drive my rig."

Lily didn't miss a beat. "Drive a getaway vehicle once and your reputation is ruined forever."

"Nice." Ethan nodded approvingly. He turned to Conner. "I like her."

Conner did, too. Too much. He stopped to reassure himself she was all right. No signs of tears. No furrowed brow. "No second thoughts this morning?"

"Now that I'm here, not even thirds." She gave him one of her radiant smiles.

It warmed him completely, not that he needed it on what promised to be a hot summer day. But it was the kind of warmth that melted hard edges inside and smoothed tough roads ahead.

"Why did the Blackwells want so many mustangs?" Ken sat next to Pepper, store creases in his new blue jeans and not a smudge on his new cowboy boots. "Pepper said you bought twenty."

"We're trying to be environmentally friendly." Ethan didn't break stride on his way back to the barn.

Conner felt compelled to explain since Lily was present. "The Blackwell Ranch leases government land where wild horses roam. Cattle and mustangs compete for the same resources—food and water. The government rounds up the mustangs and the Blackwell cattle benefit, but that means there are wild horses in need of a home."

Ethan had stopped at the barn door to listen. "Are we arguing?" He frowned. "We don't adopt out of guilt. It's a responsibility of ranching, giving back where you can. And in addition to donating my time and the ranch donating vaccines to help control the wild-horse population, we're offering them good homes, food and shelter."

"We're not arguing. We're discussing the whys and whats." A mustang kicked a post near Conner, rattling the railings and his memories. "As a Blackwell, Lily should know more than a sound bite."

"As a Blackwell, I need a photogenic horse to ride down the aisle." Pepper hung on Ken's arm. "Can we pick one out today?"

"All horses are beautiful." Ethan continued to linger. "We've got a young palomino you might ride, if Conner approves. She's a descendant of my mother's horse."

Pepper leaped to her feet. "Can I see her?"

"Sure. Give me a minute." Ethan disappeared inside the barn.

Conner hurried after him. "Hey. Katie wanted to offer ponies for liability purposes." Tall ponies, but ponies nonetheless.

"You and I both know Grandma Dot is trying to make Pepper's dream wedding come true." Ethan kept his voice down. "Dream weddings don't entail ponies. Katie might be willing to stand up to Grandma Dot over this issue, but I'm not."

Conner shook his head. "There are too many cooks on this ranch."

"If you really feel that way, you'll quit and get back to running your own spread and training those horses."

Conner glanced back at Lily. The only way he'd take on the ranch again was with someone like Lily at his side. But that seemed as impossible as riding a horse on the moon.

AFTER FALLING IN love with her wedding mount, Pepper led Natalie and Ken off to sample wedding cake, and Ethan drove into town, leaving Conner and Lily with all those horses.

They didn't talk, which was rare. Usually, they weren't at a loss for topics. But Conner felt like there was something that needed to be said. He just wasn't sure what that something was.

So he went about the business of feeding and watering the mustangs, which didn't take long. And then he hesitated. He wasn't on guest duty. Katie wasn't around to review budgets. It was just Conner, Lily and twenty horses nervously shifting in their pens. They wouldn't be nervous once they adjusted to their new roles. And they wouldn't adjust without human intervention.

With a sigh, Conner turned to the closest pen and opened the makeshift gate.

"What are you doing?" Lily moved to the corner of the enclosure.

"Keep away from the fence." Conner entered the temporary home of a sturdy brown mustang. It had a nylon rope halter on and a government tag. Fear had the horse jolting. "It's been a hard few days for these horses and it's best to get started. Sometimes gentling an animal is the most difficult part. It's best to start with a welcome."

"I thought you weren't going to train horses." Lily sounded like she was right behind him.

He didn't dare take his eyes off the skittish mustang to warn her away. "Getting them used to humans and being handled isn't serious training." Conner praised the horse when he swiveled his ears in Conner's direction.

"Really? Is this where soft words and carrots come in?"

He chuckled. "Maybe not carrots until later. Do you want the truth?"

"Always."

If only he could always give it to her. "The Blackwells want me to be involved in training the mustangs and... Good boy." The horse took a small step. "It's not a hardship to show an animal kindness."

"You need to be in the pen with it to be kind?" With every comment, she inched closer.

Too close. The horse pivoted, banging into the metal fencing.

Conner's muscle memory flinched. He stiffened. "Back up a little. There are too many humans in his vicinity right now." He waited for Lily to take a few steps away from the pen. "That's it. All I'm doing is getting him used to me. I'm measuring his acceptance of my presence. Good boy. See that? He looked at me. I'm just standing here, hands at my sides, calm voice. Good boy." An ear flicker. A head swung in his direction once more. "Good job, buddy."

"Are you scared?" Lily asked.

"My heart's pounding." He spared her a brief grin. "No more than when you look at me sometimes."

He'd crossed a Blackwell line with that tease, and he hadn't even been on a darkened dance floor.

The horse didn't feel comfortable with Conner paying attention to someone else. He pranced around his side of the enclosure, testing the fence with a kick or two.

"It's okay, fella," he said.

"Why do I feel like this is a game of chicken?" Lily's voice was pitched too high. The horse danced again.

"It's not like that. Good boy. Good boy." The horse settled. "It's like walking into a bar and taking a seat. You wouldn't march up to the first cowboy you set eyes on and ask him to dance. You'd follow him with your eyes. Maybe smile a little. Maybe exchange small talk."

"You're giving him another character test," she surmised in a much calmer voice.

Conner nodded. "And he's giving me one of his own. Good boy." The horse had looked at him again.

"Can I try?" So typical Lily, ready to jump in with both feet.

"Why don't you watch me with a few more horses first?" He backed out of the enclosure and led her to another.

Lily observed him say howdy to two more horses before succumbing to her Blackwell genetics and demanding to have a turn.

Conner faced her, placing his hands on her shoulders, willing himself not to draw her near. "First off, tell me what you learned by watching me."

"I...uh... You're quite nice to look at." Her cheeks pinkened. "But as for what I learned, I'm going to stand still, hands at my sides, slow and even conversation, positive reinforcement when I get an acknowledgment." There was excitement in her eyes, but not the hyper Pepper kind.

He nodded, kneading her shoulders a little because he was just a man who remembered how this woman felt in his arms. But he knew that he was crossing another line. "When it comes to mustangs, slower is faster. We want to establish trust and let the horse tell us what tempo they need for their training. We aren't here to break them. We're here to teach them to be part of our herd."

Lily grinned. "Wish me luck."

"I'll do better than that." He pressed a kiss to her temple. Another line crossed. It was helpful Big E had yet to return. "I'll be the good luck charm who has your back." He'd yank her to safety if anything went wrong.

The horse in the enclosure was caked in mud. His head hung low and his back was to them. Conner opened the gate enough to allow Lily inside and then stood behind her.

"Hello, big fella." Lily's voice was coarse and barely above a whisper.

The horse swiveled his ears around.

"What a good boy. He looks like he's had a bad day."

"They often do."

This was a quiet part of the ranch, a barn for working cowboys rather than the smaller stable, where guests came for their trail rides, or the main barn, where they stored equipment and Ethan had his office.

Lily and the horse worked uninterrupted for a few minutes. The mustang appreciated her relaxed approach.

"What are you doing?" Danny shouted. "Get her out of there, you stinkin' cowboy. *Now!*"

The horse spooked, bucking and kicking in the ten-by-ten enclosure. Conner yanked Lily to safety and closed the fencing just as the horse ran past. The other mustangs reacted to the emotion, tossing their heads and kicking with fear.

"Danny, not so loud." Lily rushed toward him, her voice low and urgent.

"I agree with Danny." A new voice rang out. Rudy, Lily's stepfather, marched toward her. "Elias assured me you'd be safe. And yet what do I find? You're nearly trampled by a horse. I should have known you'd find trouble."

Lily's shoulders hunched. Her chin fell. Conner came to stand beside her.

The mustangs pranced and kicked, heads high. The air was filled with their shrill voices.

"Let's all go elsewhere before you cause a stampede, Rudy." Moving with surprising speed, Big E cut Lily's stepfather off before he could reach Lily. "If you can't keep your voice down, then keep your mouth shut."

Rudy scowled at Big E and then at Lily. He gestured for Danny to come forward.

Lily jerked back when Danny tried to take her arm, recovering some of her spirit. "I'll go, but only because I don't want you to upset the horses." She stomped ahead in the direction Big E suggested.

Rudy and Danny glowered at Conner.

"She could have been killed," Rudy whispered angrily. "What were you thinking?"

"That she knew what she was doing and the choice to do it was hers," Conner whispered back. "Which is something you two seem to forget."

They huffed off.

Conner wanted to join them, but he waited

for the mustangs to settle down. They did so quickly.

He doubted Rudy Harrison would do the same.

"I COME ALL this way…" Rudy marched up to Lily in the busy ranch yard, red in the face. "Reassured by Elias that you were safe, and what do I find? You're succumbing to your impulses again. Putting yourself in danger. That horse could have killed you."

Cowboys rode up. Cowboys drove off. Hay was being transferred from a truck to the barn. Rudy didn't care who heard him rail.

"You're blowing this out of proportion." Lily felt like she was seven once more, being chewed out for an adventure-induced injury rather than comforted after a scare. And make no bones about it. She had been scared. "Rudy, I—"

"Rudy nothing." The man who'd raised her stormed closer. "I'm your father."

"And I'm Big E." Lily's grandfather stepped between them, looking like a tough sheriff from an Old West film. "Only strangers call me Elias."

"And your wife," Lily added softly, since she'd heard Dorothy call him by his given name.

"My name is *Dad*." Rudy stood at attention, so rigid that Lily stood up taller. "And I'm here to make sure my daughter is safe. Today and forever."

"She was fine until Danny boy launched himself like a firecracker." Conner entered the yard and moved to Lily's side.

I should have said that.

Lily dug deep for her backbone.

Danny pointed toward the mustang pens, his face distorted by anger and a reddish-purple bruise around one eye. "Elias—"

"Big E," her grandfather corrected, with a wink at Lily.

"—was just telling us how dangerous training wild horses could be. And we walk up to see Lily in with one. She was very nearly trampled."

"Because of you," Conner reiterated. "Lower your voice. Can't you see you're the one riling stock and the one who put Lily in danger? As usual."

Danny crossed his arms over his chest and glowered.

"The point is that the person who was supposed to be keeping Lily safe wasn't." Rudy swung a glare of his own, first at Conner and then at Big E.

The men had surrounded Lily, ringing her in and closing as if she were one of those mustangs and they wanted to direct her through a chute or into a pen.

"Stop." She burst free of the circle. "I'm not doing this anymore."

Four men stared at her. Rudy and Danny with scowls. Big E and Conner with head nods.

"I'm twenty-nine years old. I don't need a chaperone or a keeper, *Dad*. I have my own life. I'll make my own decisions from now on. And I'm not going to marry Danny. You should both just go home."

"You don't belong here, Lily," Danny said firmly. "Not with this pair." He used his thumb to gesture toward Big E and Conner.

"I'm doing fine here." There. Backbone found.

"Is that what this is about? Moving to Montana?" Rudy was beside himself. "It was bad enough you thought you could safely take people on adventures. What's next? Training wild horses? Who will you call on to help you when you can't get a jar open or put together a table you bought at IKEA?"

"Dad." Lily sealed her lips, trying to hold in what she really wanted to say, but it was

too late. "I'm not like you. And now I know why. You aren't my father," she blurted.

Rudy flinched.

"I don't have a life plan or concrete dreams I'm committed to. And yes, I explore things that interest me. This week it's horse training. Next week it might be a circus trapeze or the rodeo. Contrary to what you think, it's not the adrenaline rush that drives me to try new things the way it does Danny."

Her ex flinched.

"You know I'm never going to be a nine-to-fiver. I like to breathe the open air. I like to discover what the world of nature has to offer and, most important, decide if it's for me." She began backing up, moving away from the forces that had been so dominant in her life for so long, because she could sense the fight in her draining. "That's what I need, *Dad.*"

He flinched again.

"Do you know why I'm so open to trying new things? Because I want to find a place where I belong. And if my search leads me to Montana, so be it. Be happy for me. Be proud of me. Mom would." She turned and ran, the way Amanda had cautioned her not to, the way she'd run from her wedding five days before.

"THIS IS A mess of your making, Elias." Rudy was a tall man. He leaned into Big E's face, close enough that his forehead bumped the brim of the old man's cowboy hat.

"You're blaming this on Big E?" Conner tsked, earning him dark looks from the men most likely to make the next twenty-four hours difficult for Lily. "Lily is perfectly capable of independence. It's just not the independence you or I might have."

"I didn't catch your name." Rudy drew himself up again, like a dragon drawing in air before spitting fire. "But seeing as how you've only known my daughter a few days, I think I know what's best for her."

"Lily will be safe here, Rudy, just as I promised." Big E was showing surprising restraint. Normally, he was a master at spitting fire.

"You think I'm going to leave Lily here after this?" Rudy pointed toward the mustang pens.

"I'll stay with her until she comes to her senses." Danny was nothing if not persistent.

It was maddening.

"No!" Conner and Big E said together.

Big E stepped around Lily's former fiancé and took Rudy's elbow. "We made a deal, you and I. And we're going to stick to it."

"What deal?" No one answered Conner. He trailed behind the others, wondering where Lily had gone to. As soon as he could get away, he'd go find her.

"She wants to stay here on the ranch. At least for the time being." Big E arched a brow at Conner that told him Conner had to do better in the Lily department. "Lily is a Blackwell. She'll be surrounded by family and ranch hands dedicated to helping her in any way she wants. Isn't that what you wanted, Rudy?"

Rudy drew a deep breath and said nothing.

"I don't want you to worry, Rudy. There'll be no more horse training or risk taking of any type." Big E's voice was as stiff as weathered leather. "Conner is being paid extra to make sure of it."

"Good," Rudy said. He would agree. This was exactly the way he'd been handling Lily all her life.

And it was wrong. No more horse training? Big E could promise all he wanted. Conner wasn't promising anything. And besides, he'd fulfilled the requirement of the double bonus.

"We should get that in writing. From Conner." Danny could sometimes be smart. "I don't trust him."

Smart, but annoying.

"Right now it's more important that we find Thomas Blackwell, if he's still alive." Big E headed toward the guest ranch, but he swiveled around as if he was looking for something in the ranch yard. "We'll stock the motor home and head back to San Diego. That was our most promising lead and it's unfortunate it only came in this morning."

"Not to mention Amanda needs us to present a unified front," Rudy added.

They were on a quest to find Lily's father? That explained the need for extra days in California.

Big E stopped and turned to Conner. "Where did you park the motor home?"

"Uh…" *Uh-oh.* It seemed everyone knew about the motor-home incident except for his boss. "I'm afraid the…uh…your motor home won't be ready until Monday. Small mishap." Conner held his thumb and forefinger up until they were almost touching. "Fender bender. We're waiting on a part or two." A new radiator, brakes, grille and fender. Luckily, the frame and engine block hadn't been damaged.

Big E's frown was more severe than it had been during Rudy's outbursts. "Why didn't anyone tell me the tank was in the shop?"

Conner feigned ignorance with a shrug. "No one knew when you were returning. Katie said she tried to call." Although he'd bet money she didn't have the motor home on the list of things to discuss with Big E.

"We'll talk more about this later," Big E promised. He nodded toward the horse pens. "Get back to work."

So much for finding Lily. The message was clear—no more crossing lines.

Conner made a U-turn and returned to the mustang enclosures.

But his heart was elsewhere.

CHAPTER SEVENTEEN

LILY FLAGGED DOWN Conner as he was heading home at the end of the day. "Where are you going?"

"The Rocking H." Conner tried to focus on the straight fence posts lining the drive.

"You won't be eating dinner with us at the guesthouse tonight?" Her brow furrowed.

Conner wanted to get out and gather her close and reassure her everything would be all right. But he had yet to receive his double bonus and he'd been given a warning. "You'll be fine on your own. You handled them today."

"Yes, it's just that I…" She squared her shoulders. "I prefer not to be alone against them. They don't listen to me."

"Lily—"

"I've had enough of the Lily-ing today, thank you very much." She popped her hands on her hips. "You know, *Lily, pay attention. Lily, accept my opinion as fact. Lily—*"

"My ranch isn't exactly the safest place on earth." And Big E had been clear in regards to Lily. "Stay here. Stay inside... It's where you belong."

"You think I belong here?" Lily gestured toward the beautiful guest lodge, which had been featured in several national magazines since it opened. "Or with Danny?"

No!

Conner tapped the steering wheel with his thumb again. He needed this job.

"Conner?" Her voice cracked.

"No." He cleared his throat and clarified, "No, I don't think you belong here." But she was a Blackwell and she sure as shooting didn't belong with him.

"I'd like to meet your mom." Lily smiled tentatively. "You know, we've had some phone conversations and hit it off. I'm not pressuring you for a relationship. You know, like *I want to meet your parents* kind of deal." Color blossomed on her cheeks. "Besides, you said Pearl and Mouse were delivered to the Rocking H earlier. I'd like to see them. Please, Conner. You can show them to me and bring me right back."

It was a desperate plea. Having met Rudy

and Danny, he felt for her. Where was the harm in taking her to see her stock?

Conner glanced around. The coast was clear of Blackwells. "All right."

Lily ran around and got in. "Feels like old times, doesn't it? You, driving. Me, your co-pilot."

"You're the guest of my employer." And he'd best remember it. Funny thing was, now that the Blackwell Ranch was in his rearview mirror, all he could remember was her kiss.

They reached the main road before Lily said anything more. "Danny can't get it through his head that I'm not going to marry him. Ditto for Rudy." She sighed.

"Did you call anyone on that fancy cell phone of yours?" The one Danny had given her last night at dinner. "Try to find someone in your family on your side?"

"Just my sister Amanda."

"Did you work things out with her?"

"Kind of." Her voice was small. Her hands clasped in her lap. "She thinks my birth certificate is a clerical error or something."

What could he say to make her feel better? Nothing. He kept both hands on the wheel.

Conner drove to the Rocking H Ranch. The early-evening sun made everything look more barren. The open gate hung crookedly. The gravel road was pitted. He pulled into the ranch yard and waited while Lily gave the property a critical look. The barn was in need of a fresh coat of paint. The front porch sagged. There were chickens running loose and a cat lying in the middle of the ranch yard. Parsnip was in the pen nearest the barn with the mustangs and burro. He whinnied at Conner.

"Home sweet home." Conner wished he'd brought Lily here after dark.

"Look at how tall those trees are." She stepped away from the truck and into the middle of the ranch yard. "Your barn is huge."

It may have been large, but he barely used it. "It needs work."

"It needs hope." Lily didn't demand to be returned to the Blackwell Ranch. She headed over to the barn and her animals. "They're all together—Pearl, Mouse, Royal and...your horse?"

"I'll separate them tomorrow morning."

"Not Pearl and Mouse. They need each other." Lily picked up her pace as if eager to protect her charges.

Pearl, the burro, stuck her nose through the fence rails, begging for an ear rub.

"She's so tame. It's amazing, isn't it?" Lily cooed to the burro.

Conner didn't find the burro amazing. It was Lily who had earned that label for him. He gave the little thing a friendly pat anyway. "It's not uncommon for animals to be set free in the mountains when folks can no longer afford to keep them."

"Oh, Pearl." Lily gazed into the burro's eyes. "That won't happen to you ever again."

If Conner wanted to put distance between them—something he was desperate to do—he should ask Lily for a stabling fee. He couldn't find enough saliva to form the words.

"Good boy." Lily smiled at the big boned horse she called Mouse. He'd been looking at her. "Do I have your permission to come visit them? Mouse needs socialization."

They both glanced over to Royal, the white beauty who had won Pepper's heart. The horse turned her back to them. Royal wanted nothing to do with Conner and Lily.

"You can come as long as you don't go inside the corrals." He debated telling her about the ranch yard conversation with her family, deciding it was better to come clean about that, at least. "Big E promised Rudy you wouldn't leave the ranch or be involved in horse training."

"Did he?" That was her small voice. She must have recognized it because she said again, stronger, *"Did he?"* Lily put her hands on her hips and an uncompromising expression on her face. "And what did you say?"

"Nothing." He chuckled. "I know you too well."

"Finally." Lily gave him a sly glance. "Someone knows what I want."

"Which is?" He was inching toward that line again because he knew what she didn't want—not to marry Danny, not to leap into a relationship with him.

"The freedom to follow my heart," she said ambiguously, before adding, "I gave Danny my tour business."

"What? Why?"

She shrugged, back to being small. "He had too much of a hand in operations. I'm looking for a new line of work."

Horse training.

Big E wasn't going to like this. And Rudy… He whistled.

Parsnip trotted over to Conner and thrust his nose against his shoulder.

"Who is this handsome fella?" She scratched behind Parsnip's cheek. "He's beautiful."

"My mother named him Parsnip." He imagined even Parsnip cringed at the moniker.

"Is he the one?" She stroked Parsnip's long neck. "The one who caused the accident?"

Conner nodded, pushing the stallion's head away.

"Well, he bears you no ill will." Lily looked at Conner as if she expected him to do the same.

"Parsnip doesn't have a mean bone in his body. But he's impatient, both during training and just hanging around. Truth be told, he's waiting for me to finish making him a cutting horse."

"Truth?" Lily scoffed. "You're reading mustang minds now?"

He nodded. "He's got a long wait ahead of him."

"Conner." The way Lily said his name conveyed so much—her expectation that he put his ramshackle life back together, train the horse he loved, perhaps even keep moving their relationship along to…

"You should know something," Conner said. Something he'd vowed not to share with anyone else.

Lily stared up at Conner with trust in those clear blue eyes. A breeze lifted the ends of her dark blond hair.

"I can't go back to horse training." His words tumbled out faster to prevent her from arguing. "Everyone wants me to. But the insurance premiums are hefty. It puts the ranch at risk of being underwater financially if I can't train and sell enough horses."

Her mouth dropped open. Crickets chirped while she processed his words. "You didn't say you were afraid to train horses."

He nodded, subtly stretching the twinge in his back. Everyone thought he'd lost his nerve. "I have a healthy respect for the profession, just like I do for ranching. But a man has to realize when he's beat and focus on what he can do in life and what is foolhardy."

Conner's mother came out of the house led by Ned, who meowed like a small lion. "Is that Lily?"

"Yes." Lily turned and waved.

Two cats raced across the yard to reach Ned and Conner's mother.

"She rescues cats," Conner said half underneath his breath. "Not to mention she loves her chickens."

Lily smiled as if none of that should be in

a negative column. "You don't want to let her down."

"I'm afraid I already have," Conner admitted, being on a roll with baring his soul.

"I mean…" Lily squeezed his biceps, more than trust shining in her eyes, although he didn't dare put a name to whatever it was. "That's why you don't want to train horses anymore. Because of the money, and if anything happened to you, she'd be—"

"Are you going to make me come over there?" his mother asked. "Or am I interrupting a moment?"

Lily chuckled.

Conner closed his eyes. "My mother takes great pleasure in torturing me."

"Which makes your need to protect her that much more endearing." Lily tugged him across the ranch yard. "Hi, Karen." She trotted up the porch steps and hugged her. "I missed having our phone call last night."

"Me, too. Are you here for dinner?" Mom turned to go inside the house. "I made tomato soup with fresh tomatoes. And for dessert, I've still got cookies."

"You made soup for dinner? What about meat? Or chicken?" Conner glanced back at the free-range birds pecking in the yard.

"I don't eat chicken anymore. You know that." His mother tsked.

"She became a vegetarian after she named the chickens," Conner explained to Lily, unable to resist teasing his mother as they went inside.

"You can't eat your pets." Lily grinned. She didn't seem to care that the carpet was worn or that his mother's craft projects cluttered the living room, dining room and kitchen. She seemed at ease.

Conner couldn't remember if the clutter had been there last night. He removed his boots and hung up his hat.

Lily removed her boots, setting them next to Conner's. His ex-wife used to tuck hers out of sight behind Mom's copper umbrella stand. He'd never understood why. The two pairs of boots implied comfort and closeness.

Love.

Conner jolted to a standstill, watching Lily peer at his mother's collection of figurines in the curio cabinet.

Mom headed toward the kitchen with careful steps. "I'll grill some cheese sandwiches and roast some zucchini to go with our soup. No help needed."

Lily thanked her and picked up a picture on

an end table of Conner riding a cutting horse at a rodeo event. "Very handsome."

He'd grown up with the Blackwell brothers, who'd been quite popular with the local gals. No one ever called Conner handsome. "I suppose you mean the horse."

"She means you, honey," his mother called from the kitchen. "Don't fish for compliments."

Conner wasn't fishing for anything. If he had his way, Lily would still be over at the Blackwell Ranch. But then he'd never have seen their boots together.

Love?

"You don't have kids?" Lily wandered around the small living room.

"No." Conner began picking up the clutter. In his mother's defense, it was challenging for her to walk more than a few steps without one or both crutches. That didn't explain how she'd gotten all this stuff out. Yarn for knitting. Quilt squares. Scraps of fabric. Her sewing box. Her quilt patterns and knitting books. A couple of romances. She'd been restless today. "We never thought we could afford them. And it was probably for the best."

"Contentious divorce?" Lily's cheeks turned pink, but she didn't look away.

"No, ma'am." Conner should have left it

there, but it was important that Lily understand they could be friends but he wasn't the
kind of man she should be looking at for anything more. "I think having a child would put
more pressure on me to make this place into
something. I don't think I'm the right one to
carry the burden of generations of Hannahs
on his shoulders."

"Sounds like you gave it a lot of thought
after your accident." Lily stepped onto the
brick hearth, studying the pictures displayed
on the wooden mantel. Some were yellowed
with age and nearly a hundred years old. She
traced her finger over the trail of nail holes
made by countless Hannah parents to hang
their children's stockings. "Have you revis-
ited the topic since?"

"Recently?"

She nodded, turning to watch him.

"No. You know why." His mother.

"She'd understand." Lily made no argument. Instead, she walked toward the kitchen.
"How can I help, Karen?"

He knew how Lily could help him. She
could stop implying things could be different.

LILY SAT ON a porch rail at the Rocking H,
pretending to watch the sunset.

Instead, she watched Conner shoo chickens into their coop for the night.

"He's a good man." Karen sat in a rocking chair nearby. "Not that he'd admit it."

"He's humble. That's a trait of most good men." But being humble didn't mean Conner would open that slow door to a relationship with her. In fact, he seemed dead set against it.

"You know, when the cutting horses Conner trained began winning competitions, you wouldn't hear him crow. I suppose if he put more stock into what people thought, he'd have kept this place going after the accident."

"He cares about what people think. Big E, in particular." She'd heard him invoke her grandfather's name on more than one occasion. "And he's afraid of what might happen if he trains horses again."

Karen made a sound of agreement.

"Fear is a powerful thing." Lily concentrated on curling her fingers. "But you can't let fear win."

"I know. I know what my son fears most. Without him able to take care of things, I'd have to sell the ranch." Karen looked weary. "But things can't keep going the way they are. He hasn't been happy for a long time. And this place…"

They watched him close up the chicken coop without saying more.

Conner joined them on the porch, warm gaze finding Lily. "You about ready to head on back?"

"Let me say good-night to Pearl and Mouse first." And steal a few more minutes alone with him.

"We'll make a rancher out of her yet, Conner." His mother was getting to her feet and positioning her crutches, so she probably didn't see Conner's frown, although she probably knew she was pushing his buttons anyway.

Conner and Lily walked over to the barn paddock. Conner gave her space, although she'd have preferred he didn't.

"Tell me about the first Hannah." Lily did a slow turn as she walked, taking in the ranch, drinking in its history. "The one who settled here, built this barn and planted those trees."

"Horatio Hannah came west seeking gold, but his wagon broke down in Falcon Creek." Conner scoffed. "Not a very auspicious beginning."

"But Horatio made the most of it. Why did he call it the Rocking H?"

"Horatio married a gal who was partial to rocking on the porch. The Rocking H is kind of a *this is the life* statement, which this ranch is anything but. It needs constant work to keep it going."

They reached the corral.

She gave Pearl an ear rub. "Where did Parsnip go?"

"Who knows? That horse doesn't like to be tied down."

"Like his owner."

Conner gently took Lily by the shoulders and got her to face him. He brushed her hair behind her ears. "Don't bet on me. The Rocking H will never be as nice or prosperous as the Blackwell Ranch. The odds are stacked against me."

"Who said I wanted nice things?" Lily stared into his eyes, feeling that spark between them, trying to hide the love she had for him. "And why would you say the odds are stacked against you? That's what the doctors told Rudy after I hit my head." She flexed her fingers. "I do okay."

"You do more than okay," he said gruffly,

boots creaking as he shifted his feet. "When are you going home?"

She felt him draw away even though he hadn't moved an inch. This was a man who'd always stand behind what he thought was right. And he thought she didn't belong with him. "I haven't decided when I'm leaving. And I haven't learned anything about the Blackwells, either, other than they seem to accept me." But Conner had accepted her first.

He rested his forearms on a railing close to her. "I'm sorry the place isn't much to look at. I've pretty much decided to sell it to one of the Blackwells when Mom can't live here by herself anymore."

"Your mother is a long way off from that. And you should think twice about selling. There are probably tons of memories here and traditions to be passed on."

He stared toward the training paddock.

Lily pointed to a swing beneath an oak tree. "Yours?"

"Guilty." He was so stingy with words.

"And it looks like you had plenty of places to ride as a kid. That's how you became a good horseman, right? You rode all the time. Just you and your trusty steed, sharing apple slices and reading each other's mind."

His mouth worked, like he was fighting a smile.

"When I was a kid, I was a tomboy." She rubbed her hands on her jeans. "If things had been different... If I hadn't hit my head... I might have been a better athlete. Instead of Rudy calling me reckless, he would have called me brave."

Conner took her hand.

"I don't know what happened to Thomas Blackwell. But I have to wonder how things would have been different if I'd have grown up visiting Big E at the Blackwell Ranch. I watched some kids playing with goats this afternoon. And they weren't doing yoga." She shook her head. "If Rudy had seen them, he might have told those kids that goats are too dangerous."

"I can introduce you to the goats tomorrow. We can test out that theory if Rudy comes by." As soon as he spoke, it looked like he wanted to take the words back.

Lily brought his hand to her lips, planting a light kiss on those bruised knuckles. "I'll take you up on that offer if you give me another horse-training lesson."

His brows went up and he squeezed her fingers. "Lily, I—"

"You said you didn't promise Big E." She yanked her hand free. "Tell me you aren't becoming Danny 2.0. Tell me they haven't assigned you to be my keeper."

"The camp counselor is not going to become a horse trainer." That was no answer.

Her stomach flip-flopped. "You don't know who I could be," Lily said softly when inside she wanted to shout. She'd been so sure he wouldn't treat her like everyone else, certain enough to let feelings of love bloom in her chest. She hung her head. "I don't even know who I could be."

Conner sighed. The sun was going down and making the fringes of brown hair beneath his hat tinge a reddish hue. "I'm not Danny 2.0. I wasn't lying when I said I didn't promise anything."

"It's okay. I can read between the lines." Lily crossed her arms over her chest and acknowledged the truth. "You don't feel worthy of a Blackwell bride and I don't feel anyone will give me a chance to be more than a camp counselor." Even that had been a hard-fought battle, but it had been a false front.

"It doesn't matter to me what you do for a living," he said gruffly.

"What a lie." And he hadn't refuted the

part about her being a Blackwell. Lily's arms knotted tighter across her chest, hiding her fists beneath her elbows. "You'd feel different about me if I was an experienced horsewoman, no matter what my last name was. You'd see me as an asset, not a stray cannonball that could potentially rip apart and sink the precious Rocking H."

His eyes widened. His hands found hers. "No man would see you as a cannonball. You're an anchor. Don't talk like that. Not. Ever. Again. Or I…" Conner made that feral noise, the one he'd made before punching Danny last night. And then he swept her into his arms and kissed her.

The warm evening, the gentle breeze, the tender way he held her. Lily felt like she belonged. Here. In his arms. On this ranch. A sturdy fixture, like Horatio Hannah's buckboard.

We'd get along really well if all we did was kiss.

Her hands came up to his cheeks as she drew back. "You're like that perfect pair of jeans."

"How so?" Conner didn't roll his eyes, but he sounded like he wanted to.

"Jeans on the rack just hang there, flat with a subtle promise of greatness."

He chuckled, his breath warm on her cheek. "Where are you going with this?"

"Jeans need the right someone to come along. They need the person who touches the weave, checks out the stitching and tries them on. And then, if by some miracle the fit is perfect, you have to buy them, no matter the cost." The way she was convinced he was the man for her when they weren't arguing about limits he and others wanted to place on her life. "Do you know what I mean?"

"I do." There he went using that phrase again. "I know exactly what you're thinking."

I hope not.

She was thinking about stretching up on her toes for another kiss. She was thinking she didn't want to go back to the Blackwell Ranch. She could sleep on his couch and escape the pressure Rudy and Danny liked to bring.

"Conner? Lily?"

Conner stepped away. "My mother probably just remembered she's got kittens looking for a home in the barn."

Lily thought she was rather like the kittens, in search of a new place to rest her head.

CHAPTER EIGHTEEN

"LITTLE CHICK."

Lily froze on the front walk of the guest-house.

It was dark. The warmth of the day had faded, giving way to a cool breeze. Conner had just dropped her off, giving her a good-night kiss, fueling her feelings of love. Lights from the guesthouse glowed a warm welcome. Inside, her bed called. But a man's voice rang out from the front porch, someone she'd have to get past first.

"Lily." That was Rudy's voice. He sounded weary.

She made her way slowly up the walk and front steps to the porch. "Mom used to call us her little chicks." A shaft of grief passed through her. Mom would have wanted her to make peace with Rudy.

"Sit with me." Rudy patted the wooden arm of a rocker next to the one he sat in.

Lily did as he asked. From the porch she

could see the ranch buildings outlined against the starry sky. A horse nickered. A goat bleated. Someone laughed. The simple sounds of a simple life made her difficulties with Rudy seem complicated.

He cleared his throat. "Someone pointed out to me today that I don't listen very well."

She'd bet that someone was Big E. And although she agreed, Lily wasn't going to be the second person that day to tell him so.

Rudy shifted in his chair, making it rock back and forth. "When I married your mother, I took a post on base and was told I had a knack for keeping people in line. I've been sitting out here waiting for you and wondering if that's where I went wrong—applying what made me a success in the navy to my home life. In my defense, things were easier on your mother when you all behaved, so I tried my hardest to help you stay on the straight and narrow."

"I'm twenty-nine." Lily hesitated before expanding on that statement. "I'm past the time when you should think you have to help me stay on the straight and narrow."

"Yes," he allowed with a crisp nod of his head. "I'm beginning to see that. But beginning to see and letting go of the need to protect are two separate things. Especially when it comes to you."

"Because of my accident?" At his nod, frustration built inside her. "Everyone faces adversity differently. If Peyton had the accident instead of me, she'd have given up having adventures. If Georgie did, she'd research ways to improve her dexterity." Lily flexed her fingers.

"But it was you who wanted to fly," he said solemnly. "And if anyone tells you stop, you always just go, as if you want to stare Death in the eyes and thumb your nose at him."

Lily swallowed back her frustration, her disappointment. None of the Harrisons understood who she was today. "I admit, that's the way I was when I was younger. I didn't only want to taunt Death. I wanted to taunt you."

He gasped.

"But in the past few years, I've matured. I'm careful. I don't leave mayhem in my wake." Present wake excepted. "And yet all anyone sees when they look at me is the younger Lily, the one who leaped before she looked and was in constant need of a bandage and an ice pack. Contrary to what you might think, I'm extremely cognizant of my mortality, so much so that I don't seek out those adrenaline rushes anymore. Danny does."

Rudy didn't seem convinced.

Lily resisted the urge to tell him it was true. "You say you want to listen, but—"

"Listening is a new concept for me, Lily. I've spent nearly three decades worrying about you girls and keeping you on track. All of you little chicks."

She hated that he used their mom's nickname for them like that. She got to her feet and stomped over to the door. "Maybe you should take a real good look at Danny's hobbies and behavior before you talk to me again."

Maybe then he'd see who Lily really was and love her the way mama hen had loved her little chick.

"WHAT ARE YOU doing down here?" Katie sat on a bench near the mustang enclosure where Conner was working. She reached down to pet her dog, who'd rested his broad head on her knee. "Shouldn't you be wrangling horses for Pepper's wedding rehearsal?"

"That got rescheduled to this afternoon. I'll be bringing over several mounts to see which pass Pepper's beauty test for the bridesmaids."

Conner was choosing older horses with distinct coloring—a bay, a black Appaloosa, a brown paint.

Katie grimaced and arched her back, thrusting her baby bump forward. "That doesn't answer the question of what you're doing here. I could use some help on the books later. Have you changed your mind about training?"

"There are many factors that go into this decision, Katie." And there it was. The first time he hadn't outright refuted an invitation back into horse training made by a Blackwell.

"You sound like Chance and me. We haven't decided about a name for the baby. But when this child is born, we're going to have to decide. That much is certain." Katie patted her dog's head again. Pregnancy agreed with her. She glowed in a way that Conner hoped Lily would someday.

Not that I'll ever see it.

But Lily deserved everything life had to offer, including babies, little tykes who'd charge about the world without fear the way she had.

"Honestly, Conner. At the rate you're going, you could still be waffling about whether or not you're going to go back to the one thing you were passionate about when my baby enrolls in college."

"The onc thing," Conner murmured, ignoring her gibe. If he counted Lily, he was passionate about two things.

"You know what I mean." Katie got to her feet in a rare moment of ungainliness and a sign that the mighty workaholic needed to slow down soon. "I'll give you another week of waffling, Conner, but you and I both know by next week these horses will need a serious horse trainer." She continued on her morning rounds.

Conner stepped into the enclosure with the horse that Danny had spooked yesterday. "Hey, boy. Pay no mind to the high-strung set of personalities around the ranch. Weddings and babies tend to make people nervous."

The horse turned its head to look at him, a long look, not a quick glance.

"Good boy. The sooner we get you used to me, the sooner we can get you cleaned up."

The mud caked on his coat couldn't be comfortable in this heat. The horse brought his head around to stare at Conner once more.

"Maybe someone was nice to you," Conner said as the horse shifted, turning his back on him more completely. "Maybe you passed by a farm or a ranch and got soft words and carrots."

His big brown ears swiveled in Conner's direction.

Something made a noise behind Conner.

The horse's ears flattened.

Conner scrambled out the gate, narrowly missing being struck by a hoof. The entire herd began making noise and moving nervously, kicking out at fences and kicking up dirt. For a moment Conner was frozen, taken back to the moment when he'd been working with Parsnip and everything went wrong. This mustang had spooked, not because of anything he'd done, but because of something unexpected in the environment. It made him wonder...

"This is why we don't want Lily hanging out with you." Danny stood behind Conner, sneering. His black eye was green today and he could stare out of it.

"Do you know what I like about horses?" Conner's hands fisted. "They're a good judge of character."

Danny scoffed, but he looked around, hopefully taking in the difference between the horses now and when he'd first walked in.

"They don't like you. *I* don't like you." Conner got up into the other man's face. "If I ever catch you down here again, I'm going to do more than take one swing at you."

"WHERE DO YOU think you're going, young lady?"

Lily stopped on her way to the mustang enclosures. She put a smile on her face for her Blackwell grandfather. "Conner said he'd introduce me to the ranch goats today."

How easily the lie came to her lips. She'd slipped out of the guesthouse without seeing Rudy. She didn't want to make sneaking around the Blackwell Ranch and avoiding everyone but Conner a habit.

"Walk with me." Big E extended a hand toward her. "You can visit our goats later."

Lily came to his side. He hooked his arm through hers. He smelled like cigars and peppermint. His jeans and gray button-down weren't wrinkled today, but they were worn, as everything she'd seen him wear had been.

"It occurred to me last night—when you were missing from the dinner table and I had to talk Rudy down from a very militant ledge—that we don't know much about each other." He led her away from the ranch buildings and toward a dirt path.

"Oh." Lily nodded, looking for Conner. She didn't see him anywhere.

Wedding guests had been arriving nearly nonstop all day. She should have known that Pepper would invite a stadium-full of people. Ranch hands hurried about, but there was no sign of her cowboy.

"What I'd like to know is this." Big E ambled along at a good clip. "What questions do you have of me?"

They headed toward a cluster of trees down by the river, away from prying eyes.

She could ask him about family history. Or about Prudence. But that wouldn't reveal much about the man next to her. "Why have you been married so many times?"

"There's a question I didn't expect." He stopped, surveying the landscape, which included her. "You don't strike me as a person who changes her mind and changes it back."

"I'm not asking because I'm considering marrying Danny. I'm asking because I want to understand what shaped the stranger who claims to be my grandfather and claims to care about me."

"I see." He chuckled. "Here's the thing, honey. It took me about seventy-nine years to reach maturity." He shrugged and flashed a smile that might have charmed Pru. "And maturity builds stable relationships, while immaturity…" He held out his hands and shrugged, letting her fill in the blanks.

She didn't want to guess, but he left her no choice. "What you're saying is I'm lucky to have met you now."

He nodded. "I had a lot of fence mending to do the past few years with my grandsons and with the love of my life."

"And now? Do you have any more regrets?"

He led her toward the river. "I'd like to collect the pieces that made up Thomas Blackwell's life to discover what kind of man he is. Or was." Those last two words came out on a sorrowful note.

Big E paused at a small rise to look at her. For someone in his eighties, his gaze was sharp. "You feel like the odd man out because of those fingers Rudy claims don't work the way they need to?"

She agreed, clenching her hands into fists.

"Funny thing about belonging. It doesn't matter much unless you want to belong."

Lily smiled. "You're a cowboy philosopher."

"I'm an old man." He continued on.

The sun beat down on them, hot when the nights were cool. Unlike San Diego, this was a place of extreme weather. How hard it

must have been for the Blackwells who settled here.

"What was your father like?" she wondered
aloud.

"A lot like me, I think. And I'm a lot like
Rudy, if truth be told." Big E shook his head.
"I mean, I was like Rudy. Stubborn, thinking
my grandchildren should shape their lives to
my vision, not theirs."

"Pardon me if I admit I'm much happier
to have met the mature version of Big E
Blackwell. Two Rudys in my life would have
undone me." She lifted her chin before admitting, "I think I want to be a horse trainer."

Big E paused, studying that out-thrust chin.
"Is that because of your interest in horses? Or
in Conner?"

"Conner asked me a similar question." Lily
leaned closer as if they were surrounded by
curious people, not sparse grass and delicate
wildflowers. "He wanted to be sure I was interested in the challenge of mustang training,
not the adrenaline of working with untamed
animals. I just feel as if horse training would
be more enriching to me than taking people
white-river rafting. And I know if I tell Rudy
about my interest, he'd assume I was seeking

another rush but in a new way." Regardless of their conversation the night before.

Big E clapped her on the shoulder and gave her a wide, warm grin that showed the gold in his dental work. "You don't strike me as the type to jump a motorcycle over buses—"

"But you don't want me to get hurt." She patted his hand, grateful to be understood. "Are you so protective you'd bar me from trying? Albeit this is your ranch, after all."

"That's a tricky question." His hand fell away. "As your grandfather, I'd love to see you stick around. And training mustangs… Well, I doubt you could pursue the profession in San Diego."

"But…"

"But all this is very new to Rudy." Big E had a way of looking at her that cut to her very core. "We are leaving Monday, or as soon as my rig is fixed." Big E gave her a sly smile, and something of a blessing when it came to her exploration of horse training.

They reached the river. The level was low. It gurgled past at a leisurely pace.

"It's August." He stared toward a bridge spanning from Blackwell land to the other side. It might have been the one from Pru's photograph. "The water always becomes a trickle in August, unless there's rain in the high country. And then the water comes down in such a rush, it can wipe out everything in its path." He paused, suddenly looking sad.

There was more to learn about Big E and her Blackwell heritage.

"Tell me the truth," Lily said, thinking of the cowboy who'd always promised her as much. "You brought Rudy to Montana in exchange for information about Thomas Blackwell." San Diego was a navy town, after all, and her biological father might have served. As an active-duty naval officer, Rudy would have access to information more easily than Big E.

He chuckled. "Tell me the truth. You agreed to walk with me because you didn't want to get in another fight with Rudy."

She chuckled in turn. "I suppose we understand each other better than we thought."

Big E nodded. "Now that you've asked some questions, I have one of my own."

Lily braced herself for questions about her life choices, about her fingers, horse training, Conner.

But Big E surprised her. "What really happened to my motor home?"

"MOM?" CONNER STOOD on the threshold of the Rocking H after too many hours of wedding rehearsals, too many hours without seeing Lily.

He'd been anxious to get home and talk to his mother about the day of his accident. Could it be that Parsnip hadn't spooked because of anything Conner had done wrong? But what did it matter if something else had startled the mustang? Training wild mustangs took time. He needed a steady paycheck. Still, he wanted answers.

He'd have to wait to ask his mom. The house was quiet. The TV silent. Nothing was going on in the kitchen. Her bed was made and empty. This wasn't normal.

Refusing to let fear shake his legs out from under him, Conner made a U-turn and headed for the chicken coop. "Mom?"

She's resilient. She probably just lost track of time inside the coop talking to those chickens of hers.

The chicken coop was full of birds, but empty of his chicken-loving mama.

He drew a steadying breath, refusing to think the worst.

She's stubborn. She might have gone out to the barn to get extra oats. Enough for Parsnip, Pearl and Mouse.

The barn was empty.

Her truck sat empty.

"Mom?" Conner honked his truck horn, startling the chickens. In the ensuing silence, he listened.

Parsnip whinnied. It sounded like he was in the next pasture over, the one with the pond.

Conner ran. Unnerved, but holding it together. He was a rancher, born and bred. He'd been raised on adversity. But his mother was missing, and Parsnip hadn't run out to greet him when he'd come home.

He went through one gate and then another.

Parsnip galloped up to Conner, pranced around him and then ran toward the pond, where Conner could see his mother's overturned walker and something on the ground. Something... Someone...

"Mom!" He raced to her side.

"It's about time." She lay on her back, a small bouquet of wilted purple wildflowers nearby.

Parsnip walked over and ate her bouquet.

"Yes, you rascal." She sounded loopy. "I suppose that's your reward."

"Mom, are you hurt? Do you recognize me?" Had she experienced a dip in blood sugar or shock?

"Oh, of all the things to cap an already bad

day." She accepted Conner's help in sitting up, groaning. "You think I've lost my marbles. I was talking to Parsnip. I sent him to fetch you when I heard the truck."

Conner didn't rule out some temporary mental confusion. Parsnip wasn't a rescue dog.

"What happened? How did you get out here?" There was more than concern in his questions. There was anger. It spilled out like peat, the way it escaped from a big hole in an old bag of fertilizer. "What in the world are you doing down here? I thought we agreed you'd stick to the house and ranch yard. That you'd only do activities that are safe, like letting out the chickens and working on your indoor crafts."

"Pfft." She made no move to get to her feet, pressing her hip tenderly. "I remembered we'd had that rain while you were gone, which usually brings out the lupines. Such a stubborn flower in the high country. And so pretty." She shook a finger at Parsnip. "Bad boy."

Parsnip whinnied.

"He's not a dog."

"You think I don't know that? I told him several times to go get help. Lassie, he's not."

His mother closed her eyes. "And then to add insult to injury, he ate my flowers."

"Can we start over?" Because her story was disjointed and making no sense. He laid a hand on her forehead, but other than being sunburned, she didn't feel as if she had a fever. "You came out to get wildflowers…"

"Because I wanted Lily to see how beautiful things are here." She blinked back tears. "The Rocking H doesn't look the way it used to and I don't blame you for that. You may not realize that you've charmed her, but I do. I was hoping she was a chicken person or a cat person. But she didn't want to hold either, and so I thought we needed to win her over with flowers."

"Mom." Conner sighed and explained about Lily's challenges with holding on to things. "She's very careful about what she picks up. Remember, I had you put her soup in a cup, not a bowl."

"And she drank it two-handed." His mother's eyes widened.

He nodded. "So you came out to get the wildflowers for Lily and then what happened?"

"A bee dive-bombed me. I hit the deck." She rubbed her hip again. "I can't put weight on my left leg and I've gotten so weak from sitting too much that I couldn't push myself up." Tears spilled down her cheeks. "And the walker kept falling over. Heaven only knows where my phone's gone to. And all I could think of was that I have failed you something awful."

He wrapped his arms around her and denied it. "You're my miracle maker, the reason I had to walk again."

She clung to his shirt. "You're just saying that because I had a bad day."

"I'm saying that because it's true. If it wasn't for you, I'd have gotten rid of this place and Parsnip the day after I went in that hospital." He wiped away her tears the way she'd wiped away his when he was a little boy. "But speaking of bad days, specifically when Parsnip walloped me, I never asked, but…did something happen to spook him?" Now that she was safe, he couldn't wait for answers any longer.

"The day of your accident?" His mother sniffed. "One of the barn cats chased one of my chickens, way on the other side of the yard. But we talked about this a long time ago. And you didn't seem to think it was the reason Parsnip spooked."

"When was this talk?" Conner couldn't remember the conversation, although he knew Parsnip didn't like cats.

"Oh, gosh. It must have been those first few days you were in the hospital."

When I was heavily sedated.

"Are you getting to be forgetful, like your mother?"

"Not a chance." But the fact that his accident wasn't due to something he'd done was earthshaking. It meant his success training mustangs as cutting horses hadn't been a fluke. It meant he had more than some skill. He might go as far as to say he was a professional. And a professional horse trainer didn't take foolish risks or quit after one mistake.

"Is it important?" Mom asked. "The cats and Parsnip, I mean."

"Yes." Because it validated what people had been telling him. He should quit the Blackwell Ranch and return to his passion. Still, the idea would take getting used to. And he couldn't just flip a switch and say, *I'm a horse trainer. Now I'm worthy enough for the likes of Lily Harrison Blackwell.* He'd need proof. Months of hard work and a substantial payday. The Rocking H would need to be spruced up.

Conner lifted his mother off the ground

and sat her in her walker, which he dragged back to the ranch yard.

She shook her finger at his truck as they drew near. "Do not tell me we're going to the doctor. You know how expensive that is. I've probably just got a bruise or something."

"Don't argue." He lifted her into the truck, and they set off.

CHAPTER NINETEEN

"LILY, YOU CAN'T avoid me forever."

Lily froze, gripping the door handle of the guesthouse. A few seconds sooner and she'd have made her escape, disappearing into the growing crowd of Pepper's wedding guests.

But she'd been caught, fair and square. She turned, smoothing her hands over the dress she'd worn for dinner the other night, and faced Rudy, who was coming through the kitchen, where he'd probably been lying in wait.

"Come on." He gestured toward the do-it-yourself coffee bar in the foyer. "Let's have a cup of coffee. I'll spring for a latte." Gone was her angry father. In his place was the man she loved dearly.

"You always knew how to push my buttons." Lily came to stand next to him, smiling despite their recent differences. "Lattes are my kryptonite." That wasn't quite true. Pouring was her kryptonite, and sometimes it took all her concentration to neatly fill a cup of coffee.

"You always cared too much what people thought of you if you spilled or dropped something." He took some small caramel-flavored creamer pods—the kind that she could never open cleanly by herself. He poured their contents into a small frother-steamer and then poured them each a cup of coffee while they waited for her creamer to heat and foam. "It's okay to ask someone to help you make a latte. If people know you, they know you don't like black coffee. And look." He pointed to a dish on the next table. "Doughnut holes."

Lily narrowed her eyes. "They haven't had pastries since I've been here." Only scrambled eggs and cold cereal, which were hard for her to eat in company without looking like a toddler in need of a high chair. He'd provided those doughnut holes, all right. And she loved him for it.

"You're too thin, Lily."

"Dad."

"I like the sound of that." He chuckled. "*Dad*, not Rudy."

"Dad." He earned an eye roll.

He smiled at her as if he hadn't seen her in forever, when in fact this version of Rudy hadn't made an appearance since before her mom died. "All I'm saying is, the people who care about you don't care if you get caught up in conversation and drop food all over yourself and the floor."

"People like Danny." She took a step back, glancing around.

"There could be other people, too." He poured her hot, foamy creamer on top of her coffee. "Like that cowboy who used Danny as a punching bag."

"Dad."

"That's me." He grinned as he carried their coffees into the kitchen since the dining room was being prepared for Pepper's reception. "I wish you would have come to me when you found your birth certificate," he said wistfully.

They still had so much emotional ground to navigate. Not just the two of them, but also with the rest of Lily's siblings. "Did you know?"

He took a seat at the large kitchen island and shook his head. "I met your mother when she was pregnant with Fiona. On paper, she wasn't what a young naval officer was looking for. Four girls. Another on the way. She was waitressing at my favorite diner wearing threadbare clothes. But she had the brightest smile, like you." He sipped his coffee and stared across the room. "And she spent every penny on you girls."

"She always put others first." Lily still ached just talking about her mother.

Rudy nodded. "I fell in love. And I knew she'd been married before, but she never talked about it. About him." He glanced around the grand kitchen. "Thomas of House Blackwell."

"You've been reading your fantasy novels again."

"It passes the time." He gave her a small smile.

But she knew what he meant. The Blackwells were doing well, like fine lords and ladies of old, while the Harrisons just got by.

"I offered to adopt you, but she always had some excuse, some reason for not contacting Thomas." He shrugged. "And so I stopped asking. We were married, after all. And I loved you like a father. Why did I need a piece of paper to prove it?"

"It must have been hard for you." Lily stared at her latte, a drink he hadn't had to make for her. But he'd always been the father who anticipated what his daughters needed and tried to make their lives easier. "*I* must have been hard for you," she amended.

"You were all a challenge in your own way." Rudy took her hand. "But I wouldn't change a thing. Because although your mother and I didn't make sense on paper, we made total sense in our hearts."

Like me and Conner.

"I love you, Dad." Lily's eyes filled with tears. "I'm sorry I've been such a disappointment. I'll pay you back for the wedding." She might be able to sell her wedding dress, if she remembered to get it out of the motor home before Rudy and Big E hit the open road on this quest of theirs. "Why are you going with Big E to find Thomas?"

Rudy squared his shoulders. "I think it's important for you girls to know your biological father."

Do the right thing.

"And you've never been a disappointment to me," he said, raising his coffee mug toward her. "I bet you also want to know why Mom never talked about him."

Didn't they all?

"It must be hard being a mother." Lily gripped her coffee mug.

He put his arm around her shoulders. "You

say that like you've decided that's the one adventure you'll never accept."

"You know..." She set the mug down and held out her hands, palms up.

Rudy drew her close. "The one thing I know with certainty is that you'll be a wonderful mother when the time comes. Your mother believed it, too."

Lily leaned her head on his shoulder. "Do you really think so?"

"Lily Rose Harrison... Blackwell. You've never backed down from a grand adventure. Don't you dare start now."

She sniffed. "Would you...?" Lily stared at the layer of foam in her mug. "Would you like to come to Pepper's wedding? As my date?" She'd been hoping Conner might ask her but that hadn't happened.

Rudy's eyes teared up. "I would be honored to attend any wedding with you."

"I'M SPEECHLESS," Rudy said as he took a seat next to Lily on the aisle.

They gawked at the wedding venue, a pasture behind the guesthouse.

Not that it was recognizable as a field. There was a gazebo draped in white gauzy curtains, flanked by hitching posts where the horses the wedding party was riding in on were going to be tied during the ceremony. Rows of white chairs with red sashes flanked an aisle wide enough for two horses to ride through. There were baskets of fresh-cut flowers every few rows and ceramic pots filled with blooms at the gazebo. They'd each been given a cowboy hat. Lily's had a pink ribbon that fluttered in the soft breeze.

"I've never been to a themed wedding." And Lily was incredibly relieved that she hadn't wanted the best of everything for her canceled ceremony. The cost for Pepper's wedding had to be astronomical. She made a mental note to devise a payment plan to repay Rudy.

"I prefer less pomp and more ceremony," Rudy whispered.

Lily shushed him, glancing around to see if Conner was a guest or working. But she didn't even see her Blackwell cousins, let alone their hired hand.

Pepper had chosen midmorning for the ceremony to avoid the afternoon heat. Guests continued to fill seats. A minister took his place beneath the gazebo, and the families of the bride and groom, including Big E and Dot, found their seats in the front row. Dot wore a pale pink cowboy hat the same color as her pink dress and boots.

"Distinguished guests," the minister said. "The bridal party is about to arrive. We ask that you stay seated while the horses move through the aisle."

"Wouldn't want a stampede," Rudy whispered.

Lily didn't bother shushing him this time.

The sound of horses' hooves on pavement had everyone turning.

Ben Blackwell released his hold on the lead horse and stepped back to allow Ken center stage as he rode the big black horse toward the center aisle. Behind Ken, his groomsmen rode smaller brown horses. The groom and groomsmen wore simple black tuxedos, black boots, hats and string ties.

Three of Lily's Blackwell cousins made their way around the rows of chairs to the hitching post on the left. Ben, Ethan and Jon wore black suits and black hats. They stepped up when the groomsmen dismounted and tied up the horses for them.

Ken took his place next to the minister, staring at the far corner of the guesthouse.

Lily turned, expecting to see a mounted bridesmaid.

Conner walked next to a reddish-brown horse, holding its bridle. With a soft word, he released it and stepped back, allowing the bridesmaid to head for the aisle.

Lily should have been noticing how the cut of the bridesmaid's gray dress resembled that of a schoolmarm, if said teacher had a dress made of silklike fabric. Instead, she noted how handsome Conner looked in a black suit and hat.

He didn't seem to see Lily, being busy watching the bridesmaids ride sidesaddle down the aisle, before he and Tyler Blackwell moved around to meet them at the left hitching post.

Natalie approached. Both she and her horse had red ribbons in their hair.

"Woop-woop," Lily said softly as she passed.

Natalie grinned at her.

Soft exclamations arose from the crowd as Pepper made her entrance on a palomino guided by Chance Blackwell, the man who'd given the concert in the desert on Sunday night.

Pepper looked stunning in a simple satin gown accented by her mother's strand of pearls. Her train and long veil were draped over the horse's rump. Red ribbons were tied in the palomino's mane and tail. Her bouquet was made of white and red roses with red and silver ribbons trailing toward her toes.

Instead of letting her ride sidesaddle alone down the aisle, Chance escorted her to the hitching post. Before he could help her down, Natalie's horse reached out and nibbled on Pepper's veil.

Chuckles arose, none louder than Pepper's. This may not have been exactly what she'd planned—no white horse—but she was rising above anything thrown her way.

Ken came over to escort Pepper to the gazebo, and the wedding service began.

"You know, I was expecting to grit my teeth through that ceremony, but it was truly heartfelt." Rudy pushed his brunch plate away.

"I'm happy to call her family," Lily said, meaning it. Her gaze sought out Conner but his back was to her.

The toasts had been given and first dances made. The DJ was calling on others to find their place on the dance floor.

Rudy gestured to the ranch's long driveway. Big E's motor home sat in the far distance. "Are you going to be all right if I leave today? It seems—"

"Well, here's a surprise." Danny sat down

at their table, one eye ringed in sickly yellow. "Lily, you've been hard to find lately. I wanted to tell you ahead of time that I'm Natalie's date."

"Woop-woop," Lily murmured, although the only person who'd understand the joke was Conner, who wasn't near enough to hear.

"Did you bring a date? Perhaps your evil, hot-tempered cowboy?" Danny slurped his champagne and grinned, glancing toward the pair of Blackwell tables up front where Conner sat.

"You mean the cowboy who was kind enough to transport me back to the bosom of my family?" Really, if Danny was going to exaggerate the truth, why couldn't she?

Beside her, Rudy shifted, drawing himself up to come to her defense. Lily laid a hand on his arm. She needed to fight her own battles.

"Like Conner did it out of the goodness of his heart?" Danny was in a mood, perhaps a bit drunk. "He was *paid* to keep you on that motor-home trip for days. Away from me. And he's still being *paid* to keep you safe and happy here on the ranch for Big E."

"Enough," Rudy said sharply when Lily wanted to hear more.

Her stomach clenched as her mind put

together the pieces that she'd been too distraught to on earlier occasions. Conner speeding away from the church. Hovering nearby at every turn. Hesitating when she pressed him about Big E not wanting her to train mustangs.

Danny scoffed. "You're right, Rudy. It is enough. I made a promise when I was seven years old." He got to his feet, only wobbling a little. "I love you, Lily, but you're right. We're not *in* love. And we're different people now." He waved to Natalie, who was frowning. "Gotta go. I see my date. We're going zip-lining tomorrow."

Lily stared at Danny's retreating back blankly, brain otherwise occupied with putting two and two together. She didn't care for the sum she was coming up with.

"Ignore Danny." Rudy raised his champagne glass. "Let's toast to new beginnings and a successful search for Thomas Blackwell."

Lily refused to be put off so easily. "What did Danny mean when he said Conner was being paid to keep me out of trouble *here*? For that matter, what did you mean when you said the other day that Big E had promised to look out for me?"

Her father studied her carefully before speaking, which was never a good sign. "You want that cowboy of yours to have been nice to you because he liked you. And maybe he does. But what Danny said is also true. Conner was well compensated to watch over you and make sure you arrived here safely."

"I knew that," Lily said slowly, stomach dropping to the floor and taking her heart with her. "I could leave at any time." *That should have come out with more confidence.*

"If you say so."

She was empty. So very empty. Her fingers twitched.

"Now, Lily. Let's not blow this out of proportion," Dad said in that efficient way of his.

"It's a big deal to me. I'll blow it out if I have to." Lily leaned forward, keeping her voice down because the dining room was filled with wedding guests. "Don't you see? I can't be someone's responsibility, someone's burden, someone's charge." She stood up. "I won't be."

Across the room, Big E handed Conner something that looked suspiciously like a check. The DJ played a slow song about love but it might just as well have been a song about love lost.

"Where are you going?" Rudy asked.

"To find Conner." To hear the truth.

And to tell him a few truths of her own.

CHAPTER TWENTY

"DANCE WITH ME." Lily claimed Conner right after Big E had handed him a large check. She dragged him on the dance floor the way his mother had once dragged his ten-year-old self out of Brewster's during a clearance sale in the toy department.

"You lied to me." Lily kept her voice down as she swung around and into his arms, face flushed and eyes blazing.

Conner didn't like that look. Not at all. He held her loosely, smiled weakly and tried to avoid a scene. "Lied? About what?"

Lily smiled tensely at Pepper as she danced nearby with Ken. She pressed herself close, holding on to his shoulders, and spoke softly in his ear. "You pretended to just be a chauffeur, as if I was in charge of where I was going and when I'd get off the Blackwell bus." These weren't sweet nothings she was whispering. "You asked me if I was having second thoughts or wanted to see Danny to gauge my flight risk. You suggested I express my feelings on postcards instead of calling home. You stood behind me at the shooting range, kept me at your side during the concert, sat with me at Rustlers. You kept a close eye on me and let Pepper and Natalie roam free." Her grip on his shoulders tightened. "When I said I was considering going back to my family. When I said I was thinking about going no farther than Las Vegas with you. You said it was up to me to stay or go, but you were paid to keep me happy and deliver me here. *Paid. To. Keep. Me.*" Finally, she turned hurt eyes on him. "Deny it. Go ahead."

He couldn't deny that. "Lily, I told you I was doing a job."

"What you were doing was manipulative. Okay, it was more subtle than my family or Danny, but still." She huffed. "You really were a kidnapper. Even here at the ranch. And I thought that you and I…that we…" Her eyes filled with tears.

"Lily."

"Don't you *Lily* me!" She drew back, looking like one more hard truth would make her revert to that small, insignificant woman she'd left behind.

They were on the dance floor. Wedding

guests glanced over, as eager for gossip as the ladies who went to the beauty parlor in town.

"Let's take a moment." Conner steered her toward the door, keeping his voice down. "Yes, I was offered a bonus to deliver you here. But I didn't know you then. You've seen the Rocking H. If our situations were reversed, you'd have taken the cash."

"No." Lily lurched out of reach, shaking her head. "I wouldn't have. I would have respected your right to choose, not come up with ways to keep me placated. You're no better than my father or Big E, deciding what's best for me when you don't even *know* me."

He knew her. He knew every nuance, every strength, every sore spot she considered a weakness. He loved her. She made him want to reach for things he hadn't dared reach for in a long time—despite his mother's being laid up with a bruised hip, despite the hard road ahead and the pride he needed to swallow.

"I told Conner to ease your doubts." Big E had followed them into the large common room. He'd changed out of his tuxedo earlier and wore jeans, boots and a black shirt with a black bolo tie—his traveling clothes. Rudy appeared behind him. "Unlike most folk,

Conner doesn't bury his nose in a phone. He listens to people and I thought you could use that."

Lily grimaced. "You stuffed me into a motor home as if I were a child who couldn't stand up to the mess I'd made. I broke my word. I cost my family thousands of dollars. And now I find out the people I thought were helping me have actually been trying to direct my life. Talk about out of the frying pan and into the fire." She ran out the door before Conner could stop her.

"Wait." Conner started to follow, but Big E stepped in his way. "Let her go, son."

Rudy joined them, echoing Big E's sentiment for giving her space.

"I need to apologize," Conner said, heart breaking. "Make Lily understand my perspective."

"Your role in influencing her, you mean." Big E wasn't one to sugarcoat things. "Did you think you'd keep this a secret from her forever? Is that how you planned to play your relationship out?"

Rudy scowled.

"There is no relationship, sir." Not yet. "I have responsibilities and—"

"Stop right there." Big E brushed Conner's

excuses aside with a wave of his hand. "I have eyes. I can see how you two feel. If it's real, if it's true, who am I…who are we—" he gestured to himself and Rudy "—to stand in the way of love? If we did, we'd be the world's biggest hypocrites. And…" He squinted at Conner, which only served to push his bushy brows forward. "What was it you were saying about responsibilities? Let's be clear. Love isn't a responsibility. It's a gift. When you find the right woman, she will be a true life partner, easing your burdens, not adding to them. Unless you mean…" Big E frowned at Conner. "You think my granddaughter is a burden because of her finger issues."

Rudy made a sound suspiciously like a growl.

"No, sir." Conner held up his hands. "I meant I need to get my house in order first."

If anything, Big E's frown deepened. "Let me repeat. Love is *not* a responsibility. Do you know what responsibility is?" He didn't give Conner a chance to answer. "Responsibility is taking your friend's son by the hand and rebuilding his confidence after near catastrophe. Responsibility is finding a way to let that boy shine. Responsibility is showing your friend's son how to run a ranch."

"Stop." Conner shook his head. "You didn't hire me."

"That may be true, but after a few months, when your mother realized you planned to work here permanently, I took you in hand." The way he said it... Like he had accepted it from the very start, no thinking or fretting or deciding required. "Not that I didn't find your way with these guests that my family revels in bringing here beneficial."

"But..." Katie... The books... Stock management... Being a cowboy concierge... It was all useful information. Useful experience. But now he knew how Lily felt. Guided, cornered, trapped.

"That's right. You see it now. The bigger picture." Big E clapped a hand on Conner's shoulder. "You've bandaged your life by working here. You need to return to your own ranch and your own passions. And if Lily loves you the way I think she does, she'll understand and come back to you."

Conner lifted his gaze to the old man's. "And if she doesn't, will you orchestrate things so she does?"

"No," Rudy said.

Big E puffed out his chest, like a startled rooster about to crow with alarm. "The way things stand, my boy, that's none of your business."

An engine rumbled to life outside.

A familiar engine.

Big E lifted his head, practically sniffing the air for clues.

Conner didn't wait for the old man to put the clues together and come up with a hypothesis.

The engine was the motor home's. The shop had delivered it this morning ahead of schedule.

Considering no one else on the ranch would get behind the wheel of Big E's beloved vehicle, the driver had to be Lily.

"I AM SO STUPID." The road blurred behind Lily's tears.

She didn't even know if she was driving back into town. She just knew she had to get away from Conner, Rudy and the Blackwells. She'd hopped into the motor home in the ranch yard and driven away. Off the property. Down the road.

She approached a ranch gate. The Rocking H.

Impulsively, she turned down the driveway. Before she left Montana, she'd say goodbye to Pearl and Mouse.

She pulled into the ranch yard. Over in the corral, Pearl and Mouse lifted their heads to look at her. Parsnip leaped a fence to join them.

Nothing moved at the ranch house, although Karen's truck was there. Lily was relieved. She wouldn't have to pretend not to have a broken heart. She got out and went to the corral, where she was greeted by Pearl, ever in search of a good ear rub.

"I'm going to have to find a place for you, Pearl." She noticed Mouse looking at her. "And you, too, big fella."

Parsnip reached over the top rail and attempted to nibble her hair.

"I may feel empty inside, but I'm not made of straw, buddy." Lily patted his neck. "I wish Conner would finish your training. Don't give up on him." Not the way she was. She closed her eyes, squeezing them against the onslaught of tears. And when she opened them, Royal stood a few feet away, staring at her. "Good girl," Lily said automatically.

Royal glanced away, but a few moments later she looked back.

"Good girl. I bet Karen and Conner have been giving you a big welcome." She stepped away. It was time to go. She'd have plenty of time on the drive home to California to think about what she did next.

Maybe by the time I reach Vegas, my heart will be on the mend.

Wishful thinking.

"Hey. To what do I owe this surprise visit?" Karen stood on the porch, leaning on a walker. The orange tabby twined around her feet. She wore lived-in-looking baggy gray sweats and her hair was tousled as if she'd just gotten out of bed, even though it was well past noon. "I wish I could offer you a cookie or some lunch, but I've been on bed rest."

"Why?" Lily forgot some of her heartache and crossed the ranch yard.

"Conner didn't tell you?" At the shake of Lily's head, his mother tsked. "I had a little accident. Ventured out where I don't belong, beyond the fence where Conner thinks it's dangerous for me, given my troublesome legs. I thought I could handle it but I had a little fall. Bruised my hip." She made it sound like no big deal. But she was on bed rest. It was a big deal.

"I bet Conner was terrified." The way Rudy had been when she'd broken her arm skydiving. His face at the hospital had been white as a sheet. Karen may think it was no big deal, but Conner must have been worried sick. "Why did you do that if you knew it was dangerous?"

Karen jerked her shoulders back as if offended. "I had a good excuse."

Lily always had a good excuse when her adventures led to injury, too. She hurried up the steps. "If you're on bed rest, you should get back to bed. Let me help you."

Parsnip whinnied and galloped around the corral.

A truck approached. Conner's truck.

Lily judged the distance from the porch to the motor home and then stopped herself. "Do the right thing."

"That's always best." Karen turned her walker around and sat in it, heaving a pained sigh. "I wonder why Conner's home so early from work." She gave Lily a sly grin. "I bet he knew you were here."

"I THOUGHT YOU might come here." Conner got out of the truck first, nearest Lily.

Big E and Rudy exited on the other side.

He took advantage of the fact that they had more steps to take to reach Lily than he did. "Lily, let me explain. Please." He made it up the steps two at a time. "Mom, you shouldn't be out of bed. You could have fallen again."

"But somehow, I'm glad I came out for some sun…son." His mother would be the death of him yet. "I've got front-row seats to what sounds like it'll be a doozy of an apology."

Lily crossed her arms and stared at the corral, where Parsnip jumped the fence and trotted their way. The big horse had finally lost his patience.

"That's enough talk, cowboy." Rudy caught up to Conner, having reached the bottom step. "I'm going with my daughter back to San Diego. If that's what she wants."

"Why?" Conner blocked the man from climbing his stairs, helped by the appearance of Parsnip at his side. The big horse nudged Rudy back to the walkway, inserting himself between Conner and the two older men like a guard dog. "Why would Lily go back with you? So you can undermine Lily's confidence in herself and her job some more?" He swung Lily a look over his shoulder. "Don't go."

"I have no reason to stay. Everyone treats me like a child because of these." She held her hands up, eyes filled with unshed tears. "I can't trust anyone to stay out of my life."

"Now, Lily…" Rudy began as Big E lumbered up, having taken a moment to peruse the exterior of his motor home.

"She's right." Conner cut the rigid older man off. "None of us have given Lily a reason to trust we'd respect her independence."

"Independence is a double-edged sword." His mother gave her hip a tender pat.

"But everyone deserves to make their own decisions." Conner's gaze found Lily's. "Even when I was encouraging you to do just that, I was building a protective buffer around you, the same way I've done with my mother."

"It's too late for apologies," Lily said, holding herself as rigid as her stepfather.

"You're right." Conner wasn't going to argue with her. "You bailed on your wedding and came to Montana because you wanted to find out who you are and how the Blackwells figure into that. But really what you were doing was breaking free of everything that was keeping you from finding out who you are. I wasn't part of the solution. I was part of the problem."

"You're a problem now," Rudy griped. He extended his hand. "Come on down, honey. If you want to get away to think, we can give you a lift in the motor home. You can be back in your apartment in a few days. Then you can decide what you want to do without any pressure."

"Super idea," Big E said. "Stay or go. Your choice."

Lily gaped at Rudy and Big E. "Why would I go anywhere with any of you?"

"Because I love you," Conner said simply.

Parsnip blew a raspberry, a sound that came off like a lot of laughter.

Lily's nose reddened and she looked like she might cry. "You can't. It's too soon."

"She's right," Rudy said simply.

Big E made a noise that sounded like the one Parsnip had made.

"I can." Conner extended a hand. "I'm like a good pair of jeans, honey."

"What did you say?" His mother leaned forward, grimaced, then thought better of it and sat back. "This is not the way you ask a woman to marry you."

"She's right," Rudy said, rolling his eyes.

"You're asking me..." Lily braced herself on the porch railing. "What happened to not betting on Conner Hannah?"

Parsnip nudged Conner's shoulder.

"Not now." Conner pushed his nose away.

"Now would be the perfect time," Big E said cryptically.

Conner glanced at the old man. Words ran through his head.

Return to what you're passionate about.
Love is not a responsibility. It's a gift.
You have to make a grand gesture.

A grand gesture. That was Pepper's advice.

Parsnip had turned and started plodding toward the pasture.

"Parsnip." Conner hurried down the steps and caught up to the big black horse. He grabbed a handful of mane and swung up onto his back, guiding him with his heels until they were back at the porch steps.

Big E drew Rudy back, giving them space.

"I thought you said you had to complete Parsnip's training," Lily said in a small voice.

"His cutting-horse training." Conner didn't waste time explaining. This was a time for grand, romantic gestures, just the way Pepper had said. "I was wrong about not betting on me, Lily, or on the Rocking H. I can't carry the load here alone. I know that now."

"About time," his mother said.

"With someone like you by my side, and a bonus from Big E to give us some breathing room, I can return to what I'm passionate about—training cutting horses."

"By your side?" Lily echoed.

"Yes, darlin'." Conner embraced his cowboy heritage and slang. "You can learn to help me and we can rely on each other, just like Horatio Hannah relied on his bride. But not only that, you can learn to train mustangs on your own."

Rudy made a choking noise that had Parsnip shifting his back legs so he could see the former military man. "Now, that's going too far."

"Keep quiet, Rudy," Big E said. "You and I aren't a part of this."

"Old habits, old man." Rudy sighed.

"I know you told me you don't accept challenges anymore." Conner offered her his hand. "But I want to extend one more. Be my wife, my partner in business and in love. I love you, Lily Harrison Blackwell. I may not have done a good job of it in these early days. But I know that love is a gift you have to nurture for it to grow. From here on out, it's truth and love."

"Well done, son," Big E said, a response Conner took as a blessing.

Lily didn't move. She glanced toward her stepfather as if needing his approval.

Rudy smiled. Not a big smile, but a smile nonetheless. "Are you sure this isn't something wild? I don't want you to get hurt."

The woman Conner loved turned her attention to him and his very well-behaved but truly impatient horse. No telling how much longer Parsnip was going to help him out on this grand, romantic gesture.

"Dad, you know that place I told you I was searching for?" Lily came down the porch steps, eyeing Parsnip before turning her gaze to Conner with a jolt that was electric. "I found it. Right here. With the man I love. The man I love right down to the tips of my toes." She took his hand in both of hers the way a person who intended to stay on the ground did. "I'm not letting go."

"Good." Because Conner preferred she get on board right away. He swung her up behind him.

Thankfully, she didn't squeal. She wrapped her arms around him and held on as if she'd never let him go.

Thankfully, Parsnip showed some grace and patience, and didn't do more than twitch his tail.

"Gentlemen." Conner tipped his hat and guided Parsnip toward the pasture.

"Where are you going?" Rudy marched after them.

"To show my future bride her property."

"Let them go, Rudy," Big E said, chuckling. "You know how young people are and we've got miles to go today."

Parsnip picked up his pace, as eager to leave their audience behind as Conner was.

"Conner Hannah, you are a brave man." Lily pressed a kiss to his shoulder, her breath wafting through the thin cotton of his shirt.

"Lily, take a look around. You'll always be the bravest one in this family for taking me on. And if you weren't that brave, I wouldn't love you like my favorite pair of blue jeans."

EPILOGUE

"CAN'T THIS RUST bucket go any faster?" Rudy demanded of Elias from the passenger seat of the old rancher's motor home. "We just got passed by two old ladies in a station wagon."

"This isn't a rust bucket," Elias retorted. "It's a classic." He patted the faded dash. "And if we go over fifty, we won't make it to Elko on this tank of gas."

Rudy washed a hand over his face.

His driving companion spared him a glance. "You still shell-shocked about Conner and Lily?"

"Yeah. Ten days ago she was supposed to marry someone else."

"Ten days ago she was about to marry the wrong man. You saw her, same as I did. There was love in her eyes, more love than I saw anytime she talked about that man you wanted her to get hitched to."

Rudy didn't like the way Elias made sense when talking about his daughter. He didn't like the fact that they were going to find the man who'd been married to Susan before he was. But he didn't like loose ends. Loose ends made him twitchy. But so did worrying about his girls. *His girls.*

Will they still be mine if we find Thomas Blackwell?

Rudy gasped. "Brake-brake-brake-brake-brake!"

Elias brought the motor home to a halt just short of the station wagon with the elderly ladies who'd passed them earlier. They'd missed their exit—if their blinker and ill-advised stop just past the exit was any indication—and they were about to cause a multicar pileup on the Idaho interstate.

"I had it under control," Elias grumbled.

Rudy knew the old man often thought he had things under control. Key word being *thought.* "Like you had the situation with Lily under control?"

"Yep." Elias grinned. "I believe I'm starting to get the hang of granddaughters. They aren't much different than grandsons."

"Elias, with all due respect, you have no idea what you're talking about."

"Name's *Big E*, and I beg to differ. Beginnings are often rough, which is why you've got to have courage and learn to roll with the punches."

The old man laughed so hard his foot slipped off the brake and they rear-ended the station wagon.

* * * * *

A romance is on the cards for
Amanda Harrison Blackwell,
coming next month from
author Amy Vastine
and Harlequin Heartwarming.
Don't miss it! Big E is up to his old tricks
bringing people together yet again!

Get 4 FREE REWARDS!

We'll send you 2 FREE Books plus 2 FREE Mystery Gifts.

Love Inspired books feature uplifting stories where faith helps guide you through life's challenges and discover the promise of a new beginning.

FREE Value Over $20

Get 4 FREE REWARDS!

We'll send you 2 FREE Books <u>plus</u> 2 FREE Mystery Gifts.

Love Inspired Suspense books showcase how courage and optimism unite in stories of faith and love in the face of danger.

FREE Value Over **$20**

THE WESTERN HEARTS COLLECTION!

19 FREE BOOKS in all!

COWBOYS. RANCHERS. RODEO REBELS.
Here are their charming love stories in one prized Collection:
51 emotional and heart-filled romances that capture the majesty and rugged beauty of the American West!

YES! Please send me **The Western Hearts Collection** in Larger Print. This collection begins with 3 FREE books and 2 FREE gifts in the first shipment. Along with my 3 free books, I'll also get the next 4 books from The Western Hearts Collection, in LARGER PRINT, which I may either return and owe nothing, or keep for the low price of $5.45 U.S./$6.23 CDN each plus $2.99 U.S./$7.49 CDN for shipping and handling per shipment*. If I decide to continue, about once a month for 8 months I will get 6 or 7 more books but will only need to pay for 4. That means 2 or 3 books in every shipment will be FREE! If I decide to keep the entire collection, I'll have paid for only 32 books because 19 books are FREE! I understand that accepting the 3 free books and gifts places me under no obligation to buy anything. I can always return a shipment and cancel at any time. My free books and gifts are mine to keep no matter what I decide.

☐ 270 HCN 5354   ☐ 470 HCN 5354

Name (please print)

Address   Apt. #

City   State/Province   Zip/Postal Code

Mail to the **Reader Service**:
IN U.S.A.: P.O. Box 1341, Buffalo, N.Y. 14240-8531
IN CANADA: P.O. Box 603, Fort Erie, Ontario L2A 5X3

Get 4 FREE REWARDS!

We'll send you 2 FREE Books plus 2 FREE Mystery Gifts.

FREE
Value Over
$20

Both the **Romance** and **Suspense** collections feature compelling novels written by many of today's bestselling authors.

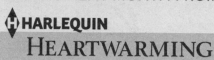

Visit
ReaderService.com
Today!

As a valued member of the Harlequin Reader Service, you'll find these benefits and more at ReaderService.com:

- Try 2 free books from any series
- Access risk-free special offers
- View your account history & manage payments
- Browse the latest Bonus Bucks catalog

Don't miss out!

If you want to stay up-to-date on the latest at the Harlequin Reader Service and enjoy more content, make sure you've signed up for our monthly News & Notes email newsletter. Sign up online at ReaderService.com or by calling Customer Service at 1-800-873-8635.

RS20